PIECES OF PINK

Copyright © 2020 Annelise Driscoll

All rights reserved. No part of this book may be reproduced in any form, except for the inclusion of brief quotations in a review, without permission in writing from the author or publisher. For permissions contact:

Grey Cap Books LLC
greycapbooks@gmail.com

Cover by Annelise Driscoll
Book Design by Annelise Driscoll
www.annelisedriscoll.com

ISBN: 978-1-7346707-0-7

First Edition

PIECES OF PINK

ANNELISE DRISCOLL

Grey Cap Books

ONE

Grey screamed as Jesse's blood sprayed across her face in a pale, pink mist. One moment, he had been kneeling beside her, his eyes saying everything his gagged mouth could not. The next, his left cheek had exploded outward, spattering shards of bone, blood, and brain onto the ground—onto Grey.

With a soft thump, his body slumped forward and crumpled into the gravel before her.

Jesse was dead.

Grey couldn't form his name through the dirty rag tied in her mouth, but she tried. She screamed and screamed, sobbing in rage and agony as the Blackcap behind her reloaded his weapon. In a moment, she would be with Jesse, wherever he was, or she would be nowhere at all.

There was a soft snap as the Blackcap cocked his gun. He pressed the barrel to the back of Grey's skull, and with one last shuddering breath, she looked at Jesse—past the pool of blood spreading out beneath him—and searched for the face she had known so well; but it was gone.

"Stop!" A frantic voice broke into the courtyard, and the cold pressure at the back of Grey's head vanished. "Stop the executions!"

Twisting her neck, she saw a boy in a glossy black helmet charging through the courtyard gate with a bright, white envelope clutched in his outstretched hand.

"Stop the executions," the boy panted as he jogged to a halt beside Grey.

"On whose orders?" the Blackcap demanded, though Grey heard him click the weapon's safety back into place.

"The captain's," the boy responded.

The Blackcap snarled and snatched up the envelope.

As the man tore the seal and began to read, Grey's eyes sank back to Jesse's limp form.

The pool of blood had reached her knees, and she could feel it, wet and sticky, as it soaked through the fabric of her pants. A silent tear leaked from her eye and dripped off the tip of her nose. With a splash, it fell into the red puddle and dissolved into Jesse's blood, as if it could join them back together again.

"All right, then." The Blackcap's voice raked through her, and he pushed the letter back into the boy's hand. "Take her."

"Yes, sir." The boy gave a sharp salute and reached for Grey's gag as if to remove it from her mouth.

"Don't bother." The Blackcap stopped him and hauled Grey to her feet. "I've got plenty of spares."

"Yes, sir," the boy stuttered out the words and saluted a second time before gripping Grey's elbow to lead her away.

When they were almost clear of the courtyard, she paused, straining against the boy's touch just long enough to gaze back at Jesse, whom the older Blackcap was lifting from the ground and dumping into a wheelbarrow. Grey's throat bobbed as she watched, and a hoarse sob cut between the gag and her teeth.

Pieces of Pink

After a moment of hesitation, the boy tugged her elbow. It was not a harsh movement, as the older Blackcap's handling had been. No, this was something soft, something gentle that seemed to whisper, *look away*.

Deep in her chest, Grey's heart strained as she watched Jesse's body wheeled away, and when her eyes drifted back to the boy—the Blackcap—standing at her side, that heart snapped entirely.

Even with his black helmet, the boy was an unconvincing soldier. He was no more suited to life as a Blackcap than Grey, to life as a Redcap, or Jesse, to life as a Pinkcap. Like them, this boy had simply been born to the wrong parents. And suitable or not, his profession—his future—was predetermined by the Code.

With her head bowed, Grey followed the boy's guiding touch through the barracks as he led her past buildings and courtyards, empty, as the majority of men and women on active duty patrolled the border wall to keep fugitives, like herself, from escaping the boundaries of Citoyen.

She wondered how many people they caught in a day; how many were foolish enough to believe that there was a place for them beyond the wall. Were there dozens? Or would Jesse be the only one to die at the hands of the executioner today?

The thought of him, alone and buried in some unmarked grave without her, sent a wave of nausea rolling through her gut. She wanted to ask the young Blackcap what would happen to the body—to know if the victims were buried or burned, or thrown into some garbage heap—but the strip of black cloth held her mute.

"Here we are," the Blackcap mumbled, more to himself than to Grey, and came to a halt outside of a small concrete building.

With a quick swipe, the boy scanned his wrist against the door, deactivating the lock with his security chip. As was the case for all citizens born into the armed forces, the microchip had been implanted before the boy was even old enough to remember.

"Watch your step," he cautioned as he placed a hand on Grey's back to guide her over the threshold.

Against the steady pressure of his touch, Grey realized she was trembling. But even through his armored glove, his touch reassured her. And to her relief, his hand remained resting on her lower back as they entered a hallway lined with cells. In the artificial light, black numbers—stenciled on the center of each steel door—stood out stark and cold.

When they reached the last door, the boy stopped and turned to look at her, as if he might be able to read her crime in her expression; might be able to find justification for the way his fellow Blackcaps had treated her, or find an explanation for why they had executed Jesse. But Grey knew he couldn't, and tears welled up in her eyes as she stared back.

An older Blackcap wouldn't have wondered at all. But the boy, barely older than twelve, was probably on his first assignment as a clerk or messenger for the captain. And the compassion that came with his inexperience was fresh.

It hurt her to consider the future that awaited him, a future of cruelty and apathy, in which the line between protecting the people and enforcing Citoyen's laws would blur until there was nothing left of the child that stood before her now.

Again, the Blackcap swiped his wrist over a lock, but this time, the door opened into a cell; and when Grey stepped inside, the boy did not follow.

"The captain will be with you shortly," he said dutifully, but hesitation remained in his eyes. "And . . ." he paused, "I'm sorry about your friend."

With a click, the steel door closed, and Grey sank to her knees.

Friend. It was too simple a word for what Jesse had been to her.

A breath rattled through her throat, and she curled into herself as the grief crashed over her. Unable to remove the gag or wipe away her tears with hands still bound behind her back, she gave in to the pain and screamed, her cry muffled by the unfeeling walls.

With every ounce of energy, she clawed for her memories of Jesse, willing herself to see his soft, brown eyes and quirky smile, aching to hear his outrageous laugh, and straining to feel the warm touch of his skin against her own. But the only image that remained was a broken face with a ragged hole torn through one half. Fragments of exposed molars, bones, and sinuses flashed through her mind, and lightless, dead eyes stared past her into nothingness.

- ♦ -

When the cell door opened again, Grey was curled on her side, still shivering against the images in her mind. She did not look up, even as a pair of elegant, brogue shoes stepped casually toward her. Beyond them, a second pair of shoes—black boots—stood planted in the doorframe.

"Thank you, Captain." The male voice that drifted over her head was cool and smooth, almost carnal. "But this isn't Jesse."

Grey closed her eyes, and a noise—guttural and aching—split through her chest.

"They were traveling together." The captain's tone was cold and hard, as though she hadn't just heard Grey's heart breaking.

"Ah." The man remained conversational—pleasant, even—as he plucked the gag from Grey's throbbing jaw and dropped it around her neck.

"Where is Jesse?" he asked.

"Dead." The truth croaked from Grey's dry mouth before she could stop it.

"Well, if this isn't the Pinkcap you're looking for," the captain said, sharp and emotionless, "we'll dispatch her."

Grey could hear the black boots striding toward her, but she kept her eyes squeezed shut, still trying to find one beautiful memory of Jesse. She had to find him, had to see his face one last time before she died.

"Just a moment," the man interrupted, coy and confident. "Before you do, I'd like to find out why, exactly, I just lost one of my best Pieces."

The captain sighed impatiently but grunted her permission and stepped back.

"Open your eyes, darling," the man cooed in Grey's ear. His soft fingers brushed down the side of her cheek. "Tell me who you are."

Grey didn't move.

"At least," he teased, "tell me who you are to Jesse?"

Grey sucked in a breath. *Who you are to Jesse. Are.*

The word repeated itself in her head, over and over.

As a Redcap, she had watched plenty of families grieve the loss of a loved one and witnessed the brutal reconciliation of past and present. She understood the time it took for people to transition into using the past tense—the discomfort it caused them—and knew that such a simple tense shift was often the first step of letting go.

And this man was not ready to let go.

Grey opened her eyes, still stinging with the salt of her tears, and looked up. The man crouching on the floor beside her smirked slightly, but the expression didn't quite reach his eyes. They were bright blue—so much more severe than she had expected—and tucked above high, sharp cheekbones. But it wasn't the man's eyes that Grey recognized, or the pink lips, like Cupid's bow, or even the mop of tousled, black curls, uncovered by any colored cap. It was his chunky, purple scarf—a symbol of his rank and his defiance—that told her who had come for Jesse.

"Lock," she breathed.

He blinked once, as though startled by the sound of his name on a stranger's lips, and feigned shock lit his eyes.

"Do you know her?" the captain demanded.

"I can't say that I do." The grin remained etched across Lock's face. "But she seems to know me."

Directing his attention back to Grey, Lock smiled to reveal a row of straight, white teeth. "Have we met?"

It was a game, and Grey didn't know the rules.

She shook her head once.

True, they had not met, but he knew who she was. As Jesse's Purplecap, Lock had been the kingpin of their attempted escape. It was only with his help that they had even made it this far. And although she had never met Lock personally, Jesse had spoken highly of him. Jesse had called the man just and fair, and of all the brothels in Citoyen, he had been glad to end up in one of Lock's. Nowhere else were Pinkcaps—Pieces, as they called themselves—treated with the respect that Lock had given them.

"You know my name," Lock simpered, "so it seems only fair that I should know yours as well."

He was lying. And although his words were even, there was an urgency in his eyes that compelled her response.

"Grey," she whispered, "Grey Alcott."

The last name, Jesse's last name, still felt strange on her tongue. And though it was not legally hers—nothing about her marriage to Jesse had been legal—it was the name she had planned to bring with her to the Pinelands.

"Alcott?" Lock raised a coal-black eyebrow.

Grey nodded, hoping he understood her plea.

"I see." Abruptly, Lock stood and turned toward the captain, who was still waiting at his back, watching with narrowed eyes.

"It seems," Lock frowned, "that my Pinkcap ran away with this, this—" he waved a hand at her. "What are you?"

"A Redcap," she answered.

"This Redcap," Lock repeated her rank.

"And?" The captain crossed her arms over her broad chest and tilted her head expectantly. The black beret perched neatly on her smooth, brown hair didn't budge.

"It's her fault he's dead," Lock shrugged.

The words cut into Grey. What was he saying?

"As I see it, she's the one who broke the Color Code. It's her fault that I've lost a considerable portion of my income. So, if it's all the same to you," Lock smiled at the captain, "let her punishment be to take his place."

The breath hitched in Grey's throat as the truth of Lock's claim crashed into her. Jesse was dead, and it was her fault. If she had never met him, never cared for him, never loved him, none of this would have ever happened. He would still be alive, and she would still be—she whimpered—what would she be without him?

"Make her a Pinkcap," Lock said.

Grey's stomach knotted. This was not what she wanted. She wanted to be buried with Jesse, not to take his place.

The captain hummed, then spoke. "Granted," she agreed. "We'll process her, and once you've settled the new Pinkcaps in the barracks, you can come and pick her up."

"Thank you, Cap—" Lock began, but the captain held up a hand to stop him.

"But take her back to the city with you." The captain's eyes turned deadly. "And keep her there. If she ever comes near the border again, she'll be shot on sight."

"Of course, Captain." Lock smiled. "You have my word."

The captain gave him a sharp nod of approval, and Lock followed her from the cell without a second glance at Grey, who was still lying on the floor.

Pieces of Pink

- ◆ -

Grey's arms were still bound behind her back when two Blackcaps—one male and one female—led her into a large, tiled room. In the center of the floor, there were three open drains, and a small ditch ran around the perimeter to catch excess water. Four or five hoses hung coiled on each wall, and six large bars crisscrossed overhead for curtains, which were pushed open.

With a sharp flick, the male Blackcap opened a switchblade, and instinctively, Grey shrank away.

"For the zip tie," he nodded toward her wrists, then reached for them. "Hold her still."

Without hesitation, the female gripped Grey's forearms, as her partner snapped the zip tie with a deft sweep of his knife. The pair worked as one—a carefully honed unit—and with their black helmets shading their faces, they were almost indistinguishable.

"Spread your feet and hold your arms out at your sides." The man yanked the broken zip tie from her wrist and pocketed his knife.

Although her shoulders ached from hours of being bound, and her fingertips prickled painfully with the steady flow of blood returning to her hands, Grey obeyed.

"Do you have any concealed weapons or jewelry?" he asked while the second Blackcap remained standing behind her.

"No," she shook her head.

"Ring," the woman behind her grunted.

"Again," the man repeated, "do you have any concealed weapons or jewelry?"

"No weapons," she frowned. "Just my ring."

Her wedding ring, a thin silver band, had been Jesse's pledge, and she fought not to whimper as the Blackcap twisted it off of her finger and slid it into the breast pocket of his bulletproof vest.

Tears prickled in her eyes at the sensation of the ring's absence, and she wondered what had happened to Jesse's ring. Perhaps the executioner had kept it for himself. Or maybe it had gone unnoticed and would remain with his body, wherever it was.

"Do you have to take it?" Grey whispered the words, fighting back the sob that bobbed in her throat.

The Blackcap did not answer but began to pat her down, searching for anything else that she may have hidden in her clothes. She didn't bother to tell him she had already been searched multiple times since being caught. And even if she did, she doubted it would make a difference. When he was finished, the Blackcap reached for the zipper on the front of her jacket and pulled.

"What are you doing?" Grey shrieked and stepped quickly out of his reach, only to collide with the Blackcap still standing at her back.

"We have orders to process you," the man explained flatly. "You'll be stripped, checked for contraband, and washed. Then, you'll see a Redcap for a physical exam, complete some paperwork, and we'll release you to your Purplecap."

Without waiting for her response, the man reached for Grey's jacket a second time, and she shuddered but did not resist.

Layer by layer, the two Blackcaps stripped her. First, they removed her jacket, shirt, and undershirt, dropping the travel-stained clothes into a pile on the floor. Then they took her boots, socks, and pants, and finally her bra and panties—carefully checking all pockets and seams for weapons—until she was standing barefoot and naked, with her arms still outstretched.

"You can put your arms down," the man instructed as he headed toward the far wall.

The woman, who had been standing at Grey's back, scooped the dirty clothes into a bag and moved out of the way as the first Blackcap began to twist the small brass valve on the wall. There was a soft rushing sound as the hose filled, then a sharp spray of water shot toward her.

Grey gasped, teeth chattering against the freezing stream, and the Blackcap hosed her down. The water pressure stung her skin, and she instinctively turned her head away and held up her hands when he aimed the blast at her face.

"Put your hands down," he ordered.

"It's too strong," she bleated through the deluge.

"It has to be strong," his voice was so impassive, she almost didn't understand, "to get all that shit off of your face."

Her eyes widened as realization struck, and she raised a shaking hand to her cheek.

"Don't—" the woman began, but it was too late.

Something sticky met her fingertips, and when she pulled it away and saw the piece of flesh with a small tuft of brown hair attached to it, Grey dropped to her knees and vomited.

The rest of the washing passed in a blur. If the Blackcaps had given Grey orders, she did not hear them. She only knew that at some point, they had turned off the hose, wrapped her in a hospital gown, and deposited her in an exam room, where she now sat perched on the table, waiting for another Redcap to come and inspect her.

Through the small window in the door, she could see the two Blackcaps stationed in the hallway, stoic and unmoving. As a Redcap, Grey had seen blood before. She had been covered in things much more horrifying than the clump of skin and hair that had been plastered to her cheek. But those things had never belonged to her husband. No, they had been pieces of strangers, patients she had been trying to save. She had never known them—never *loved* them.

The door creaked loudly, and Grey looked up to see a short woman in a white lab coat striding into the room. A thick red headband—marking her as a Redcap—held back the woman's black hair, and a clipboard nested in the crook of her elbow. The Redcap barely glanced up from her medical charts before heading to the sink to wash her hands.

"I see you were a Redcap?" the woman asked as she ground her fingernails into a bar of soap and scrubbed.

"Yes," Grey nodded, "I was."

"Good." The woman yanked a fresh, white towel from the stack on the countertop and dried her hands. "Then we can skip the small talk. You know what to expect."

She tossed the rag in a small laundry bin under the sink.

"But for the sake of full disclosure, I'm required to let you know, you're here for a physical exam, bloodwork, chip installation, and a copper IUD for birth control."

Grey frowned. "I haven't given consent for any of that." She shook her head slightly, in disbelief that the Redcap could skip such a crucial step in an exam.

"And you won't need to." The woman tapped the clipboard still tucked against her elbow. "I have your Purplecap's signature for all of the procedures."

A pit formed at the base of Grey's throat, and her cheeks flushed. How could she have forgotten? After all, it was a statute she, herself, had enforced more than once—a law she'd enforced the first time she saw Jesse.

Finally, the woman raised her eyes to look at Grey, who sat in silence, waiting.

"Shall we get started, then?"

Grey nodded.

Pieces of Pink

"All right, go ahead and remove your gown." The Redcap stared at her with bored, if not impatient eyes, waiting for her to obey.

Grey hesitated for a moment before pulling her arms free of the sleeves. And for the second time in as many hours, she sat naked, completely exposed to the eyes of a stranger.

- ♦ -

Once the Redcap had finished Grey's procedures and disappeared down the hall, the Blackcaps tossed her a bag. She didn't catch it, and it tumbled to the ground, dumping clean clothes—if they could even be called that—on the floor.

"Get dressed," the man ordered, and his partner smirked as Grey bent to pick up the clothes.

Wherever the Blackcaps had found them, it was clear that the transparent, PVC corset and miniskirt had once belonged to another Pinkcap—probably from the brothel that Lock himself had been visiting at the barracks—though, mercifully, they were lightly used.

"They should be a perfect fit for a Pinkcap," the woman sneered as Grey reluctantly slipped out of her hospital gown and struggled to squeeze herself into the PVC contraption.

Even in the cool air of late summer, the plastic fabric stuck to her skin and made her sweat. And when she drew the laces, it pinched under her armpits and around her waist. Grey fidgeted in discomfort as she shimmied the matching skirt up around her thighs. But when the Blackcaps tossed her a pair of pink, platform heels, she made her stand. Unable to bend over in the corset, she squatted, swept the shoes off the ground, and hooked the ankle straps over her fingers.

"Put them on," the man ordered.

Grey shook her head. "No."

"Fine," the woman snatched them back. "Go barefoot then."

With that, the Blackcaps led her from the exam room and out onto a loading dock at the back of the building. In her plastic corset, Grey stood like a life-sized doll, waiting for Lock and his driver to bring the car around and take her back to the city, far away from whatever remained of Jesse.

A small group of Blackcaps—off duty—passed by, and a few stared pointedly at Grey's chest, where her nipples pressed against the clear fabric like shriveled peaches. Self-conscious, she crossed her arms over her breasts, and her fingertips grazed the raised bump on the inside of her wrist, where the Redcap had implanted her chip.

Pinkcaps and Blackcaps were the only citizens to carry a chip—Blackcaps for clearance, and Pinkcaps as a means of making non-cash transactions—but the chips for both were also tracking devices.

Before they'd decided to run, Grey had carefully removed Jesse's chip and tossed it into the river, which had carried it south. In the weeks that had passed since then, if any Blackcap had been alerted to the tracker's movement, they would have assumed it was a suicide. After all, those were common enough among the Pinkcaps.

"He's here."

Grey jumped at the voice of the Blackcap behind her. Bleary-eyed and exhausted, she had forgotten her guards were still there.

"This way." The female Blackcap took her by the elbow and led her off the loading dock as a black car with tinted windows pulled into view. No sooner had the driver put the vehicle into park than the back door swung open, and Lock stepped out with a pale, pink cap clutched in his hand.

"Oh, my." He sauntered over to her with a smug grin, and his black eyebrows quirked up. "Don't you look exciting."

Exciting was not the word Grey would have chosen, but she didn't protest. Delicately, Lock placed the cap on her head and turned to address the Blackcaps.

Pieces of Pink

"I picked up the paperwork from the office." Lock patted the inner pocket of his coat. "Is she ready to go?"

"She is," the man nodded.

"Well, in that case," Lock shrugged out of his long coat, "thank you for your services."

With a dramatic sweep, he draped the coat over Grey's shoulders and led her to the car. As she climbed in, he turned back to give the Blackcaps a final nod of appreciation, then sat beside her and closed the door, blocking her from the watchful eyes of her guards.

As the car rolled forward, Grey sank gratefully into the privacy that the coat offered. Lock's flippant personality had surprised her at first, but when she glanced up at the man seated beside her, she saw no trace of the coy Purplecap he had been moments before.

Now, in the car, with no one but her to see him, Lock's playful expressions had vanished, and he stared silently out the window with a grim look on his face. He was older than she had expected—probably in his late forties—and without his mask of smiles, the creases at the corners of his eyes and along his forehead were evident. After a moment, the Purplecap sighed deeply and turned to look at her.

"Alcott." The name seemed so familiar on his lips. "So, you were married, then?"

Grey nodded.

"I'm sorry for your loss." There was no teasing in the man's voice. "I hoped you two would make it."

She looked down at her lap, at the goosebumps rising on her thighs, and pulled the coat tighter around herself. It took her a moment to respond, and when she did, the words sounded hollow, even to her own ears.

"Sixty seconds."

Lock's eyebrows pinched together. "What?"

"If you had been one minute sooner," she struggled to speak as her throat clenched with tears, "we both would've made it. Jesse would be alive."

There was a moment of silence.

"Yes, he would," Lock's words were soft, almost pained, "but you wouldn't be. I couldn't have saved you both," he shook his head. "Not after you were caught. They would have let me take Jesse, but not you. You were a Redcap, not one of mine, and with Jesse alive, there would have been no argument to keep you."

"It wouldn't matter if I were dead." Grey's voice was hoarse.

Tenderly, Lock laid a hand over hers.

"It would have mattered to Jesse."

A tear slid down Grey's cheek as Lock drew his hand away and reached into the pocket of his silk vest.

"These belong to you."

There, resting in Lock's open palm, Grey's wedding band sat with Jesse's nestled beside it.

Sobbing, Grey scooped the rings from Lock's hand and clutched them against her chest. And in that moment, the images of the morning receded, and she remembered a glimpse of Jesse's smile.

TWO

It was dark when the car rolled to a stop in the dead-end alley. Through the tinted glass, Grey vaguely recognized the neighborhood as they had driven in, but it wasn't one she had visited often. She was not being placed in the same brothel where Jesse had lived. That much was clear.

All around them, the buildings stood windowless, except for one—a brick townhouse—whose front door faced the alley.

"We call it the Base," Lock said, following Grey's gaze. "It's where I stay when I'm not visiting my other units."

Internally, Grey scoffed at the word, but she was too exhausted—too broken—to make the noise outright. It seemed silly to skirt around the truth, to call the buildings anything other than what they were. They weren't units. They were whorehouses.

"So, I guess you could say it's home." Lock offered a weak smile.

Grey didn't respond as she stepped from the car, and Lock turned his attention to the Bluecap in the driver's seat.

"Thank you," he said, handing the driver a fold of bills.

With a tip of his hat, the Bluecap rolled up his window, made an impossibly tight turn, and drove back down the alley.

When the taillights disappeared, Lock glanced at his watch—large on his slender wrist—before turning to Grey.

"It's late," Lock said, stepping toward the circular portico that jutted from the building. It was strange how the Base had been hidden with no access to the main road, but it was not the first brothel Grey had seen constructed with such discretion in mind.

"I'm not sure who will be home," he said, "but we'll find someone to get you situated."

Pulling Lock's coat tighter around her shoulders, Grey followed the Purplecap up the steps and through the ornate wooden door.

Although the exterior hadn't been a surprise, the interior was a shock. From the foyer, a staircase with an emerald carpet and intricately carved banister swept up to a second-floor balcony. Mahogany wainscoting flanked the walls, and oil paintings, illuminated with brass lights, hung to the ceiling. To the left, Grey saw a large room lined with books and filled with plump chairs. And to her right was a dining room with three long tables and benches.

"It's from an older time, I know." Lock stood with his hands in his pockets, staring up the staircase. "And it's not necessarily better, but it's home."

She glanced at him.

"In the past, clients used to come to us, not the other way around. And while there are certainly disadvantages to welcoming clients into your home," his eyes drifted to the dim hallway behind the stairs, "it's easier for Purplecaps to keep the Pinkcaps safe. Sometimes I wish they hadn't changed it."

Grey frowned. She had heard enough from Jesse and had seen enough from making house calls as a Redcap, to know that many Purplecaps did not maintain the same sense of duty that Lock seemed to uphold.

"Now, there," a deep female voice slid from the darkness behind the stairs, "is a handsome man."

Pieces of Pink

An involuntary grin broke over Lock's face as the owner of the voice stepped into the light. Grey's swollen eyes widened as she took in the woman standing before her. She was around Grey's age, but that was where the similarities between them ended.

Standing well over six feet tall in a pair of black, knee-high boots, the woman was unlike anyone Grey had ever seen. Her bleached blonde hair, slightly dark at the roots, was pulled into a tight bun that rested at the crown of her head, drawing her pink-dusted cheekbones into sharp mounds.

Her eyes, hazel brown, glinted like honey as an almost dangerous smile tipped up the corners of her deep red lips. And as she strode toward them, Grey realized that under her black, fishnet dress, the woman wore absolutely nothing.

"Roz!" Lock laughed her name aloud. "I'm glad you're home. I didn't expect anyone to be here!"

"I have a day-booking tomorrow," the air around the woman pulsed with energy as she moved, "so I'm taking the night off."

Grey frowned. Wearing *that*?

"Well, that's lucky for us." Lock placed his hand lightly on Grey's upper back. "Because Grey could use a friend to help get her settled. And also," he grimaced, "to help her find a different outfit."

Roz turned her predatory gaze toward Grey and took a step closer. Reaching out a pale hand, tipped with deep purple fingernails, she snagged the opening of the coat and drew it aside to reveal Grey's plastic corset.

"What's wrong with what she has on?"

Lock rolled his eyes.

"Not everyone can be as . . ." he hesitated, searching for the right word, "comfortable as you are."

"Oh, that's what we're calling it now?" She purred, "I like it."

"I'm sure you do," he teased.

"So, she's moving in with us?" Roz asked.

"Yes." Lock nodded. "She's a new Piece."

"And does she have a name?" Roz's eyes locked with Grey's. She wasn't asking Lock.

Grey scowled at the woman. "Grey Alcott." Her voice came out weaker than she had intended, but at least she had responded.

Roz raised her eyebrows, accepting the unspoken challenge between them. "Which unit is she from?"

Lock shook his head. "She's a *new* Piece."

Almost imperceptibly, the woman's eyes softened.

"Would you mind prepping a room?" It was a genuine request, not a veiled command. Regardless of the Code, Lock didn't treat his Pinkcaps like property.

"Of course." Roz lightly trailed a fingernail down Lock's cheek. "I'd love to."

"And Roz," there was something unspoken in the look he gave her, something she seemed to understand without further explanation, "play *nice*."

"I always do." Roz winked, caught Grey's hand in her own, and dragged her up the stairs.

- ◆ -

Grey stood in the center of Roz's bedroom, watching as the woman pulled clothes out of her closet and tossed them on the floor. It was a simple room, nothing like the vivacious young woman who occupied it, with only a bed, a chair, a dresser, and a small table.

"Too big," Roz threw a pair of pants on the ground. "Too long, too scandalous." A dress and a sheer, lace shirt followed in quick succession. The woman let out a huff of annoyance and turned her sharp eyes to scan over Grey. "I don't think we'll find anything that fits you in here."

Pieces of Pink

Roz blew past Grey and strode into the hall, hanging a sharp left around the doorframe as she went. In silence, Grey followed her into the room next door.

"I think," Roz smiled as she flicked on the light, "we'll have better luck with Selene's wardrobe."

The room beyond Roz was in complete contrast with her own. Selene—whoever she was—had crammed the small space full of clothes, jewelry, and makeup. An assortment of brushes, combs, scissors, and other hairstyling tools sat on an ornate vanity, and the chair beside the bed was draped in evening gowns. A pile of shoes spilled out of the open closet, and the dresser drawers sat open, too full to close properly.

A part of Grey—the last piece of common courtesy she could muster—wondered who Selene was, and questioned whether she would mind sharing her clothes. But Grey couldn't find the energy to ask.

"Selene's an App," Roz said casually as she beelined for the dresser. "Most of this crap is just given to her by different clients. They expect her to dress a certain way, you know? Maintain appearances and all that bullshit."

The Apps—Apicals, as Grey had always known them—were the most expensive Pinkcaps. And if Selene was an Apical, then she was sure to be stunning, intelligent, and—most importantly—reserved for the exclusive use of Whitecaps, the highest-ranking inhabitants of Citoyen.

Even as the lowest rank of the Color Code, the Pinkcaps still had their own internal hierarchy. Based on the way she dressed, Grey could safely assume that Roz was a Dom, one step below an App. Jesse had been a Rag—an Average—and below him, in the worst position of all, were the Dispensable. Dispensable, or Pences, as they called themselves, were cheap. Most had some kind of mental or physical abnormality, and they were often abused by their clients.

Grey had seen the treatment of the Dispensable firsthand during her rounds as a Redcap, and the memories of it still made her skin crawl. But the worst thing was knowing that if they lived to see old age, all Pinkcaps became Dispensable.

"She's also our resident hairdresser." Roz's voice pulled Grey from her thoughts as the woman waved a hand toward Selene's vanity. "With our hours, it's a lot more convenient than going to a Bluecap, and we don't pay her, so it's technically legal."

When Grey didn't answer, Roz turned her attention to the dresser and began to rummage, irreverently stirring the neatly folded clothes into a heap.

"Here we go!" Roz yanked a gray sweater from the drawer and tossed it across the room.

With Lock's coat still draped over her shoulder, Grey fumbled to free her arms and caught the garment just in time to see a pair of black pants flying toward her.

"Selene hasn't worn these in ages." With a bump of her hip, Roz pushed the drawer half-closed and headed for the door. "She won't even miss them."

Booted feet hammering into the hardwood floor, Roz strode into the hall, not waiting for Grey to follow.

"Your room is on the fourth floor," Roz called over her shoulder. "It's a little bare at the moment, but I'm sure Lock will have things fixed up for you in no time. He's good about that."

The steps creaked underfoot as Grey followed Roz into the stairwell. In the early days, only the first two floors would have been meant for clients, and although the Base had been remarkably well-maintained, the upper floors showed its age. Here and there, obvious repairs had been made: a floorboard that didn't quite fit, a paint job in a slightly different shade, a light fixture too new to match the original pieces.

Pieces of Pink

"Here you go." Roz halted abruptly at the top of the stairs, and Grey almost ran into her back. "This will be your room."

Peaking around Roz's shoulders, Grey stared into the room. It was small, with a pitched ceiling, barely high enough to fit the single bed tucked in the far corner, and the walls were stark and bare.

"Not an ideal design, I know." Roz shrugged as she stepped inside. "But at least you're not next to the bathroom. Plus, it has a nice view."

Grey followed Roz inside and glanced around. Along with the bed, there was a dresser, a chair, and a small nightstand with a lamp. And as Roz had said, the large garret window overlooked a courtyard, just visible in the dim glow of the streetlights.

"All right, then." Roz's eyes glinted playfully, and she grinned. "Let's get you out of those clothes."

Without hesitating, she stepped toward Grey, snatched the pink cap off of her head, and tossed it on the bare mattress. Roz's movements were smooth, almost practiced, as she slid the coat from Grey's shoulders and draped it over a wooden chair.

Instinctively, Grey crossed her arms over her chest, covering as much of herself as she could through the translucent fabric.

"I'm guessing you didn't dress yourself up like this?" Roz asked as she spun Grey around and began to pull the corset laces free. With each tug, Grey felt a gulp of air—air that she didn't know she was missing—rush into her lungs.

"Well, I know Lock didn't make you put this on," Roz continued when Grey didn't answer. "So, what I'd like to know," she pulled the final loop free and turned Grey around to face her, "is how the hell you ended up here."

Grey remained silent.

"But since your new," Roz gripped the top of the busk with her dark nails and unlatched each of the tabs with a soft click, "you're probably smart to keep your mouth shut."

She peeled the corset away from Grey's skin and dropped it on the floor. Immediately, Grey pulled the hand-me-down sweater over her head, grateful that it was long enough to cover her bottom, and shimmied out of the skirt. As she did, the two rings she had stowed in her pocket slipped to the hardwood floor and rolled.

Before Roz had a chance to react, Grey lunged between the woman's legs, snatching up the silver bands before they were lost in the cracks between the boards.

"What the hell?" Roz growled as she stumbled out of the way, but when her eyes fell on the rings in Grey's open palm, her voice softened. "Wedding bands?" she asked.

Grey nodded.

"Since you're new to being a Pinkcap, here's a piece of advice," Roz frowned as if she had bitten into something sour. "The Base doesn't get inspected very often, but when it does, valuables tend to disappear. Beaks take whatever they like."

Beak, the Pinkcap word for a Blackcap, was not new to Grey. Though Jesse hadn't taught her all of the Pinkcap slang—code, really—he had told her a few words, and she had no doubt they would come in handy over the next few days.

With a nod of understanding, Grey slid on the pants Roz had taken from Selene's room and tucked the rings into her pocket.

"So, I guess," a lightness returned to Roz's voice as she gathered up Grey's discarded clothes and draped them over her long arm, "the only thing left to do now is to show you the bathroom and get you some clean sheets."

Pivoting on her toe, the Dom walked out into the hall, and Grey followed her without a word.

- ♦ -

Pieces of Pink

Grey squirmed against the blankets and tugged at her pillow. The sheets—clean and crisp—still retained a pleasant scent of detergent. In the past, Grey would have enjoyed the feeling of a freshly made bed. But after so many weeks of sleeping on the ground, the mattress was too comfortable, and the sheets were too soft.

More likely, it was the absence of Jesse that kept Grey awake. Earlier in the night, when she had closed her eyes, horrible images had flashed through her mind: images of Jesse's blood, his body, the clump of skin and hair that had been plastered to her cheek. And with those memories came tears, some silent, others sobbing.

At one point, she managed to cry herself to sleep. But when she woke and reached across the empty bed for Jesse, she found herself alone, and the truth slammed into her gut with a force that sent her scrambling to the bathroom.

She vomited—though there was no food left in her stomach—and remained curled on the checkered tile floor, clinging to the edge of the toilet, and imagining how things could've ended differently.

Maybe if they had waited an hour longer before leaving their hiding space that morning, or left an hour sooner, maybe if they had cut further south, or maybe if she had just accepted that Jesse was a Pinkcap, and she was a Redcap, Jesse would still be alive.

It wasn't until Grey heard footsteps and voices moving downstairs that she crept back to her bedroom. Curled in the darkness under the covers, she listened as the Pinkcaps found their beds after a long night of work.

Muffled voices crept through the stairwells and floorboards; some laughing, others exhausted. Through the old pipes in the walls, Grey could hear the showers turned on, bathtubs filled, and toilets flushed as the other residents cleaned themselves up and settled in for a morning of sleep.

By the time the voices faded, the pale, pink light of dawn was slipping through the garret window, casting a warm beam of sunlight across the floor. Silently, Grey slipped out of bed and crept barefoot into the hallway and down the stairs. If there were ever a time to explore the Base—to plan an escape—it would be now, while everyone else was too exhausted to care what was going on outside their bedroom doors.

After everything they had been through—everything they had fought for—it would be an insult to Jesse's memory to stay here and become a Pinkcap.

Holding her breath, she made her way to the second floor and slipped into the laundry room. Along with detergent, an ironing board, and an iron, a small toolbox sat on the shelf above the washer and dryer. Carefully, Grey pulled it down and peered inside. Most of the tools were too heavy to take on a long journey—even to use as weapons—but there was a small multi-purpose tool, equipped with the essentials she would need on the road, so she made a mental note and moved on.

From room to room, Grey crept on her toes as she formed her checklist: a first-aid kit, an old pair of women's boots, a basket of clothes for mending, a thick piece of tulle—perfect for making a net—spare blankets, darts from the game room, and even a flask. It would take days to find everything she needed and to learn the schedules of the other Pinkcaps, but she would do it. And when the day came for her to run, she would take what she needed and disappear for good. Whether it ended in escaping Citoyen, or in her death, Grey wasn't entirely sure she cared.

As she descended the grand staircase to the first floor, the sound of the front door handle jiggling froze her in mid-step. Grey stared ahead, heart pounding as the door swung inward, and a small dark shape appeared. Framed by the morning light, she couldn't make out the person's face, only their body. And it was ruined.

The torso and hips lilted to one side at a sharp angle, an indication of severe and untreated scoliosis. Short arms dangled by the figure's side, and the hands—with few fingers between them—were barely more than claws. Whether it was a case of phocomelia, or maybe symbrachydactyly, Grey couldn't tell without her diagnostic tools. But one thing was certain: this Pinkcap was a Pence.

Grey's foot found its place on the next step, and as she moved closer, the figure looked up.

"Who are you?" he said, startled but unafraid.

"Grey Alcott." The words—the only ones she'd spoken since arriving at the Base—sounded stale. "I'm new."

"Well, I'm Arik." He closed the front door, and without the morning light streaming in behind him, she could finally make out his face.

The man was pale, almost sickly looking, with jet black hair that stuck out from under his pink cap and hung over his forehead in thin strands. His face was covered in scars and bruises—some fresh, others still healing—and his small nose looked as though it had been broken more than once. But there was still light in his narrow, black eyes, which tilted up at the corners as he smiled at her.

"Which unit are you from?" he asked as he bent down, unlaced his shoes, and slipped his feet free.

It was the same question Roz had asked Lock.

"I was a Redcap," she answered.

Arik looked up, eyes wide with surprise.

"So, I take it," he said as he picked up his shoes and took a few steps toward her, "you're not quite used to the sleeping schedule around here, then?"

Grey shook her head. "Not yet."

"That's all right," Arik shrugged. "You'll get there eventually. Honestly, sometimes I think it's easier to sleep with the sun shining in on you." His eyes drifted as if he were thinking of faraway things. "It feels safer, you know?"

Grey forced herself to smile, though it made her heart ache to look at this small, broken Piece.

"When did you get here?" Arik stepped up the first few stairs.

"Late last night," Grey answered.

A grin flicked across his face. "So, Lock's home, then?"

Grey nodded.

Arik leaned over the railing and glanced toward the end of the hall as if hoping Lock might appear.

"He's been traveling a lot lately," Arik explained. "We miss having him around."

Seeing no sign of Lock, Arik continued to climb the steps one at a time, carefully gripping the railing to steady his unstable body, and Grey fell into place beside him as he limped his way up.

Even with the help Lock had given Grey and Jesse, the idea of a Pinkcap being able to feel such affection for their own Purplecap seemed strange.

Though Jesse had tried to explain it, Grey still struggled with the reality that all of Lock's money—all of his power—came from the suffering of those beneath him.

"Why do you miss him?" she asked.

"Things aren't as easy when he's not around." Arik shrugged.

"What do you mean?"

"Just the little things," he answered. "It's harder to get a hold of what we need: clothes, medical stuff, someone to talk to a client for us. He always leaves Jax in charge when he's gone, but Jax can only do so much."

Grey nodded as if she understood, but she didn't. Not really.

"Who's Jax?"

"He's one of the Apps. People say he's the best in Citoyen." Arik smiled a little. "I don't know if it's actually true, but I know he's High Chancellor Lachlan's favorite."

She raised an eyebrow. "And he lives here?"

"Mm-hmm," Arik nodded. "He and his girlfriend, Selene. They work together."

Grey tugged at the hem of her sweater. Hopefully, Selene wouldn't mind that Roz had raided her wardrobe.

"I'm guessing they put you on the fourth floor?" Arik asked.

"Yeah," Grey grimaced at the thought of living at the Base permanently, but if everything went smoothly, she wouldn't be here for long. And this time, she would escape without any help but her own. "I'm in the room at the top of the stairs."

Arik nodded knowingly. "I'm right next door. It's a long climb, but it's worth it for the view."

It was impossible not to smile at the man by her side as Grey made her way back up to the fourth floor. Every word was so full of optimism, hope, and appreciation for those around him. And when they reached the top landing and stepped into the hall, Arik paused and reached out a tiny hand.

"It was very nice to meet you, Grey.

"You too." She shook his hand.

"Oh, and breakfast is at noon," he added. "But don't worry, I'll be sure to wake you."

"Thank you." Grey smiled, and Arik disappeared into the adjacent room. Alone again, Grey slipped into her own room and shut the door behind herself. Her escape plan would have to wait.

- ♦ -

As promised, Arik woke Grey for breakfast, though she hadn't been sleeping. Instead, she had been planning her next move, running over the list of items she would need and how she would acquire them. But a meal was the perfect way to determine what food was kept in the large kitchen behind the dining room.

Surrounded by a few dozen groggy strangers, Grey eyed the platters, which had been prepared by a small staff of Bluecaps who worked for Lock. There wasn't an excess of food, but there were a few things that would be useful.

"Eggs?" Arik leaned toward her with a small plate of scrambled eggs stacked in a precarious mound.

Although the eggs would keep, they would be too fragile to bring on a journey. But the cured meat, potatoes, and thick slices of homemade bread would be perfect.

With a tight-lipped smile, Grey took a small scoop and thanked him. She wasn't particularly hungry, but it was important to gather her strength before making a second attempt at escaping Citoyen.

As Grey ate, she scanned the room. Lock was nowhere to be seen, but his Pinkcaps, although tired, had marked his return with her presence. A few pointed at her—not so discreetly—but she pretended not to notice.

"The people here are pretty friendly," Arik said, following her gaze. "Once they get to know you a little, they'll accept you."

She wasn't planning on staying long enough to be accepted, but Grey could see what Arik meant. While the rest of Citoyen lived and worked within the rigid boundaries of the Code, the Pinkcaps didn't seem to care about their own hierarchy. Pences, Apps, Rags, and Doms sat side-by-side, chatting in friendly conversation, with no clear rationale behind their seating choices.

"Good morning, Lydie," Arik said, smiling across the table as a young woman with thick auburn hair plopped down, put her elbows on the table, and sleepily rested her head in her hands.

Lydie smiled back, her expression dazed.

"Thank you," she whispered.

Grey frowned and glanced at Arik. The woman was obviously high, but no one seemed to care.

"Eggs?" he asked the redhead and ignored Grey's glance.

"No," Lydie sighed dreamily. "The chickens will miss them."

Arik tried again. "How about some toast?"

"Waffles," Lydie murmured, her glazed eyes drifting to Grey.

"No waffles today," Arik shook his head, and Lydie's eyebrows pinched together in confusion.

"But I can smell them," Lydie said. "I'm sure they're here."

Grey exchanged a furtive glance with Arik, then took a piece of toast and set it on Lydie's plate.

"There you go." She did her best to smile. "Last waffle left."

Lydie looked down at the toast and grinned.

"Awesome." She picked up a fork and knife and slowly cut the bread in half. "I love waffles."

Content with the food on her plate, Lydie began to eat, and Arik raised his eyebrows in surprise.

"I've never tried that before," he whispered.

Grey shrugged. "It worked on a patient I had once."

Arik's head cocked to the side, and he was just opening his mouth to ask a question when a cold voice—directly over Grey's head—interrupted them.

"Who are you? And why are you wearing my clothes?"

Grey turned around and froze.

Selene was gorgeous. Her jade-green eyes stood out bright against her dark, brown skin, and a halo of black corkscrew curls, meticulously styled with honey highlights, framed her face.

"I'm Grey," she answered, then glanced down at her clothes. "Lock asked Roz to—"

At the mention of Roz's name, Selene held up her palm, cutting Grey short.

"Fucking Roz," Selene hissed and stormed over to a table on the opposite side of the room, where a man—as handsome as Selene was beautiful—sat talking with a Dom.

Without hesitation, Selene interrupted the conversation, and while her words were too quiet to hear, her gestures were unmistakable. Selene flung an accusing finger in Grey's direction, and the man turned to see where she was pointing. His chiseled face was topped with a crown of chestnut hair, and his eyes—though darker than Selene's—were a brilliant green. Whether he had a personality to match his girlfriend's, Grey wasn't sure, but even without asking, she could tell this man was Jax.

A few moments of heated discussion passed before Selene finally settled into a seat. The woman was obviously still fuming, but she was trying to keep it to herself.

"Don't worry," Arik said. "It's not about you."

Grey raised her eyebrows.

"Roz has a habit of—" Arik paused. "Well, you've met her. She's very open. Selene," he nodded across the room, "is not."

It was easy to see that it wasn't Grey's clothes that had upset Selene, it was the fact that someone—specifically Roz—had been in her room and invaded her personal space without permission. And considering the life of an Apical Pinkcap, Grey couldn't blame her.

It was nearly sunset when the Pinkcaps began to prepare for the night. Some, like Arik, wore simple clothes. Others, like Jax and Selene, dressed in elegant formalwear. But Grey remained in her borrowed sweater and pants.

No one had approached her about working yet, so as far as she was concerned, no one would notice her absence, at least not for a while. And by then, she would be long gone.

Once the house was empty of all but Roz—who was sleeping off her dayshift—Grey made her way from room to room, filling an old backpack with the essentials for the journey. She had a pocket knife, the med-kit, a coat, socks, boots, and every other useful item she could squeeze into the small satchel.

All that remained was to steal some food and sneak out the door before any of the Pinkcaps returned. If she could manage that, nothing but a bullet would stop her from crossing the border and leaving Citoyen forever.

Halfway down the staircase, a sound on the front porch sent her receding into the darkness of the second-floor landing. Grey watched, holding her breath as the wooden door creaked open, but when she saw the man who crawled over the threshold, she gasped and dropped her bag.

Arik was on his hands and knees, inching his way into the Base, tears streaming down his cheeks.

Instantly, Grey shucked off her jacket, ran down the stairs, and crouched beside him.

"What happened?" she asked, quickly assessing any damage she could see with her eyes. "Where are you hurt?"

His nose had clearly been broken, and a ribbon of dried blood still clung over his lips and chin. His arms and hands seemed to work well enough—all things considered—but still, he was crawling.

"Is it your legs?"

"No," Arik gasped in pain.

His ribs, then. "Are your ribs broken?"

Arik nodded. "I think so."

"Let me help you," Grey reached for him, but he shook his head.

"Roz," he sobbed. "Get Roz."

Carefully stepping over him, Grey closed the door and draped her jacket over his back before sprinting upstairs. On the second floor, she grabbed her bag. And skipping two steps at a time, she rushed to the fourth floor and chucked it under her bed before descending to Roz's room.

When she reached the Dom's door she pounded once, a courtesy warning she had used as a Redcap, before flinging it open.

Completely naked, Roz sat up and snarled, "What the fuck?"

"Arik needs you."

Without demanding any further explanation, Roz leapt from her bed, grabbed a black robe from the back of the door, and flew down the stairs with Grey close at her heels. But as she neared the landing of the second floor, Roz halted, quickly smoothing her hair, as if to erase the panic dripping from her.

She spun on Grey. "Be calm for him."

Grey nodded, ignoring the irony, and watched in silence as Roz quickly made her way to Arik's side and knelt down.

Roz tutted, and her shoulders stooped forward in dismay as she took in Arik's situation. Then, she gently reached out to stroke his misshapen hand. Arik was still sobbing.

"It's all right," Roz cooed. "We've been here before."

As she spoke, his sobs lessened, then faded to whimpers.

"You know what we'll do, right?"

Pained, Arik nodded and reached a trembling hand for her knee.

"That's it," Roz encouraged as she helped to steady him. "Nice and slow."

Grey watched as Roz eased her forearms under Arik's armpits and pulled him upwards in a carefully choreographed embrace. How many times this had happened before, Grey couldn't tell, but it was clearly too often.

Once Arik was on his feet, Roz looped an arm around his curved shoulders. "This is the worst part, I know," she assured him, "but we'll get you upstairs and clean you up, and then you can rest."

In as smooth a motion as she could manage, Roz lifted Arik into her arms and cradled him against her chest as she steadily ascended the stairs. Step after step, she carried him up until finally, they reached the fourth floor.

Pieces of Pink

"I'll get some warm water and washcloths," Grey said as Roz carefully laid Arik in his bed.

Roz didn't answer. She simply nodded. The full weight of the woman's attention rested solely on Arik, and Grey doubted there was anything that could shake it.

Alone, Grey made her way into the bathroom and found a small bucket with clean rags, and a few medical supplies tucked in the closet. Her heart sank as she saw just how sparse the kit was. There were no bandages, barely any antibiotic ointment or disinfectants, no gloves, and an empty bottle of anti-inflammatories. Sighing, Grey filled the bucket with steaming water, and with the few available supplies from the closet, she brought it back to Arik's room.

"Set it on the dresser," Roz instructed, and Grey obeyed.

With her mouth clenched in a hard line, Roz turned her back from the crumpled form, lying in the bed, and dipped a clean washcloth into the steaming water.

"They didn't pay." The words barely made a sound as they slipped from Arik's lips, but Roz heard them well enough. She froze, and the look of rage that flashed through her eyes was enough to make Grey step back. But when the Dom turned to face her patient, her expression melted back into a look of sympathy and care.

"It's all right," Roz assured him as she gently wiped at the dried blood from his chin. "Jax will make sure everything is accounted for. You just rest."

"I—" Grey stuttered, and Roz looked up. "I was a Redcap." She offered up that precious information, that story that still felt too raw to share. "Before I came here, I was a Redcap."

Roz blinked.

"I could examine his injuries."

"Thank you." This time, Roz did not meet Grey's eyes, and when she turned her attention back to Arik, there was something icy in her tone. "But we can take it from here."

Annelise Driscoll

With a nod, Grey backed out of the room but paused a moment before returning to her own.

"I'm here," she offered softly, "if you need me."

With that, she turned away, slipped into her room, and sank onto the bed. Gripping the edge of the mattress, she stared down at the floor. That morning, becoming a Pinkcap had seemed like an insult to Jesse's memory. But now, seeing how little care they were given—how few medical supplies they had—Grey wondered if the greater insult would be to leave them behind. Tomorrow, Grey resolved, she would find Lock, and they would fix this.

THREE

Determined, Grey marched across the dining room and knocked on Lock's office door.

"Yes?" To her surprise, his response was instantaneous.

Lock's work had kept him out of the Base ever since Grey's arrival two days prior, and his sleeping schedule was anyone's guess. A part of her hadn't expected him to be home at all.

With a deep breath, Grey pushed open the door and stepped inside. The office was much smaller than she had expected. It was an unassuming room off the side of the kitchen, just large enough to fit a desk, a pair of chairs, and a few high shelves, full of books and papers.

"Please, sit down." He waved her forward without looking up. "I'll just be a minute."

In what little space there was, Grey squeezed around the chair opposite him and took a seat. Even with the chairback pressed against the bookshelf behind her, Grey's knees still brushed the front of the desk as she watched Lock work. He scribbled notes in a small ledger, cross-referencing a larger notebook until finally, he stacked his paperwork and slid it into a drawer.

"So," Lock looked up with a smile and clasped his hands over the old wooden desk, "I see you've decided to stay with us?"

"I—" Grey hesitated, then sat up a little straighter.

"Don't worry." Lock's eyes were bright but gentle. "You're not in trouble."

Grey relaxed—barely.

"And after everything you've been through," he frowned, "I can hardly blame you for trying to escape again. Love is a difficult thing."

She swallowed.

"Even more so when it's illegal to feel it." There was an edge to his tone, and Grey had the distinct sense that Lock was talking about something greater than Jesse.

"How did you know?" Grey had been so careful to make sure no one was watching when she'd gathered her supplies the previous night. Her eyes darted to the corners of the room, searching for cameras, but there were none.

Lock sighed, "Arik may be a Dispensable, but he's not an idiot. He saw your clothes and your bag."

A lump formed in Grey's throat.

"He was afraid for you." His gaze was firm but reassuring. "And he told me because he didn't want you to get caught or killed. Of course, he doesn't know that you have a proclivity—let's say—for covering long distances without being noticed."

Grey's throat went dry. Even with a broken nose and cracked ribs, Arik had noticed her. He had worried and wanted to keep her safe, and Grey couldn't help but feel a pang of guilt for being so willing to leave the Base behind.

Lock raised his black eyebrows slightly as if hoping she might tell him more, but Grey kept her mouth shut.

"And since you didn't ask me for help with last night's escape plan," Lock smirked, "is it safe to assume that you didn't come here to discuss treason?"

"No," Grey lifted her chin. "I'm here to talk about medical supplies. For being the best brothel in the capital, this place is outrageously understocked. There's nothing here for emergencies."

Lock shifted in his chair, and somehow Grey found the voice of the Redcap she had been.

"You have Pinkcaps living under your care who need regular medical attention, and there are less supplies here than you would find in a household medicine cabinet." She persisted. "Hell, a Greencap's garden would be more useful than the med-kit I used last night."

It was the most that Grey had said since she'd lost Jesse, and the effort of it almost took her breath away, but Lock didn't seem surprised. He simply tilted his head to the side, listening.

"Honestly," she pushed onward, "I can't even think of a good explanation for it. I've done plenty of rounds to visit Pinkcaps and provide treatment, and—"

"And you always brought your own medical supplies." He cut her off. "Correct?"

Grey frowned but conceded. "Yes."

"I agree with you completely." Lock's face grew serious, his blue eyes dark. "But getting clearance for high-quality medicine and supplies—even regular appointments with Redcaps—it's difficult."

"Why?"

Her eyes narrowed on his. It was common knowledge that Lock was one of the wealthiest Purplecaps in Citoyen, and of all people, it should be easy for him to get whatever he needed.

"In the months that you and Jesse were trying to escape," Lock lowered his voice, "the Whitecaps started diverting medical supplies to the Blackcaps."

Grey shook her head in confusion. "What for? We're not at war."

"Not officially," Lock answered. "But there are rumors."

"Rumors of what?"

Lock leaned forward, but a knock interrupted their conversation. Before he could even utter a response, the door swung opened.

"Oh." Jax stopped in the doorframe with a box in his arms. "I thought we had a meeting."

"We do." Lock offered him a warm smile. "Come in."

Grey watched the App as he stepped gracefully inside and shut the door. Even in the cramped space, his movements were fluid, like an expertly choreographed dance. In a way, he reminded her of the surgeons she'd observed during her classes. Every movement was precise and calculated.

Jax glanced between Lock and Grey. Up close, it was easy to see why he was an Apical. Strands of copper ran through his brown hair, shining where the light touched it. His jaw was chiseled, and his square chin had a slight cleft in its center, barely more than a dimple. His pink lips were full and smooth, and his skin was flawless, aside from a light dusting of freckles that ran across the bridge of his nose. But his eyes were the most striking feature of all. Dark and sea green, they shone with a hard intelligence.

Then again, to hold the attention of a man like the High Chancellor, Jax would not only have to be gorgeous, he would have to be brilliant. For Whitecaps, it was common to bring Pinkcaps to social functions to display their enormous wealth and power. Those exceptional Pinkcaps were expected to be clever and witty, and naturally, the High Chancellor would only have the best.

"What's that?" Lock nodded toward the box, and Grey followed his gaze.

"Selene pulled together some clothes that she doesn't want anymore." Jax handed the box to Lock without a second glance at Grey. "For the Rougie."

Grey frowned. She had been called Rougie before. It was Piece slang for a Redcap. But as a rule, Pinkcaps only used the term amongst themselves. To a Redcap's face, it was meant as an insult.

Pieces of Pink

"Well, in that case," Lock peeked inside the box and shrugged as if he hadn't heard Jax, then passed it over to Grey, "this is yours."

It was heavier than Grey had expected, and as the weight of it settled into her lap, a different heaviness grew in her chest. These were her clothes now—the clothes of a Pinkcap—and whether the other Pinkcaps called her a Redcap, a Piece, or a Rougie, it didn't matter. There would be no more lab coats or ID cards, only hand-me-downs and a tracker chip.

"Thank you." Grey forced the words through her teeth, but her throat was tight, and her expression was a grimace at best.

"You've been wearing the same clothes for three days," Jax's frowned down at her. "Selene didn't just do it for you."

"On that note," Lock rose and stuffed his hands in his pockets. The motion was casual, but there was a point to it—a command to end the hostility—and Jax backed down.

"Jax and I have some paperwork to go over," he said. "But, if you wouldn't mind, I'd appreciate a list of those supplies we were talking about. Drop it off later. I'll do my best to make sure I get what you need."

"Of course," Grey nodded.

"Excellent, thank you." He glanced at Jax. "Oh! And I almost forgot. I'll be in and out of the Base for the next few weeks, so Jax will be in charge of your training."

Grey's stomach knotted, and she barely managed to swallow the bile that rose in her throat with the thought of working as a Pinkcap.

"I think we'll have you shadow with Lydie—she's one of our Averages—and also Roz. And once you have a feel for the policies, you'll be all set to start working."

The warmth leaked out of Grey's hands, and sympathy crept into Lock's gaze. It was the same look she had seen in the car on the way from the border.

"But thank you again for your suggestions. I think you'll be an asset to the Base."

"Thanks," Grey mumbled as she stood, and Jax stepped aside just enough for her to skirt around the shelf. When she slipped out the door, the App closed it behind her with a loud thump.

-◆-

When Grey emerged at the top of the stairs, she glanced down the hall. The door of Arik's room stood slightly ajar, and through the crack, she could see Roz slouching in a chair beside the bed. Setting down the box of clothes, Grey gently pushed the door open and peaked inside.

Roz stirred at the sound of the old hinges and turned to press a finger to her lips, silencing Grey. Over Roz's shoulder, Grey could see Arik sleeping, a rare reprieve for someone with broken ribs, and she paused in the doorframe.

Silently, Roz stood and crept to the door, pushing Grey out into the hall alongside her. Using both hands, she eased the door shut and tugged Grey further down the hall. It wasn't until they had passed the bathroom that Roz stopped abruptly and turned on Grey with her arms crossed over her chest.

"So, you were a Redcap?" Roz's voice was cold, but not icy as Jax's had been.

Grey nodded. "Yes."

"What the hell happened to land you here?"

"Nothing good." Grey held her ground.

Thoughtfully, Roz nodded, and her posture relaxed.

"How's he doing?" Grey glanced back toward Arik's door. "Did you call a medic?"

Pieces of Pink

"After it happens so many times, you learn what to do." Roz scoffed, "I mean, how often did you treat the same Piece twice?"

Grey shifted on her feet. Jesse had been one of the only ones she'd visited more than once. At first, it had only been because her supervisor had misdiagnosed him, and Grey had come back with antibiotics to keep the whole brothel from catching strep throat. After that, she had simply found excuses to visit.

"It gets to a point," Roz continued, "where there's nothing you people can do to help. With cracked ribs, you just poke and probe, and we already take enough of that from our clients."

"What about painkillers?" Grey suggested. "If you call another Redcap, they could at least give him something for the pain."

"They won't give them out anymore," Roz scowled. "They say it's because too many Pieces abuse them. And you can hardly blame them. I mean, have you seen Lydie?"

Grey *had* seen Lydie, and one thing was sure: regardless of any shortages, the woman clearly hadn't run out.

"Well, where does she get her supplies?"

"I don't ask," Roz said. "Some things are better left unknown."

"It doesn't make sense." Grey shook her head. "There are rehab facilities for people like Lydie, and taking away medications from people who genuinely need them is just—"

"It's all lies," Roz cut her off impatiently. "It's not about drug addiction or rehab. That's all just some convenient bullshit that helps the Whitecaps cover up the truth from the other caps. They've started rationing medical supplies. And whenever rationing starts, Pieces are always the first to notice."

"I don't understand what's changed," Grey frowned. "We haven't had medical supply rations in years."

"Where have you been the last two months?" Roz threw her hands in the air. "Living under a rock?"

Grey glanced at the floor and didn't answer.

Without pressing her for more information, Roz raised a perfect, black eyebrow and explained.

"The High Chancellor is dying," she said. "He has no children. No legitimate children, anyway. And the other Whitecaps are stockpiling resources."

"What for?" Grey asked.

Roz shrugged. "To buy each other out," she sighed. "You know how it is. Everything's about money and power, and who has what. If one Whitecap can get the majority of medical supplies or guns, or whatever, the other Whitecaps will *need* them. Whoever can buy up the commodities will become the new High Chancellor."

"How do you know all this?" Grey frowned.

"I paid attention in school." Roz rolled her eyes.

"No, not that." Grey shook her head. "How do you know the High Chancellor's dying?"

"The Apps keep us all in the loop," Roz answered. "And there are plenty of Whitecaps with kinks." Her lip curled in disgust. "You'd be amazed what people will tell you when they're begging you to piss on them."

"You—"

Roz waved a hand in the air, silencing Grey as her honey eyes narrowed, and her ruby mouth twitched up in a smile. Like a cat, the woman took a step closer and trailed the backs of her fingers down Grey's cheeks. Grey shivered, and Roz leaned forward until her lips hovered, mere millimeters from Grey's right ear.

"You'll do shit you never even dreamed of, Rougie."

The word didn't have the same bite when Roz said it. From her lips, it was the name of a lover, not an outsider.

"And if I were you," she purred, "I would get some sleep. You're in for a long week."

Grey stared in silence as Roz strode back down the hall and disappeared into Arik's room. There was something wild about the woman that she couldn't quite put her finger on—something that flirted with the edge of sanity—and whatever it was, she liked it.

- ♦ -

"This is your schedule for the next week." Jax pushed a piece of paper across the table, and Grey looked down at the neat handwriting. "Since you'll probably be a Rag, I'll have you shadow Lydie tonight. There's an old Perp who enjoys—"

"It means Purplecap," Roz interrupted over the din of voices in the dining room, and Jax shot her an annoyed glare.

"There's an old Purplecap," Jax repeated himself, "who enjoys spending time with Lydie, and she doesn't mind extra company."

"Her name's Ama," Roz cut in. "She gets a real kick out of the physical pleasures of life."

Roz glanced at Lydie, who was seated beside Jax. The Rag's eyes closed, and she bobbed her head to music no one else could hear.

"And the metaphysical pleasures too." Roz tapped the side of her temple and wiggled her eyebrows. The implication of her words was clear enough to Grey. Ama was Lydie's dealer—one of them, at least—and that meant she might have a link to medical supplies.

"Can I finish?" Jax scowled at the Dom.

Roz threw her hands up defensively. "Just trying to help."

With an impatient sigh, Jax turned his attention back to Grey.

"I don't expect you to learn much from Lydie," he admitted. "But Ama has a thing for training new Pinkcaps, and she's good at it, so listen to her."

"She certainly taught us a thing or two." Roz grinned and winked at Jax. "Do you remember that first week with you and Selene? When we all—"

"Yes, Roz," Jax cut her off. "I remember."

Roz's eyes shimmered as she puckered her aubergine lips and blew a kiss across the table. Grey lifted her brows and glanced between the pair, but Jax ignored her and pointed to the next date on the schedule.

"After tonight, you'll spend the rest of your week with Roz."

"I thought you said I'd be a Rag," Grey frowned.

"Probably," Jax nodded. "But most of the Rag's clients don't appreciate onlookers."

"But, mine do," Roz smirked. "And since Arik can't work, I need someone to fill in as my assistant."

"Isn't he a Pence, though?" Grey asked.

It was one thing to shadow a Dom temporarily, but it was another thing to end up with a broken nose or cracked ribs before her first week was even up.

Jax scowled, "Is that a problem?"

"Don't worry," Roz said before Grey could answer. "Arik wasn't with a Dom when he got hurt. Unfortunately, we don't need assistants every night, and if no one asks for his help," she shrugged, "he's stuck as a Pence for the night."

"Lock usually asks the Doms to give Pences preference as their assistants," Jax explained. "It leaves them some time to recuperate between shifts."

"Most Doms," Roz's glare narrowed on Jax, "don't need to be asked. We give them preference because we're not assholes."

"Jax!" A voice shot across the dining room, and Grey turned to see Selene rushing through the doorway.

The App was wearing a green sundress—the same color as her eyes—and she clutched a small white envelope in one hand. In her other, she held a satin gown.

"Damn," Roz whistled. "That's new."

Selene whirled on Roz.

"Keep your claws off of my clothes," she snapped, curls bouncing around her carefully made-up face. "I know you were in my room the other night. My drawers were a mess."

"Your drawers are always a mess," Roz smirked at her own innuendo and arched her brow in a silent challenge.

Selene's lips curled back over her perfect teeth, but instead of fighting back, she spun on Jax and held up the envelope.

"Change of plans," she said. "They've requested us for the garden party, not just the gala. We have to leave. *Now*."

With a jolt, Jax shoved back from the table and stood.

"Roz, you can handle the rest of this, right?" he asked with an anxious edge to his voice that had not been there before.

"Handle what?" Roz asked. "I think it's pretty self-explanatory."

"Just," Jax huffed in frustration as he backpedaled out of the dining room, "tell her when to be ready and what to wear."

When Jax was out of site, Roz looked down at the schedule and rolled her eyes.

"You can read, right?" she asked.

"Of course." Grey nodded.

"Excellent," the Dom grinned. "In that case, be ready when the schedule says to be ready, and don't forget to wear clothes."

"Thank you," a hint of sarcasm crept into Grey's voice. "I'll try to remember that."

Feral glee flashed in Roz's eyes, and she smiled.

"I think we'll get along just fine," she said. "And once you're trained up, people will forget you're a Rougie. After all, we were all new once."

Grey's smile faltered a little as she glanced around the room. Most of the Pinkcaps were around her age. But in the few days since her arrival, Roz and Arik were the only two she had spent any real time with. And most of their interactions had been coincidences.

"So, did you all train together?" Grey asked.

"No," Roz shook her head. "There are four or five different groups that arrived at different times."

Roz turned to look at a small cluster of Pieces on the far side of the room.

"Like, Nic." She pointed out a Dom with dark, wavy hair that fell to his jawline.

Beside him sat two brothers with deep olive skin and inky black hair. Physically, the men were identical in every way, but one—affectionately leaning into Nic's side—was dressed as an App, and the other, as a Dom.

"He—and Megz—came up with the twins," Roz explained.

Across from Nic and the twins, a small woman sat laughing. Her hair was soft brown with highlights, but when she turned her head, Grey saw that her lip was severely cleft. Below the nostril, the woman's teeth grew in a cluster, and her nose—flat without the full support of her septum—twisted to the side.

It was no secret that Lachlan had made life easier on the Pinkcaps in the decades since he had become High Chancellor, but still, the discrepancies between the caps were painfully obvious.

Born into another color, Megz would have been provided with immediate access to the best surgeons and healthcare. But as a Pinkcap, she had simply been forced to live with her condition.

"But I grew up with Arik, Jax, and Selene," Roz went on. "And Lydie trained with us later."

They both glanced at the redhead—still lost in a drug trip—as she swayed back and forth.

"Lydie came from a different Perp," Roz explained. "She was transferred over to Lock once she was old enough to start working. But she came to the Base at the same time as we did. So, for now, we're the oldest ones here. Speaking of age," Roz's eyes narrowed. "What are you? Like, twenty-five?

Grey nodded.

Pieces of Pink

"So, it's safe to assume you're not a virgin anymore, right?"

Heat rose in Grey's cheeks. "No," she shook her head. "I'm not."

"Good." Roz's shoulders relaxed.

"Why?"

"It means there won't be a bid on for your first night." Roz's lips twisted in disgust. "There are some sick fucks out there who pay fortunes for virgins. But we have certainly done our fair share to make sure the Rags and Pences never have to go to auction."

Grey's eyes widened at the implication, but Roz laughed.

"Trust me, if you were a virgin and you didn't want to be auctioned, even Jax would take care of you, no questions asked."

"But what about the Apps?" Grey asked. "You'll only do it for Rags and Pences?"

Roz frowned. "There's no choice for them. If you want to be an App, you have to go to auction. If you don't want to go to auction, Dom is the highest rank you can have."

"Is that why you're a Dom?"

"No." The word was gentle, but Roz's eyes were dark. "No one really starts as a Dom. It's something you become. I was trained as an App . . ." her voice trailed for a moment, "but it wasn't for me."

"Oh."

Roz smiled, but the light didn't touch her eyes.

"And on that note, I should probably bring Arik some food." She swung her long legs over the bench and stood. "So, if I don't see you before you leave, have a good night, and good luck with Ama."

"Thanks." Grey forced a tight-lipped smile.

"Bye, Lydie." Roz blew Lydie a kiss—it went unnoticed—and beelined from the dining room.

Once Roz was out of sight, Grey slipped away from Lydie and made her way to the little room beside the kitchen. She knocked, and when there was no answer, she opened the door. Lock's office was empty.

With a sigh, Grey reached into her pocket and pulled out the list she had made for him. Roz's hint about Ama's drug use had been clear enough, but if Lock could get labeled medications—obtained from a Redcap pharmacist—it would be better than resorting to the black market.

Grabbing a paperweight from the corner of his desk, she laid the list down, secured it, and left. Whether or not Lock would actually be able to get the supplies, she had no idea, but it was worth a shot.

- ♦ -

In the full-length bathroom mirror, Grey's clothes were utterly ordinary. She had found a cream top and a simple black skirt in Selene's box of hand-me-downs, and even though the outfit had barely been worn, it still felt strange to see herself wearing someone else's things. Without her hat, there was no indication that Grey was a Pinkcap; but she didn't feel like a Redcap either.

"Ready?" Lydie's voice—dreamy and lethargic—curled under the door. "We should probably go."

"Coming." With a sigh, Grey grabbed her pink beanie off of the counter, pulled it over her head, and opened the bathroom door.

In the hall, Lydie leaned into the wall as if she couldn't quite remember how to stand on her own. Although she was more alert than she had been at breakfast, her eyes were still sleepy and glazed.

"You look nice." Lydie slurred and slowly extended her arm to link elbows with Grey.

"Thank you," Forcing herself to smile, Grey staggered as the redhead leaned heavily against her. "You look nice too."

Lydie giggled at the thought as they trudged down the stairs. "I always look like this."

"Oh," Grey frowned. "Okay."

Pieces of Pink

"But, I'm usually by myself." Lydie reached for the front door of the Base and pulled. "I wonder if we look different together."

"I don't know," Grey shrugged. "Maybe."

A chill ran down Grey's neck as they walked down the steps and into the alley. It had been days since she'd left the Base, and even longer since she'd walked freely through the streets of the city, and there was something off-putting about the silence around her.

The streets were quiet, apart from the stream of Pinkcaps tricking out of brothels. By this time of night, most people were at home with their families, finishing dinner or watching the news. And those who were planning to hire a Piece had either booked in advance or would wait until the rest of the world had drifted off to sleep before creeping into the arms of a Pinkcap.

It was strange to think of all the Pieces just beginning their shifts for the night. Somewhere across the city, Selene and Jax were working a party for the Whitecaps. They were probably being passed off from one hand to the next—like a cocktail glass—or stuck on the arm of their client like a shiny jewel for others to admire. Either way, it sounded better than being a Pence or a Rag.

For Pinkcaps like Arik and Megz, there were no guarantees of safety unless they were with a Dom. And Roz—wherever she was—seemed more than capable of taking care of herself.

"Here we are." Lydie's voice was almost ethereal in the darkness as she stopped in front of an old stone building and pulled Grey up the tall stoop. But before they even reached the top step, the front door flew open, and a short woman appeared in the doorframe.

She was old and draped in floor-length silk robes. Gaudy rings shone on each of her gnarled fingers, and a garland of beads clacked around her wrinkled neck. On her head, the woman wore an ornate purple turban, and a frizzy burst of orange hair stuck out beneath it.

"Lydie!" The woman gestured dramatically, then turned her attention to Grey. "And you must be Lock's new Piece. What's your name, sweetheart?"

"Grey."

"Well, it's lovely to meet you, Grey. I'm Amaryllis, but you can call me Ama." She bowed her head slightly. "And Redcap or no, we'll make you a proper Pinkcap in no time."

Grey forced a smile and climbed the final steps to the door. When she reached Ama, she could see makeup caked into the deep agelines that cut across the woman's face. Ama's eyebrows—what was left of them—were penciled in with practiced strokes, and her bright, red lipstick bled into the wrinkles around her thin lips.

"Come in, come in," she simpered with a sweep of her arms. "Don't be shy."

Without hesitating, Lydie slipped inside, and with a deep breath, Grey followed.

The foyer of the apartment was draped in swaths of royal purple, orange, and red fabric, and large floor-pillows were piled in every corner. Beaded curtains hung in the doorways between the rooms, and they jingled lightly when Ama passed by.

"Lydie," Ama smiled, "Go get my box—you know where it is—and bring it here."

Obediently, Lydie disappeared through a beaded curtain.

"Grey, love," Ama reached out and clasped Grey's clammy hands in her own. "Oh, you're trembling! Are you cold? Here, let me get you a sweater."

Ama dropped Grey's hands and turned toward the closet.

"No, thank you," Grey said. "I'm not cold."

"What is it then?" Ama's lips curled up at the corners. "I hope you're not nervous, dear. After all, you're here to learn how to act, not how to fuck."

Grey raised her eyebrows.

"Oh, Jax." Ama scoffed. "He never explains anything, does he?"

At that moment, Lydie burst through the curtain, and the beads shivered up and down the doorframe. There was a small tin box in her hands, which she carefully held out to Ama as though passing over a small baby bird.

"He had to leave for work," Grey said. "So, Roz to fill me in."

"Well, that explains it." When Ama smiled, her dried lipstick cracked. "Thank you, Lydie. Go find yourself a comfortable spot. I'll be with you in just a moment."

Dreamily, Lydie tripped off toward a mound of pillows and sank into them. In silence, Grey watched as Ama popped open the tin and removed an eyedropper and a tiny slip of white paper, no larger than her fingertip.

"You're here to learn to compartmentalize," Ama said as she unscrewed the lid on the eyedropper. Holding the slip of paper with her pointer finger, Ama squeezed a tiny drop of clear liquid onto its surface and walked over to Lydie. "Open up."

Lydie's eyes were still glassy—from whatever she'd taken that morning—as she tipped her head back and stuck out her tongue. Carefully, Ama placed the paper in Lydie's mouth and turned back to Grey.

"Most of us," Ama glanced pointedly at Lydie, "need something to take the edge off every once in a while. But it's better if you don't depend too much on substances."

With that, she packed away the eyedropper into the tin, closed the lid with a sharp click, and slipped it into the pocket of her robe.

"So, tonight," draping an arm over Grey's shoulders, the old woman led her into the far room, "you're going to build an alter-ego for yourself."

Grey glanced back over her shoulder at Lydie, who was sprawled on the pillows and gazing up at the ceiling in awe. It wasn't compartmentalizing or building an alter-ego that worried her. As a

Redcap, she had already learned to tuck away her emotions. What worried her was what the rest of the world would see when they looked at her, and how it would make them treat her.

But when Ama drew back the beaded curtain, Grey found herself face-to-face with her own reflection. The entire room, from floor to ceiling, was covered in mirrors. In the corner, a small vanity, littered with makeup and powder brushes, sat crammed beside a rack of costumes. A few of the outfits were like the clothes that Ama herself wore, but others were more suited to Roz.

"Look at yourself in the mirrors." Ama positioned Grey so that she could see herself from all angles and stepped away. "What do you see?"

Turning her neck, Grey looked at her reflection. She was thinner than she had been when she and Jesse had first run away together. Too thin, really. And her shoulders slumped forward as if the cap sitting on her head was crushing her under its weight. There was no smile on her pallid face, and her brown eyes looked sunken in defeat. She bit her lip. Exhaustion lingered in every expression she made.

"I see someone whose courage is just a little frayed." The old woman's voice was gentle.

It was true. As a Redcap, she had been confident, so confident that she had honestly believed she and Jesse could escape Citoyen without being caught. Now, she wasn't even sure she could survive the next few weeks, let alone a lifetime.

"And it's perfectly all right to feel exhausted and unsure of yourself. It's all right to feel afraid," Ama assured. "Just don't let the clients see it. Whether you're tired, or hungry, or your heart is breaking inside your chest, you can never let them know."

Frowning, Grey pulled her eyes away from her reflection and turned to face Ama.

"As a Redcap, I'm sure you put on a different face for your patients. As a Pinkcap," Ama crossed the room and paused in front of the vanity, "you'll do the exact same thing, only your mask will look a little different."

The woman selected a tray, full of lipstick tubes and slid it from the vanity.

"And I don't know about you," the old woman returned to Grey and extended the collection of samples, "but for me, the right shade of lipstick can set the mood for a whole day."

Grey scanned the colors. Ranging from red to purple and silver to black, there were too many shades to choose from. After a moment, Ama sighed thoughtfully and reached for a muted raspberry red.

"Here, try this." She offered the lipstick to Grey. "And when you put it on, become someone new. Don't be calm, be coy. Don't be serious, be sweet. Don't be afraid, be fierce."

Heaving a sigh, Grey took the tube of lipstick and stepped toward the mirror. Coy, sweet, fierce; it was a lot to fake. With a pop, she pulled off the lid and twisted the stick upward. Then, she leaned toward the mirror and carefully drew the color over her lips.

The motion felt strange, somehow. As a Redcap, she had rarely ever worn makeup, but even without a practiced hand, the color slid on smoothly. When she was finished, she stared at her mouth in silence. Where her lips had been thin and tight, they now looked fuller, softer somehow, in the dim-lit room.

"Of course, pretending to be sexy is the hardest part of the act," Ama patted Grey's shoulder and smiled. "After all, you won't feel your best every single day, but you'll still have to work. So, the first thing to remember is: keep your chin down and your eyes up."

Grey obeyed.

"Perfect," Ama nodded. "Now, let's have a little smile at the corner of the lips."

Her cheeks twitched up, but her eyes didn't match expression.

"The eyes feel hard at first," it was as if the old woman had read her mind, "but they're the most important part. You have to make them sparkle."

Ama reached out a wrinkled finger and touched Grey's lower lashes, tickling the sensitive skin.

"Feel this here?" she asked, "That tear-duct sensation?"

Grey nodded.

"Tighten it a little."

When Grey tried, the smile dropped.

"Ah, ah," Ama warned, "not too much. It should barely be perceptible. And don't forget your lips! There, that's it. Now, look in the mirror."

When she looked, Grey saw a flash of the Pinkcap Ama had created. For a moment, there was no hint of the heartbroken woman she was on the inside; no trace of the husband she had just lost. But in an instant, the false smile faded, and with a blink, Grey returned to herself.

"That's the key." Ama's own eyes had grown sad as she watched. "Practice every day. Learn to wear your mask without a mirror. Do it until it becomes second nature.

"And when the night is over, and it's time for you to go home, take off your makeup and find your true self again. Cross your eyes, stick out your tongue, make yourself as ugly and horrible as you possibly can. And once you remember who you really are," Ama patted Grey's cheek, "only then do you sleep."

-♦-

At dawn, they returned to the Base. While Ama had given Grey hours and hours of instruction on how to please her clients, Lydie had flown through a drug trip, and even as they'd walked home, Grey could tell the woman was still soaring.

It was only after they climbed the stairs to their rooms, and Lydie collapsed in bed that Grey had a moment to herself. After slipping into one of the bathrooms, she stripped down, tossed her clothes on the floor, and stepped into the warm steam of the shower.

Without the right supplies, it took time to scrub away the mask of makeup that Amaryllis had painted there. And now, without mascara or blush to cloud her skin, there were no faces left to make. She couldn't conjure a snarl or frown, or even the hint of a smile, just a dead, exhausted stare.

Still staring at nothing, Grey hugged her arms around her naked body and curled in on herself, crouching in the bottom of the tub as hot water pulsed against her back. Maybe that was all she was anymore: dead exhausted.

"Almost done in there?" A sharp tap on the door startled her to her feet.

"Two more minutes," she yelled back, and her voice cracked with the strain of facing one more person before she could crawl away and sleep.

Quickly, she scrubbed her hair, turned off the shower, and wrapped herself in a clean towel, before snatching her dirty clothes off the floor and stepping into the hall.

"It's all yours," she said without meeting the eyes of the Rag waiting outside the door.

"Thanks." The man smiled at her, but Grey only returned a weak nod as she shuffled to her room.

When she was finally alone, she paused in front of the mirror, preparing to find herself as Ama had instructed. But a box on the dresser made her pause. Narrowing her eyes, she picked it up and brought it over to the bed. Then, she carefully lifted the lid and removed a small piece of folded paper.

"'This is what I've been able to find so far,'" she read. "'Still working on the rest of your list. Thank you for your suggestions.'"

Tossing the note aside, Grey rummaged through the package. There were needles, medical thread for sutures, a scalpel, tweezers, multiple tubes of antibiotic ointment, iodine, and one precious bottle of painkillers. And while it certainly wasn't everything from her list, Lock had managed to pull together some valuable supplies.

Grey grinned, even as tears of relief slid down her face. Ama was right. Being a Pinkcap was only an act. What Grey really was—what Jesse had fallen in love with—was a healer. And as a healer, she could make a difference.

Wiping the tears from her eyes, she hid the supplies in the back of her dresser—along with her wedding rings—then collapsed into bed. And for the first time since she'd arrived at the Base, Grey slept in peace.

FOUR

Grey held up the black, leather corset and frowned. Even if she wore it over her clothes, she would never fill it out.

"You're right. Too big." Roz snatched it from Grey's hand and tossed it on the end of Arik's bed, where a pile of discarded outfits was rapidly growing. "What about this?"

Roz handed her a fishnet dress covered in buckles and snaps. Grey twisted it around, searching in vain for the opening.

"What's wrong?" Roz demanded.

"How do you put it on?" Grey asked.

"Never mind." Rolling her eyes, Roz took the dress away.

From his place in bed, Arik chuckled, then winced in pain.

"I mean, is it really necessary to dress like . . ." Grey paused.

Roz's eyes narrowed. "Like what?"

"Like you?" Grey grimaced as Roz's lips pursed in a sullen pout. "What's wrong with the way I dress?"

As Grey searched for an answer, her eyes trailed over Roz's outfit. The Dom's bleached blonde hair was pulled up in her signature bun. A thick, black choker stood out in stark contrast around her long, pale neck. For a shirt, she wore a tube top, barely large enough to fit her ample chest. And her black pants were so tight, Grey could tell that Roz wasn't wearing anything underneath.

Roz considered it loungewear and had already picked out a different outfit—every bit as fearless—for work. But Grey knew, even without trying anything on, that even on her best day, she could never pull off Roz's style.

"There's nothing wrong with it," Grey admitted. "You look fantastic—but I'd look ridiculous."

"You'd be fine." Roz stuck out her tongue. "Plus, you're just observing this week, so you might as well live a little. Figure out what you can get away with before you start going out on your own."

Roz bent down and pulled a black sheath dress out of the box. She shook it out and held it up to the light.

"Here." She threw it to Grey. "Try this on. It's always been way too small for me."

Grey caught it and was almost surprised by its weight. Compared to the clothes she was used to, it was still a little flimsy, but of all the outfits Roz had brought upstairs for her to try, it was the first one that had seemed remotely wearable.

"Okay." Grey nodded and slung the dress over her forearm. "I'll be right back."

She reached for the door handle, but Roz stopped her.

"Where are you going?"

"What do you mean?" Grey paused, her hand still on the knob.

Roz repeated her question slowly as if Grey couldn't understand the words, "Where are you going?"

Grey frowned. "To change." She held up the dress as a reminder. "You just told me to try this on."

For a moment, Roz's eyebrows pinched together, then they arched upwards in surprise as realization washed over her face.

"Holy, shit!" Roz exclaimed, and a wolfish grin curled up her dark lips. "No way."

"What?" Grey scowled, though she could feel a flush rising in her cheeks. She glanced at Arik, but he was painstakingly adjusting his pillow, too preoccupied to care about what Roz was doing.

"You're afraid to change in front of other people! You really *are* such a Rougie, aren't you?" Roz laughed, but the teasing words were playful, not cruel.

"No, I'm not." Grey shook her head.

As she did, her memory flashed to the Blackcaps who had stripped her naked and hosed away the chunk of Jesse's face. In a burst of red, the image of Jesse's body exploded back into her mind.

Her skin grew clammy as her mind began to drown. She still didn't know what had happened to his body after they had loaded him in the wheelbarrow. Maybe Lock knew. After all, he had gotten Jesse's wedding ring. Or maybe the executioner had simply picked the ring off of Jesse's corpse and given it to the Purplecap.

"Grey?"

Jesse had barely been dead for a week. Six days ago, they had been together, so close to slipping over the border of Citoyen and leaving the Color Code behind forever. But now, she was a Pinkcap, and he was nothing. Jesse was dead.

"Hey, Rougie." Roz took a step forward. "Grey?"

Grey blinked away the images flooding through her mind. When she looked up at the world around her, Roz was staring, forehead twisting with concern.

"Are you okay?" she asked.

"I—" Grey nodded. "Yeah, I'm fine."

"You know," Roz's voice was gentle now, the way it had been when she'd carried Arik up the stairs a few nights before, "even when you're raised to do this, it's scary sometimes, especially when you're new. So, if you want to change in the other room, that's fine."

Roz reached for Grey but stopped halfway as if trying to decide how much contact was too much. The Dom's fingers skimmed the back of Grey's hand before she closed them in a fist and let them fall back down at her side.

"But it can be easier," her voice was steadier now, "to try and break your fears around friends." Roz turned to look back at Arik. "Don't you think?"

Arik's dark eyes turned to Roz as he nodded and grimaced against his ribs.

"It's better to learn who you are with friends," he took a small breath, "than to learn who you're not with strangers."

"Look," Roz said, "we don't know what happened to you, or how you ended up here. But we do know what it means to be a Piece. So, don't be afraid to let us help you. Rougie or no, you're one of us."

Grey looked down at the dress in her hands and took a shaking breath. They were right. Whatever she had been before, that life was over. And if she wasn't going to run—if she was going to stay in Citoyen—she had to start acting like a Piece. Glancing at Roz, she slid out of her pants, pulled her shirt over her head, and tossed her clothes on the floor.

Cold air rushed around Grey's thighs as she walked. The outfit had been a good pick on Roz's part. It was just long enough that she didn't feel completely exposed, but when paired with thigh-high boots—borrowed from Lydie—a few inches of skin were still visible beneath the bottom of the hem. To complete the look, Roz had loaned Grey her black choker and a cuff bracelet. And of course, the Dom had pulled Grey's hair into a high ponytail in emulation of her own favorite hairstyle.

"No sex," Roz assured her as they strode down the lamplit streets. "You'll only be there to observe. So, keep in mind, every situation is different. If you start to feel uncomfortable or don't know what to do, just remember, I'm the Dom, you're my assistant. It's literally your job to do whatever I tell you. If I don't give you a cue, just watch."

Grey nodded.

"Hell, you can pretend you're a mute if you want," Roz scoffed. "Some clients might get a kick out of it."

"Okay," Grey breathed heavily as she jogged to keep up with Roz's long legs.

Standing well over six feet, Roz was an absolute force of nature, and even though Grey was nervous, with Roz at her side, she wasn't as terrified as she had expected to be.

"I know you did a house-call with Lydie last night," Roz didn't miss a beat as she walked, "but since shit can get a little kinky, most of my clients prefer to use the pods instead."

Roz paused for a moment to glance down at Grey.

"Have you ever used the pods before?" she asked.

"Sort of." Grey shrugged as her mind drifted to the first few weeks she had spent with Jesse. After he'd recovered from strep and Grey had run out of excuses to visit him as a Redcap, she'd resorted to visiting him as a client.

They hadn't done anything in the pods—not at first—but it wasn't safe to invite him to her boarding house. And without a medical reason, she couldn't visit him in the brothel. So, they had agreed to meet up in the small, portable structures located in discreet areas throughout the city.

In the beginning, she had simply hired him when they wanted to spend time together. They had talked and laughed, and little by little, they had gotten to know one another.

Of course, with time, things had become physical. But initially, the pods had only served as a hideaway, a secret place to meet up with a new friend, regardless of the Code.

Looking back, it was a strange arrangement. But it was better than the alternative. Admitting to a friendship—a relationship—outside of the Color Code could prove extremely dangerous.

"Grey?" Roz's voice cut through her thoughts.

"Sorry." Grey nodded, "Yes, I've used the pods before."

"Then you know about the blood sample?" Roz pressed. "And the cleaning mechanism?"

"Yes."

A simple prick of the finger tested the blood of both users, inhibiting the transmission of diseases throughout Citoyen. Then, after each session, the pod would run a self-cleaning cycle, ensuring a sanitary environment for the next Pinkcap and their client.

During her training as a Redcap, Grey had done a research paper on the efficacy of the pods, which had been the first major public health project under High Chancellor Lachlan's administration. And while they certainly had flaws, most Redcaps agreed that the pods were responsible for the sharp decline in Pinkcaps contracting—and inevitably spreading—incurable viruses and diseases.

"So, you're not afraid of needles?" Roz confirmed.

Grey shook her head. "No."

"Good." Roz veered down a dark alley, too narrow for a vehicle. "There's always someone who passes out on their first night. I'm glad it won't be you."

The end of the alley opened into a wide alcove. At one point in time, it had likely housed dumpsters, but the receptacles had been replaced by a row of five, interlocking pods.

Soft red lights already glowed above three of the doors, signaling that they were occupied, but two pods—both with green lights—were empty.

"We'll use this one." Roz stepped up to the pod on the far end and scanned her tracker. The device beeped, and a small hatch—just large enough for a finger—opened beside the door.

Without hesitation, Roz inserted her pinky finger and provided a blood sample. The machine whirred softly as it reset a clean needle, and Roz stepped aside.

"Your turn."

Following the Dom's lead, Grey scanned her tracker and pressed her pinky into the machine. At the sharp stab of the needle, she flinched, withdrew her hand, and quickly sucked the droplet of blood off the end of her finger.

"Tip for the future," Roz suggested as the steel door slid open. "It helps if you switch up your fingers every night. Keeps them from getting raw."

With that, Grey followed the Dom over the threshold, and the door slid shut behind them.

Inside the pod, there was just enough space for three people to stand—four if they pressed in tightly—and there was an antiseptic smell that turned Grey's stomach. Against the wall was a low table, covered in a disposable sheet. While it wasn't designed for comfort, the slab was large enough to fit two people, and it did have an adjustable heating and cooling mechanism, which could be controlled by both Pinkcaps and clients.

"By the way, if I'm bitchy," Roz cracked her neck, "remember, I'm just playing a role." She looked Grey in the eyes. "It's nothing against you, okay?"

"I know," Grey mumbled.

"Any minute now." Roz stretched her arms, one after the other, and as if on cue, the pod beeped. Stooping to see the internal screen, Roz read the client's request and sneered. "It's a regular."

Before Grey could ask more, the steel door slid open to reveal a short, bald man in a sweater vest that stretched taught over his round belly. He had already removed his cap and was now clutching it in his hands. Between his swollen fingers, she could see a tuft of orange fabric. He was a businessman.

Though short, the man was wide enough to fill the doorframe. His face was red and sweating from the exertion of walking down the alley, and below his chin, the man's tie looked uncomfortably tight, as though he had cinched it to form the illusion of a neck. His small eyes glanced warily from Roz to Grey, then back to Roz again.

"Who's she?" The man's voice was distorted. Though Grey briefly wondered if it was caused by his tie, she knew it was really due to an excess of soft tissue in his throat.

"She's my new toy." Roz's eyes flashed, dark and commanding under her long lashes. "She's mute," the Dom slipped in, and Grey bit the inside of her cheek to keep herself from snorting. "But she likes to watch."

Wheezing, the man nodded and stepped into the pod. Then, the door closed behind him.

- ♦ -

In silence, Grey and Roz watched the orange light blink while the pod cleaned itself. The machine's process took a few minutes, but until it was finished, they waited a short distance away; close enough that they wouldn't lose the pod to another Piece, but far enough that clients could come and go without feeling watched.

Roz's confidence and quick thinking had eased the tension in the pod, but for Grey, watching had still been difficult. At first, she was surprised by just how many props Roz had been able to hide in her outfit. There was a riding crop tucked down the side of each boot, a ball gag hidden in the center of her high bun, and a blindfold slipped under the hem of her corset. Even the woman's thick bracelets had unraveled into black cords for tying up the client. And whenever the fat man glanced at Grey, Roz had whipped him for daring to do anything without her explicit permission.

"Poor bastard." Roz sneered, and Grey glanced away from pod. "He never gets hard unless I make him cry."

It was true. The man was in tears by the time Roz fucked him.

Fucking. That's what it was. It was too cold to be called sex, and it certainly wasn't making love. No, Roz had fucked the weeping man until he was finished, and then she had untied him and watched him skitter from the pod, like some kind of frightened rat.

"They're not always that blubbery." Roz frowned, crossing her arms over her chest, and Grey wasn't sure if she was referring to the man's weight or his tears.

"Sometimes," Roz went on, her eyes focused on the orange light like a moth to a candle, "clients try to hit, or switch roles. As a Dom, you can kick them out based on the rules of the contract they select when they pay. And the best part is, if they break the contract, they don't get a refund."

A dark grin twisted up the corners of Roz's lips. "In a way, it's the best kind dominance." She glanced at Grey. "Don't you think?"

Grey shrugged. "There are worse things."

"Too true." Roz's smile faded. "Like being a Pence. I mean, I've never understood why the regulations aren't the same for all Pieces." She was silent for a moment. "I guess whatever sick assholes were in charge of writing the laws wanted to make sure they could still get their rocks off."

Grey nodded.

"But I try to bring Arik as an assistant whenever I can. And I know Nic takes care of Megz. If we pair up with the Pences, at least we can keep an eye out for them. Unfortunately, people aren't always willing to pay for two."

"What happens then?" Grey tucked her fingers under her armpits to keep them warm.

"If people book me in advance, there's not really anything I can do," Roz shrugged. "Arik just has to go out on his own. Sometimes he's fine, and sometimes," she shook her head, "he comes home the way he did the other night."

"What if people don't want to pay for two this week?" Grey asked. Her fingertips tingled with the slow rush of cold panic spreading from her chest. "What will you do with me?"

"Oh, they're not paying for you this week," Roz said. "You're a freebie, so you stay with me. No matter what."

Grey felt a slight surge of relief, but there was still the question of what would happen when training was over.

"The light's back on." Roz nodded toward the pod, where the signal above the door had turned green.

"Come on," Roz waved her forward, and with a deep sigh, Grey followed the Dom back into the pod.

- ♦ -

Seated in the chair across from Lock, Grey fidgeted. Beside her, Roz perched on the corner of his desk, and in front of the closed door, Jax stood with his arms folded across his chest.

"How's everything going so far?" Lock clasped his long fingers on the desk and flashed a soft smile at Grey.

"Not bad," Roz answered before Grey had a chance.

Jax shifted closer and asked, "Is she Dom material?"

Grey's heart slammed against her ribs. She expected to be a Rag—like Jesse had been—and the thought of wearing corsets and pulling whips out of her underpants was enough to make her sweat.

"No one's Dom material when they start." Roz snapped at the Apical. "But I think she could learn . . ." she paused and glanced at Grey. "Eventually."

Lock scanned the three Pinkcaps thoughtfully, and his blue eyes came to rest on Roz.

"So, a Rag for now, but on track to become a Dom?" he asked. "And you're willing to train her?"

"Of course." Roz sighed deeply, "I mean, if it were up to me—"

"It's not," Jax cut in.

"You don't even know what I was going to say," Roz growled.

"Jax." Lock shook his head slightly, and Jax backed down.

"If it were up to me," Roz hissed, glaring at Jax, "all Pieces would be Doms."

"Wouldn't that be nice?" The sarcasm was thick in Jax's tone as he waved a hand toward Grey. "But is *she* capable of doing it?"

Roz shrugged.

"I don't see why not."

"Seriously," Jax shot Roz a withering glare. "Have you seen her? Look how shy she is. We're standing here, deciding her future, and she won't even speak for herself."

Roz held up a hand, like she might strangle the App, then clenched it in a fist and dropped it back down to her side. Whirling on her heel, she spun to look at Grey.

"Well, what do you think, Rougie?" she asked.

There was a challenge in Roz's last word, almost a plea, and her eyes commanded, *fight for yourself.*

"Could you be a Dom?"

"I—" Grey thought of the men and women she had seen with Roz over the past few days. She had tried to understand why they wanted to be hurt like that, and how Roz could do it.

The idea was so against everything she had ever been taught as a Redcap—how to ease pain, not cause it—that she wasn't remotely convinced she was even capable of being a Dom.

"I'd like to try." The words surprised Grey as they left her lips, but they were the truth. She was willing to attempt it. Whether or not she would succeed was another matter, but she would try if only to hang onto whatever small piece of autonomy she could.

"Excellent." Lock leaned back in his chair. "You'll start as a Rag and work with Roz once a week, as long as she continues to see progress. Then, when you're ready, we can reassign you to work on your own. Does that sound reasonable?"

"Yes," Grey nodded. "It does."

A grin cracked on Roz's face, and Jax, defeated for the moment, just frowned at her.

"Well, it's settled then. Roz, Grey," he nodded at each of them in turn, "you can go and enjoy the rest of your afternoon."

When they stepped into the hall—leaving Jax behind—Roz shut Lock's door and strode toward the kitchen.

"You look like you could use a snack," Roz she said over her shoulder. "Come on."

Lunch was long over, and there was still time before the Bluecaps arrived for dinner preparations, but Grey hesitated. As a Redcap—with constant exposure to sick patients—the main kitchens had always been off limits.

"What's wrong?" Roz asked. "Aren't you hungry?"

"Are we allowed to go in there?" Grey asked.

"Of course," Roz laughed and bumped open the kitchen door with her hip. "You think I could survive off of two meals a day?"

With a shrug, Grey followed her inside. The space was large enough to fit multiple refrigerators, freezers, and prep tables. And along the far wall, the old sink had been replaced with stainless steel.

Pieces of Pink

Roz yanked open a small, white fridge and pulled out a loaf of bread and a block of cheese.

"Listen," the Dom said as she slid open the silverware drawer and grabbed a knife. "As much as I hate to admit it, Jax is right."

Grey frowned. "About what?"

"If you want to be Dom, you'll have to find a way to break out of that whole 'shy' routine." Roz pulled out a few slices of bread and slapped them down on the prep table.

"And I know this is new to you," she continued, "but I'm not the only one you have to convince. I can stick up for you for a while, but at some point, if you don't want to be a Rag—and maybe you do, I don't know—but if you don't, you'll have to show it."

"I know," Grey sighed. "It's just . . ."

She shook her head.

"I guess I . . ."

Patiently, Roz listened, and unexpectedly, Grey felt the sting of tears prickling at the corners of her eyes. She cleared her throat, trying to hold them back.

"The past few weeks have been a nightmare." Grey's voice cracked and Roz turned away from the sandwiches she was making.

"Do you want to talk about it?"

"No," Grey answered.

The wound was still too raw—too open—and if she told Roz about Jesse, and the border, and everything in between, the reality of what had happened might just swallow her whole.

"That's okay," Roz said. "But you can't spend the rest of your life in tears. All of these things you're feeling—whatever they're about—you can't keep them bottled up forever."

Grey wiped her eyes with the edges of her sleeves.

"So, however you want to deal with it—take it out on the clients, talk to Lock, write it down, whatever—that's fine. But do it. Okay?"

Roz's golden eyes narrowed as she took a step toward Grey.

"And when you do become a Dom, you take whatever's left in here," Roz tapped Grey's chest—just above her heart—and her lips curled back in a grin, "bring it with you, and shove it up their asses."

- ♦ -

Even though its location was different, on the inside, the pod was indistinguishable from any other. Of course, there were benefits to using multiple locations, and Roz had explained them all during the walk from the Base. First and foremost, it helped to eliminate stalkers. Second, it provided a slight reprieve from the regulars. But mostly, it just kept things interesting.

"Do you want to watch," Roz cracked her back, "or are you ready to participate?"

"I don't want to talk to them." Grey shook her head. "Not yet."

"All right. We can still pretend you're a mute if you want." Roz hitched her long leg up over the edge of the table and leaned forward, stretching her hamstring. "For now, at least."

In the past week, Grey had seen Roz sleep with over a dozen men and women, and the one thing that had remained consistent for every session was the pattern of stretches Roz completed before each client arrived.

At first, Grey had simply thought it was a way to limber up, to avoid cramps or pulled muscles. But day after day, Grey had watched, and slowly one thing had become clear: Roz wasn't stretching, not really. She was completing the ritual that allowed her to maintain the barrier between her work and herself.

Unlike so many of the other Pieces Grey had met, Roz was always a Dom. In every conversation and action, even in the clothes she wore, there was an energy around her that dominated the room.

Pieces of Pink

She didn't differentiate between work clothes and loungewear, and she was comfortable in anything—or nothing—no matter where she was or who she was with. Where the others had costumes and personas to help them delineate their behaviors—just as Ama had taught Grey with her tube of lipstick—Roz only had herself. So instead of playing a part, Roz played a game. And like any good athlete, she stretched before her clients arrived, and once more when they walked off the playing field.

"Mute sounds good," Grey affirmed.

"Do you want to tie them up?" A wicked light flashed through Roz's eyes, and in the dim glow of the pod, her grin looked feral.

Grey hesitated, but finally gave in. "I guess."

"Wonderful," Roz beamed and unbound the bracelet around her wrist just as the pod beeped.

"Here." She handed the long, thin rope to Grey, then bent down to read the screen. "This one's pretty basic." She glanced back up. "You've got this, Grey."

With a slight screech, the steel door slid open, and a lanky man—nearly as tall as Roz—stepped inside. As the door closed behind him, Roz slid the riding crop from her right boot and slapped the table.

"Sit," she commanded.

Immediately, the man sat.

"Tie him up." She snapped an impatient finger in Grey's face.

Hands quivering slightly, Grey gave a sharp nod and stepped toward the man.

"Lay down," Roz ordered, and he did.

Here in the sterile pods, Grey could imagine that she was in a hospital room, and this was a patient who needed to be restrained on a gurney, but still, she fumbled as she looped the rope around the man's wrists, then ankles, binding him to the table like a starfish.

When Grey was finished, Roz flexed the riding crop in her hands, then pointed it at the man's face, and slowly—so slowly—traced a line over his forehead, down his nose, across his lips and chin, until she reached the top of his buttoned shirt.

"Buttons," Roz commanded.

This time, the order was for Grey.

Grey still trembled but didn't hesitate as she reached for the top button and began to undo them one by one until the man's chest was laid bare.

Skimming the crop over his skin like a feather, Roz glared down at the client.

"Why are you here?" she asked.

"To be punished," he gasped.

With a sharp flick, she hit his chest with the crop. It was hard enough to leave a patch of flushed, pink skin, but no welt.

"And why do you need to be punished?"

He licked his lips and swallowed, eyes glazing over with pleasure. "Because, I'm stupid and pathetic."

Again, Roz slashed the crop across his chest.

"Yes, you are stupid," she hissed. "And pathetic."

She hit him again, still careful not to leave permanent marks.

Through his pants, Grey could see the bulge slowly swelling.

"You disgust me," Roz spat on him and hit him again.

Lash by lash, she worked her way down the client's torso until she reached his waistband. Eyes cold, she glanced back up at Grey and said, "Pants."

Hands now clammy, Grey undid the man's zipper and pulled his pants down to his ankles, avoiding looking at his cock as it sprang free and slapped against his stomach.

"That will be all," Roz instructed, and Grey stepped back against the wall, watching as the Dom stroked his genitals with the crop. When Roz finally mounted the man, Grey stared past the pair, focusing instead on a small square of light, reflecting off the cold silver walls.

Still, she couldn't shut out the sounds. The man's groans were choked as Roz rocked her hips back and forth and pressed the riding crop hard against his clean-shaven throat.

Whatever fire burned in Roz that allowed her to be a Dom also helped her make quick work of her clients. Soon the man grunted, and Roz quickly slid away, leaving him to come all over his own stomach instead of inside of her.

As he lay gasping on the table, she pulled her skirt back into place and untied the bonds. When he had recovered himself, and disappeared into the night, Roz wrapped the rope back around her wrist and stepped outside for the pod to complete its cleaning cycle.

Grinning, Roz turned to Grey. "Your knots were awfully tight."

"Too tight?" Grey asked, frowning.

"Never." There was pride in Roz's expression. "You'll be a Dom in no time."

And as Grey stood beside Roz, staring at the dim orange light pulsing above the pod, she wished she could believe it.

FIVE

The air had grown chilly with the onset of autumn. But in the squares of sunlight scattered around the courtyard, pockets of warmth could still be found. Meandering through the garden with Arik and Roz, Grey made her way toward a large oak tree that leaned against the brick wall, separating the Base from the outside world. Although its trunk was trapped within the confines of the property, the twisting branches reached out over the wall and shaded the narrow street beyond.

Roz inhaled deeply as she led Arik over the uneven brick pathway beneath their feet.

"I love fall," she sighed and smiled like a cat in a window.

"Only because it makes the PVC," Arik took a ragged breath and grinned, "less sticky."

"You just wish you could pull it off," Roz said, raising her dark eyebrow in a challenge.

"I know I could pull it off," Arik teased back.

Although it was still painful for Arik to walk, Grey had insisted that he keep moving to minimize the buildup of mucus in his lungs and decrease the risk of pneumonia while his ribs healed.

Pieces of Pink

The first few days, he had managed to walk up and down the hall easily enough, but this was the first time he had felt strong enough to brave three flights of stairs and walk in the garden.

"It's nice to be outside." Arik's expression was peaceful—almost blissful—as he closed his eyes and lifted his face to the sunlight. "I wish the weather was like this all year."

"That would be nice," Roz agreed, pausing to wait for him.

When Arik was in bed, it was easy to forget just how small he was. Surrounded by covers, his arms didn't look so short, and the severe curvature of his spine was less noticeable. But here in the courtyard, standing beside Roz, he seemed almost childlike.

"I feel like I can finally breathe again," he said, letting Roz guide him to a low stone bench.

Arik gritted his teeth as he eased himself onto the seat, but once he was comfortable, the smile returned to his face.

With a sigh, Grey paused beside a flowerbed and stroked the petal of a deep pink zinnia. Even with fall upon them, new buds were still bursting from the plant's thick, green stalks. They were hearty flowers, and they would last a few more weeks—maybe even months—depending on when the frost set in.

"What do you think, Grey?" Roz asked as she plopped onto the bench beside her friend.

"About what?" Grey let go of the flower and turned to face them.

"This." Roz waved her hands in the air, motioning to the courtyard and the garden. "Do you like it?"

Grey glanced back at the flowers and forced a smile.

"You know," Roz pushed, "it's okay to find *something* you like about being here."

It didn't have as much to do with the place as the people. Even with the bonds slowly forming between Grey and the other Pinkcaps, it was hard to love a place when the person she loved most couldn't be there with her.

"For example," Roz braced her hands on the bench, kicked her feet out into the walkway, and lounged back, "I like raiding Selene's room." The Dom's lips curled up to reveal her bright, white teeth. "And Arik likes the library in the lounge."

"The garden, too," Arik amended. "But in the winter, the Bluecaps keep a fire burning in the lounge, and there's nothing as good as curling up with a new book when it's snowing out." His dark eyes grew dreamy. "You can almost just melt into another world."

Grey nodded thoughtfully. She hadn't pegged Arik for a reader. Then again, she didn't actually know that much about him. And maybe it wasn't reading that he loved, so much as escaping from his current situation.

"Do you ever . . ." Grey hesitated.

"What?" Roz asked.

She bit her lip. "Do you ever wonder what it might've been like if you hadn't been born a Piece?"

Arik's brow furrowed, and the smile faded from Roz's lips as her eyes narrowed. The Dom took a deep, slow breath. "We don't usually talk about things like that."

"Why," Grey asked cautiously.

Roz remained silent, so Arik answered for her.

"It's just not worth dwelling on," he said.

"But what if—"

"What if what?" Roz snapped. "What if I had the chance to be a Beak, or a Bluecap, or a Rougie, like you?" She scowled. "Honestly, I probably would have tried not to fuck it up!"

Surprised, Grey took a slight step backward into the flowerbed.

"It's okay, Roz," Arik's voice was soothing as he reached a twisted hand for the Dom. "I think about it sometimes."

He smiled, and for a moment his black eyes locked with Grey's before he turned his full attention back to Roz.

"If I could choose," he said, "I'd want to be a Yellowcap."

"A teacher?" Roz's shoulders slumped forward—just slightly—as the tension eased.

Grey kept her mouth shut. Somehow, she had overstepped a boundary with Roz, but whatever Arik was doing, it was bringing the Dom back down, calming the storm that had been stirring behind her fiery eyes.

Arik nodded. "They have the most freedom."

There was a painful truth to his words.

"They get to pick the subjects they want to learn," he explained, "and teach in their preferred fields."

"And what subject would you have picked?" Roz asked.

"Literature, I think." Arik leaned toward her and rested his tired head on her shoulder.

"You'd make an amazing teacher," Roz smiled again, but there was something bittersweet in her gaze as she looped her arm around his shoulder. "But you're already amazing as you are."

"Not nearly as great as you," Arik grinned.

Roz chuckled and gave him a gentle squeeze.

After a moment, he returned the tentative question, "What would you have been, Roz?"

"I don't think there *is* anything else for me," Roz sighed and leaned forward to rest her elbows on her knees. "I'm just a Piece."

Though Grey was only a few feet away, the space between them felt cavernous. She wasn't a Redcap anymore, but she certainly didn't feel like a Pinkcap.

She only knew that if she could have, she would have chosen to spend this day in the garden with Jesse—chosen to live in a world where loving him wasn't a crime. Casting her eyes away from Arik and Roz, Grey turned back to the flowers.

- ♦ -

Grey glanced at the clock hanging on the wall as she slipped through the back door and into the kitchen. One of Lock's chefs—a Bluecap—was carefully slicing a mound of green peppers on the prep table. If he noticed Grey, he didn't acknowledge her. Instead, he remained focused on the sharp blade flashing uncomfortably close to his knuckles.

It was strange to think that this man—and other Bluecaps like him—were now above Grey, yet they prepared her meals, cleaned the Base, and even washed her clothes. And if it meant that she didn't have to go out with the other Pinkcaps, she would have gladly taken his place and scrubbed the Base from cellar to attic.

But there was no choice. No choice over what she did or what she ate, no choice over where her money went or how it was spent, not even a choice over who she slept with. The only choice she'd had was to run, but for some reason, she had chosen to stay.

A part of her wanted to believe she really had stayed to help—that seeing Arik suffering had made her feel useful to Lock and the Base—but so far, no one had even needed her. No one but Arik, at least. And deep down, she knew the truth: she was just too exhausted to run.

She had spent weeks and weeks hiding and starving with Jesse, and without him—on her own—she wasn't sure she had the strength to make it anymore.

Grey stared at her feet as she walked out of the kitchen. Jax had asked her to meet him for a quick briefing before they left for the night, and although she didn't feel it was entirely necessary, there was some small comfort in knowing that she hadn't been forgotten.

When Grey reached the lounge, she stopped in the doorway. Jax and Selene were standing in the sunlight by the side window with their lips pressed together in a gentle kiss. They drew apart almost instantly but didn't immediately turn to face Grey. Instead, they smiled at each other, sharing some secret message that only eyes could convey. And when they did finally acknowledge her, there was no shame or embarrassment on their faces. They were in love, and it didn't matter who knew.

"I'll see you later," Selene crooned, trailing a finger across Jax's chest as she turned and sauntered toward the doorway.

Quickly, Grey stepped aside and blushed—absentmindedly running her thumb over her tracking chip—as Selene passed by.

Like Roz, Selene was comfortable in her own skin. She had an undeniably magnetic quality. Every movement was elegant, almost dramatic, but the mask she wore to hide her true self was unlike the Dom's. Where Roz was friendly and blunt, Selene was leery and watchful—as if she always knew something that no one else did—as if she had a secret that she wasn't willing to share.

"Thanks for meeting with me." Jax was curt when he spoke. "I just wanted to make sure you were all set for tonight."

Grey nodded. "I think so."

"Good." His eyes drifted over Grey's shoulder, following Selene as she walked up the stairs. "Also, since you're new, you'll start slowly." His gaze returned to focus on Grey. "You'll just have one client tonight and tomorrow night. Roz will continue to assess your progress, and you'll gradually increase to a full workload."

Although the thought of what she would be doing that night sent a spike of cold down her back, knowing that she would only have to do it once was a relief.

"I've selected your client schedule for the week, based on the recommendations of other Pieces," Jax explained. "We want to make sure things go smoothly, so I asked everyone for a few clients that are easy to please."

"Okay," Grey frowned.

"And since you're a Rougie," Jax rolled his eyes slightly, "I also just wanted to make sure you know how payment works."

Grey had heard enough about it from Jesse, and Roz had told her even more, but the thought of only being paid through her chip still made her cringe.

"When you scan in at the pod," Jax said, "It will automatically register Lock as your Purplecap. So, when the client pays, all of the money will be transferred directly into Lock's account. He'll be able to see who earned it and which unit they live in, then he'll transfer a portion of it into your allowance."

"And how do I spend it?" Grey scowled.

"Most of the local shops have chip readers," Jax answered. "Roz can take you around."

Grey's heart sank. Over the past two weeks, she had only left the Base with Roz for observations. As a Pinkcap, she had never walked into a shop or stopped in a restaurant, and the thought of being forced to scan her wrist for every purchase was humiliating. As if the pink cap on her head wasn't punishment enough.

"Anything else?"

Jax shook his head, but when Grey turned to go, he stopped her.

"Oh, and Rougie?" he added.

She glanced back.

"Good luck tonight."

- ♦ -

Grey smoothed her hair into a high ponytail and slid the wide, pink headband—a permanent reminder of what she was—behind her ears. When it was situated, she took the tube of lipstick Ama had given her and carefully traced the bright color over her lips.

She was not Grey Alcott, she reminded herself. She was an actor, a Rag, and this was just a role she had to play. Unfortunately, as a

Rag, she wouldn't have the level of control that Roz was able to wield over her clients, but at least the night would be over quickly.

Whoever Jax had booked, he or she would find Grey's pod through her tracker, they would fuck, and she would come home. And when she did, she could wipe it all away and be herself again.

That was it.

Grey heaved a breath and stared at her face in the mirror. She pursed her lips lightly and tried to force some light into her eyes, but they felt heavy and dull. She felt no spark—no coy playfulness—and despite what Ama had suggested, Grey still wasn't entirely sure that it could be faked.

With a sigh, she tugged on the bottom of her black miniskirt, grabbed her jacket off the end of the bed, and headed for the stairwell. It was still difficult to walk in the high, black boots, and even as other Pinkcaps zipped past her, she gripped the railing tightly as she descended.

"Good luck, Rougie." The twins—Arden and Taryn—called out as they passed. Even though they were identical, one—the App—wore a tux, and the other was dressed as a Dom. But which one was which, Grey still wasn't sure.

She tried to smile at them—at the well-wishes that seemed genuine enough—but she could only manage a nervous, wholly unconvincing laugh.

"Don't be afraid." Megz's lisp was easily recognizable, and Grey glanced up as the young woman fell into step beside her. "We all had to go through the first night once."

"Thanks," Grey flashed her a weak smile.

"Plus, I'm sure Jax picked a good client," Megz added. "He tries hard to make things easy for us when Lock's not around."

Grey nodded, but even with all of the reassurance, she still felt clammy and lightheaded. It wasn't until she reached the bottom of the stairs and saw Roz, that her panic finally ebbed. The Dom was standing in the foyer leaning against the wall with her arms crossed over her chest. And she was grinning.

"Look at you," Roz whistled as she stalked toward Grey, her boots clicking on the hardwood floor. "Love the headband."

"Thanks." Grey tugged her miniskirt, which had ridden up almost indecently high during her journey down the stairs.

"Of course," Roz reached out a hand and lightly pulled her aside. Then, her smile faltered. "Listen, Grey," she lowered her voice, "I wanted to apologize about the garden."

"For what?" Grey shook her head.

"I shouldn't have snapped at you the way I did," Roz said. "Thinking about how life could have been—talking about the what-ifs—it's just not something I do, you know?"

"It's okay," Grey assured her. "I shouldn't have kept pushing for an answer."

Roz shrugged. "Either way, I wanted to give you this." Roz pressed a small bottle into Grey's hand and motioned toward her cleavage. "Store it in there for now. It's just lube—but it'll help."

Grey stared at the bottle for a moment before sliding it down the front of her shirt.

"Also, I just wanted to let you know, I'll take the pod next to you tonight." Roz's eyes narrowed. "I know you're only starting with one client, but if something goes wrong, or if you need help, I'll be right there, okay?"

In relief, Grey finally cracked a genuine smile. "Thank you, Roz."

"Don't mention it." A wicked grin stretched over the Dom's face as she gave Grey a light slap on the butt. "Let's do this, Rougie."

- ♦ -

Pieces of Pink

Alone in the pod, Grey waited. Since she had been booked in advance, no one but the client Jax had arranged would be able to enter. They would only need to scan their ID to pay, and the doors would open for them, whoever they were.

She glanced at the screen, waiting for it to beep and show her the client as it had done with Roz. But the screen made no sound. Nervous, Grey paced and wiped her clammy hands on her skirt.

Maybe she would get lucky, and the client would get stuck at home, or fall in a ditch, or get hit by a car. If that happened, she supposed she could just wait out the night and leave with Roz, who—as promised—had taken the pod beside hers. And while she couldn't see or hear the Dom, at least it was a comfort to know she was there.

Underneath her skirt, Grey was already sticky. She had applied the lube Roz had given her, and as strange as it had felt to do it alone, it was better than doing it in front of the client.

A sharp beep made Grey jump. Her stomach heaved as she crossed the pod to glance at the display screen, but unlike the complicated list of instructions and kinks clients left for Roz, the screen simply read: *Yellowcap, Male.*

Swallowing down the dryness in her throat, Grey tried to steady her breathing as the door opened to reveal the man on the other side. He was taller than her—and a little older, too—with dark hair and hazel eyes, accentuated by the yellow, knit cap on his head.

"Hi." With an awkward flap of his hand, the Yellowcap waved, then shoved the offending appendage into his pocket as if instantly embarrassed by what he had done. "Sorry."

"It's all right," Grey stuttered as the man stepped over the threshold, and the pod closed them inside together. "Um, I—"

"I know you're new," his words were quick and nervous as he spoke. "Your Purplecap, well, I guess he wasn't your Purplecap. He was another Pinkcap—but, Jax. Jax said you were new."

Grey nodded.

"And he thought we might be a good fit because I'm new too."

She blinked and raised her eyebrows in surprise. Jax had found her a virgin?

"Oh, no!" The man read her expression and waved his hands in the air as if he could erase what he'd just said. "No, no, no. I don't mean I'm *new*, new. Like, I'm not a virgin or anything. I just, I mean, I've never . . ." he pointed at Grey then at himself. "You know?"

"You've never hired a Pinkcap?" she asked.

"Yes, that." He smiled in relief. "Exactly."

"Okay." She took a step toward the steel table, but the man made no move to undress.

"My wife," he chattered nervously, and Grey couldn't help but think it was cruel for Jax to pair this poor man with her. He needed someone with experience, someone who knew what they were doing, who could reassure and calm him—not her.

"My wife," he repeated the words again. "She, um . . ."

Grey waited.

"My wife died last year."

When the words finally came out, Grey's forced smile faded from her face completely.

"She had cancer, and the Redcaps did what they could," he glanced at the floor, "but she didn't make it."

"I'm so sorry to hear that," A hard lump formed in Grey's throat.

It seemed that the cosmos had turned on her in some sick joke. Unless Lock had told him, there was no way that Jax could have known about Jesse—known that Grey had just lost her husband—but if he did, then this went beyond cruelty.

"That's terrible," she murmured.

The man took a breath and pulled off his yellow cap. "At least there was time to say goodbye." He wrung the hat between his hands. "I know that's more than some people get."

Pieces of Pink

A spray of blood flashed through Grey's memory, and she bit down hard on the inside of her cheek as if she could hold back her emotions with her teeth alone.

"She was a teacher." He laughed at himself as he squeezed the yellow hat. "Obviously."

"Oh, what kind?" Grey feigned interest even as darkness crept in around the corners of her eyes.

Not here, not now, she couldn't fall apart.

"Art." The man smiled wistfully.

She forced out the words, "And what about you?"

"Oh, I teach literature."

Literature. There was a tether. Grey lashed out for her memories of Arik and Roz, clinging to their earlier conversation like a lifeline.

"I have a friend who loves to read," she smiled.

The man's shoulders relaxed a little. "What does he read?"

In the dead center of the Color Code, Yellowcaps had the most flexibility of all the caps, and though they had ranked below her as a Redcap, it was easy to envy them.

Teachers could choose a subject that sang to them. They could find fulfillment in their work, because even if it was small, they were given some choice.

"Fiction, mainly, I think." She answered.

"I can't blame him there." The man took a breath—calmer, now—and finally looked up to meet her eyes, still rimmed with the threat of tears.

"Oh." He took a step toward her, and she froze. "I'm sorry. I think I upset you. I shouldn't have brought up my wife."

"No, no." She shook her head and lied, "It's all right."

As much as her heart screamed for it, she couldn't tell this stranger about Jesse. She couldn't commiserate with him or find consolation. It would be suicide if people found out that the government had spared her—a traitor—on Lock's request.

"I just thought maybe it was time for me to move on." He sighed and looked back up at Grey. "Not to forget her, of course. Just to let myself live," he paused, "without her."

Grey took a step toward the Yellowcap. She had to make him stop talking—stop telling her these things—because if he didn't, she was going slip back into her memories—into her hell—and she wasn't sure she would be able to crawl back out.

"Is that wrong?" He looked up, and Grey took another step.

"No," she shook her head. And though her words felt strange, they were real. "When someone leaves us, the only thing we can do is cling to the memories."

She reached for his hands, still clutching the yellow cap, and trailed her fingers softly over them.

"And you're right. Even if we want to, we can't just stop living."

Her fingers traced up to his wrists.

"We have to survive."

Slowly, so slowly, her hands made their way up his arms and over his chest until they reached the top button of his shirt.

"They would want us to find a way to be happy without them."

She undid the first button and found the next.

"Just like we would want them to find happiness."

The Yellowcap had finally stopped talking.

As Grey undid the last button of the man's dress shirt and pushed it open to reveal the white undershirt beneath, he dropped his cap. She pulled the shirt down his arms, and he let it fall to the floor.

Trembling slightly, Grey shrugged out of her jacket, tossed it down, and reached for the man's belt. With a deft motion, she slipped the tongue free of the buckle and began unzipping his pants.

She had undressed patients in the emergency room more times than she could remember, and she let herself cling to that familiarity as she pulled the man's pants to his ankles and left him standing in his briefs and undershirt.

Pieces of Pink

Reminding herself over and over that it was just a job, she raised her shirt over her head and tossed it beside the growing pile of clothes on the floor. Then, she reached around her back and unhooked her bra.

Following her lead, the Yellowcap removed his undershirt, and they stood face-to-face, topless in the stark pod. Slowly, the man lifted a hand to cup her breast. Grey shivered at the thought of what was about to happen as he ran a thumb over her nipple, hard in the cool air. She laid her hands on his shoulders, watching as his eyes skimmed down her bare torso to the skirt and what was beneath it.

Without allowing her gaze to focus too long on any part of his body for too long, she hooked her fingers around the band of the man's briefs and pulled them to his ankles. Quickly shimmying out of her skirt, she kicked them to the side. And fighting every emotion in her body, Grey slid onto the steel table, pulled the man between her legs, and guided him inside of her.

He shuddered as he entered her, and even though she tried to relax, her muscles remained rigid. Silently, she thanked Roz for the bottle of lube as the Yellowcap slowly began to move back and forth, sinking deeper and deeper inside of her.

The man gasped as he adjusted their position and gently laid her flat on the table. Pressing his body into hers, he buried his face against the smooth skin between her neck and shoulder, either too shy or too heartbroken to look at this woman who wasn't his wife.

As Grey listened to his ragged breaths and felt the strangeness of his shape inside of her, she found the pulse of his heart. And with one hand resting against his chest and the other wrapped around his back, she began to count.

One, two, three, four.

She ignored the thrusts, and the breathing, and squeezed her eyes tightly shut.

Five, six, seven, eight.

Her first night with Jesse had been on a table like this, but she had brought blankets.

One, two, three, four.

And as much as she wanted to, she hadn't been able to afford booking him every single night.

Five, six, seven, eight.

So, he had still been forced to take other clients.

One, two, three, four.

Even though Jesse had loved her, and was willing to risk everything for her . . .

Five, six, seven, eight.

He'd still had to live.

A tear squeezed from the corner of Grey's eye and rolled back into her hairline as the Yellowcap shuddered and went still.

There was a moment of silence before the man climbed off of her and quickly bent to pick up his clothes. As he dressed, Grey stiffly rose from the table—glad he wasn't looking at her—and found her bra.

Between her legs, she could feel his semen leaking out with the pull of gravity, and she fought the urge to dry-heave. Quickly snatching her skirt off the floor, she pulled it around her hips as a trickle of warm fluid slid down her legs.

The Yellowcap didn't wait for Grey to pull her shirt back over her head before he stepped toward the door to leave. But as it slid open, the man paused and glanced back at her—only for a moment—and she saw that his eyes were lined with tears.

"Thank you." His voice cracked.

She nodded once, and the Yellowcap disappeared into the night.

When the pod door sealed shut behind him, Grey hoisted the skirt up around her waist and scrambled for the tissue dispenser mounted on the wall. Yanking tissues out by the handful, she scrubbed between her legs until it felt raw.

Pieces of Pink

But still, she didn't feel dry. Desperate to wash him off of her—out of her—Grey gathered her belongings, dashed from the pod, and ran for the Base.

- ◆ -

Alone in the darkness, Grey sat on the edge of her bed and sobbed. Strands of wet hair hung over her shoulders and dripped to the floor with her tears. Even after two showers, she still felt dirty. Maybe she always would.

Clutching her wedding bands tightly in her fist, Grey held them against her chest as if squeezing them hard enough could somehow bring Jesse back to life.

Her breath stuttered when she sucked in a mouthful of air. She had been crying for so long, it almost seemed impossible, but somehow the tears continued to flow. The skin under her eyes felt raw and puffy, and the edge of her nose was sore from wiping it on her sleeve.

A soft noise in the hall made Grey look up just as someone opened her door.

"Grey?" It was Arik.

In the darkness, she could just make out his shape as he limped toward her.

"Are you all right?"

Even though he couldn't see it, Grey shook her head.

"No." The word scratched from her throat.

"What happened?" Slowly, Arik found the edge of the bed and sat down beside her. "Did the client—"

"It's nothing," she whispered, quickly wiping the snot from her nose with the inside of her shirt. "Everything was fine." A hollow laugh escaped as she glanced toward Arik's dark outline beside her. "I made him cry."

"Oh." Though he tried to hide it with shock, Grey could still hear the amusement in Arik's voice. "Well, maybe you could be a Dom after all."

"Yeah," she chuckled darkly and dabbed at her damp eyes with her free hand. "Then again, he made me cry too."

"That bad, huh?"

Grey sighed in response as Arik reached his small hand across the space between them and patted her back.

"It's just," she let out a shaking breath, "before I became a . . ." she hesitated. "Before I became a Piece, I had someone—someone I loved—and now he's dead."

Arik listened in silence.

"And tonight," her voice trembled, "was the first night that I've been with someone else since I lost him. And I never really got to say goodbye."

The tears were flowing now.

"I don't even know where he was buried—if he was buried at all." She held her breath for a moment, just trying to keep the sobs from spilling out of her chest. "I mean, for all I know, they threw him in a pit or burned him."

Her shoulders shook.

"And now he's gone." The words heaved out of her. "And I'll never see him again."

For a moment, Arik said nothing. In silence, he listened as Grey wept into her hands. But when her tears died away, and she caught her breath, he laid his hand over hers.

"Whatever happens to our bodies," Arik whispered. "It can't really hurt us."

Grey sniffled.

Pieces of Pink

"All of this skin and bone and blood—it's just temporary—just something to hold us for a while," he said. "And when it wears out, and we're gone, we'll live on in the water, and the trees, and the starlight. We'll be a thousand pieces of the universe."

"But how do I say goodbye?" she murmured. "How do I live, knowing that I'll never touch him, or see him, or hear him laugh? How do I *live?*"

"You live, because you have to," Arik answered.

In her hand, Grey could feel the heat of the wedding bands—the weight of them—as they pressed into her skin. She took a deep breath and looked up.

"There's something I need to do

Arik nodded in understanding, and slowly, Grey stood. In the darkness, she made her way down the stairs, one flight at a time, until she reached the door to the courtyard and shouldered it open. Without the sun to warm it, the air outside was cold; but by the light of the moon and a nearby streetlamp, the garden path was clear.

Each step was deliberate as Grey marched toward the massive oak near the garden wall. When she reached the edge of the path, she paused a moment, scanning the ground until she found a rock—about the size of her fist—and picked it up.

Then, with feet like lead, she stepped off the path and made her final procession toward the tree. At its roots, Grey dropped to her knees and began to dig. Clawing the cold earth away with her hands, she formed a small hole—less than a foot deep—and carefully lined it with the leaves, black in the darkness. And when she was finished, she placed the wedding rings inside.

In silence, Grey stared at the overlapping bands, glinting in the moonlight. They were meant to be Jesse's promise to her—the promise of a lifetime—but now they rested at the bottom of a hole. And as much as wished for it, there was no way to change the past. Arik was right. She had to live.

Heart aching, she scooped up a handful of dirt and sprinkled it over the rings. It pattered onto the leaves like rain, partially obscuring the silver bands. She took a second handful, then a third, and slowly filled in the damp earth.

With shaking hands, she patted the ground smooth and carefully placed the rock over the final resting place of everything that might have been. Then, taking a deep breath, Grey stood and turned back toward the path.

SIX

Holding back, Grey slapped the man across the face.
"Harder," Roz instructed.

Grey struck again, and the man whimpered.

The client, her last of the night, didn't come for sex—not in the traditional sense, at least. He was a Browncap, and after winning a high-profile case, he just wanted to be hit over, and over, and over again—wanted a Dom to slap him—while he pleasured himself.

Although Grey wasn't strictly a Dom yet, she still accompanied Roz once a week for additional training, and as strange as it felt, being with Roz was better than being a Rag. As an Average, clients only wanted one thing: sex. But for Doms, sometimes penetration was the last thing on a client's mind.

"Hit me," the man groaned as he stroked himself.

"Did she give you permission to speak?" Roz growled from where she stood, observing in the corner.

The Browncap snapped his mouth closed and shook his head.

Roz took a step toward him, then bent down. Her teeth hovered dangerously close to his earlobe. "Then, shut up," she hissed.

Nodding his head vigorously, the man bit down hard on his lower lip, but his eyes were still begging for it. Grey kept her expression cold and slapped the man again. A part of her didn't mind doing it. When she thought of every client she had been with over the past week—every man and woman who had asked her to take off her cap, so they could pretend they weren't paying for it—she found the strength to hit this lawyer again.

Grey focused her energy into a final backhand. And as their skin made contact, the man grunted and finished on the ground in front of her booted feet. He hovered there for a moment, panting and swaying slightly in the aftermath of his orgasm. But before he had a chance to collect himself and stand, Roz scooped the Browncap's clothes off of the floor, shoved them into his arms, and pushed him outside of the pod into the cold autumn night.

The two women stared him down in silence as he scuttled on his hands and knees, clamoring to dress until the pod door slid shut and obscured him from view. When Grey was sure the Browncap couldn't hear her anymore, she spun on Roz.

"Are we allowed to do that?"

"What?" Roz asked.

"Throw them outside naked?"

"Trust me," Roz smirked, "he loved it."

Grey frowned but shrugged it off. Carefully avoiding the ejaculate on the floor, she stepped around Roz and reached for her jacket and scarf, hanging from a peg on the far side of the pod.

"You did okay tonight," Roz said, stooping to pick up her jacket.

"Yeah?" Skeptical of the Dom's praise, Grey raised her eyebrows.

"Well, better than last week's session." Roz grimaced a little. "At least you've stopped apologizing to the clients."

"Fair enough," Grey said, pulling her scarf from its peg. But as she slipped it over her head, she knocked the hot pink headband out of her hair. Tumbling to the ground, it rolled, then teetered and fell on its side—directly into the puddle of come.

"Oh, that sucks." Roz stuck out her tongue as she bent and plucked Grey's headband from the floor. A thread of semen clung to the pink fabric for a moment, then snapped as the Dom lifted it and handed it back to Grey.

Sighing in frustration, Grey snatched a handful of tissues out of the dispenser and tried to wipe the satin clean, but a splotch of dampness remained.

"Shit," she growled under her breath, then glanced up at Roz. "Do you have a spare?"

"Not with me." Roz shook her head apologetically.

Grey groaned and slipped the come-stained headband back into her hair. There was no choice. Without some kind of headpiece to signify her cap, Grey could be fined or even arrested by the Blackcaps patrolling the streets.

"We can stop by the shops and get another one tomorrow," Roz suggested. "I know you hate hats."

"Yeah," Grey agreed. "That would be good."

"Anyways." Roz ducked out of the pod and stepped out into the darkness. "It's nice to see you making progress."

Grey rolled her eyes. "I bet."

"No, really." Roz's boots clicked against the cobblestones as they headed toward the Base. "I'm glad you haven't fallen apart. Some people—even people who are born Pinkcaps—just sort of crack."

"Oh yeah?"

"Yeah." Roz shrugged. "Just look at Lydie. She started using as soon as she came to the Base. Honestly, I never even really got to know her when she was sober."

Grey frowned and slid her cold hands into her pockets. It was too bad that no one had sent Lydie to a clinic. After all, there were plenty of facilities run by Redcaps, and with a little love and attention, maybe she could get clean. Then again, the past few weeks had made one thing painfully clear: Pieces didn't trust the other caps, and Grey could hardly blame them.

"And Jax and Selene," Roz grumbled. "Don't get me wrong, I love those two, but being Apps has made them so uptight."

"Why?"

"Too much time watching their significant other fucking someone else," Roz answered. "That's my guess. Either that or they know way too many government secrets. I mean, sure, the Apps get a few perks, but in the end, the bullshit outweighs the benefits." The Dom's eyes grew dark. "I was an App for *one* night, and it wasn't worth it."

Grey glanced at Roz but didn't push for more information. Some things were better left unsaid.

"And then there's Arik," Roz said. "He's worse off than any of us, but he never complains about it. Nothing gets to him."

It was true. By far, the Dispensable—the lowest ranking in all of Citoyen—lived the worst-case scenario. But somehow, Arik had clung to compassion and friendship. He was open, without the bravado that Roz used to get by, but also quiet and reflective, without being cold or tense, like Jax and Selene.

"What about you?" Grey finally broke her silence.

"What about me?" Roz flashed a teasing smile.

"Did you change when you started working?" Grey probed gently, unwilling to have a repeat of the day in the courtyard.

"I've grown up a little," Roz hummed thoughtfully to herself. Then a wicked grin broke over her face. "I mean, look at these." She pushed up her breasts, hidden—for once—under her jacket. "They're more magnificent every day."

Grey chuckled.

"But, no. I don't think I've changed." A smile lingered on Roz's dark lips as she draped her arm around Grey's shoulders. "I've always known what I am."

Grey leaned into Roz to keep from losing her balance. "And what are you?"

"I'm a badass."

Laughing, Grey looped an arm around Roz's waist, and together they wound their way home.

- ♦ -

"Do you want a waffle?" Grey held the platter toward Lydie, but the redhead only stared at her breakfast with glassy eyes.

"I don't like waffles," she sighed.

Grey raised her eyebrows. "I thought they were your favorite."

She glanced at Arik, who was watching Lydie skeptically.

Lydie frowned, "No. I don't like waffles. I'd rather have toast."

"Take mine." Roz dropped two slices of bread on Lydie's plate and reached for the waffle platter. But when Lydie moved to pick up the toast, Roz froze, and her eyes narrowed.

"Lydie?" She asked, "What happened to your finger?"

Grey leaned forward to see, as Lydie lifted her hand and held it up in front of her face.

It was perfectly fine.

"What finger?" Her voice was sleepy as she tipped her head to the side, and her glossy auburn hair slid over her shoulder.

"Not that hand." Roz shook her head.

Grey shifted her gaze to the hand resting on the table and then, she saw it. Lydie's ring finger was bent toward her pinky at a sharp, right angle.

"Did a client do it?" Roz hissed. "If you tell me who, I'll report them to Lock. He can block them."

Confused, Lydie looked down. "No, I don't think so."

"What do you mean?" Roz demanded. "How did it happen?"

"I'm not sure." A little grin danced over Lydie's face as she held up her hand and reached to stroke the finger.

"Don't!" Roz commanded, but Grey was already up and reaching across the table to stop Lydie from mishandling her injury.

"Lydie." She switched on the calm and patient voice that she had mastered as a Redcap. "I think you might have broken your finger."

"Hmm," Lydie cooed softly to herself as Grey quickly skirted around the table and intercepted Lydie from poking the finger a second time.

"Do you want me to take a look at it?" Grey asked.

"What's there to look at?" Lydie's head bobbed as she spoke.

"Your *finger*."

The sleepy smile remained on Lydie's face as she said, "Oh," and reached for the water glass by her elbow.

"All right." Grey hauled Lydie to her feet. "We're going upstairs to straighten this out."

"Okay." Lydie's voice was dazed, but she stepped away from the table without protest and followed Grey out of the dining room.

Grey held Lydie's hand as they walked to the fourth floor, careful to ensure that the woman wouldn't cause herself further injury. But at the top of the stairs, Grey hesitated. If she took Lydie into her room, the woman would see where all of the painkillers were kept. Then again, if she left her alone, she might hurt herself.

Clenching her jaw against her own better judgment, Grey steered Lydie into the bathroom and sat her down on a low stool that was kept under the counter.

"Stay right here," Grey instructed. "I just need to find something to splint your finger with, okay?"

Still smiling, Lydie nodded, and Grey dashed to her room.

Over the past few weeks, Lock had brought home more supplies every time he had returned from a business trip. And each time, Grey had taken an inventory of what she had and stocked everything in her bedroom closet. So far, nothing had been touched, but she wasn't willing to risk Lydie discovering the supplies. Quickly, Grey grabbed a splint, medical tape, and a small bottle of disinfectant.

When she returned to the bathroom, Lydie was standing in front of the mirror, staring at herself, and slowly running the fingers of her good hand through her long, red hair.

"Can you sit back down for me, Lydie?" Grey asked.

Lydie nodded, but didn't turn away from the mirror.

Grey took the woman's elbow and guided her to the seat. As she went to the sink to scrub her hands clean, Grey watched Lydie over one shoulder. And when she was finished, she knelt beside the woman and held out her open palm.

"Can I see?" she asked.

Silently, Lydie placed her hand in Grey's.

It was a relief to see the injury up close. From the surface, it appeared to be a dislocation, not a fracture, but Grey checked the bone—as well as she could without an X-ray—just to be sure.

Turning the hand over and pressing lightly along the length of the finger, she felt for any sign of damage beyond the dislocation of the proximal interphalangeal joint. But it would be difficult to tell if any ligaments were torn until it was realigned. Even then, Lydie's drug use might impact her ability to feel pain. And without pain, any injury would be difficult to fully diagnose.

"Okay, Lydie." Grey massaged the base of the finger. "I'm going to put this back into place. Do you feel all right?"

Lydie nodded.

Gently, Grey pulled her way toward the tip, slowly reducing the dislocation until the finger straightened back into place. As she worked, Lydie reached for Grey's hair with her free hand and trailed her fingers down the brown strands.

"You should try something new with your hair," Lydie mused.

"Oh, yeah?" Grey focused on the finger. "Like what?"

"Maybe add some color." Lydie didn't even notice when Grey finished working.

"Can you move it?" Grey asked.

With her expression still set in a blissful smile, Lydie finally looked down and wiggled her fingers.

"Perfect." Grey grabbed the medical tape off of the countertop. "I'm just going to splint it," she explained. "And then we can go downstairs and get you some ice to help with the swelling."

"What about the pain?" Lydie asked. "Do you have anything for that?" Blinking her eyes lazily, she watched Grey bend the splint into the proper shape and fit it against the injured finger.

"No, I don't have anything," Grey lied. "Why? Does it hurt?"

Lydie nodded.

"Well, it's normal to feel some soreness," Grey said.

"So, nothing for the pain?" Lydie's eyes remained sluggish as they traced Grey's movements.

Grey shook her head a second time. The last thing she needed was Lydie tearing through her room looking for drugs.

"Are you sure?" Lydie asked.

She nodded.

"That's okay," Lydie sighed. "I'll just ask Ama."

Grey raised her eyebrows in disapproval but remained silent as she wrapped Lydie's finger and helped her stand.

"Okay, Lydie. You're all set." Grey forced a smile. "Go finish your breakfast. I'll be down in a minute."

Still smiling, Lydie traipsed out of the bathroom. Listening to the woman's footsteps, Grey gathered her supplies and stood to leave. But when she saw her reflection in the bathroom mirror, she hesitated. She had learned a lot about makeup over the past few weeks, but her hair was still the same dull brown it had always been.

Maybe Lydie was right. She ran her fingers through her limp hair. Even Roz had dyed her hair blonde, and to be honest, Grey wasn't sure the Dom would have the same effect without her smooth, bleached ponytails and buns. Grey twisted a brown strand around her finger. If nothing else, it could definitely stand to be trimmed, and for that, she would have to talk to Selene.

- ♦ -

Lock smiled as Grey entered the office and took a seat across from him.

"How are the medical supplies working for you?"

"They've been great so far," Grey answered. "But I haven't really used them much."

"You will soon," Lock grimaced slightly. "Arik starts working again tonight. He'll be with Roz until he's back to himself again, but eventually, he'll end up on his own again."

Grey frowned. Lock was right. Without Roz by his side on a nightly basis, it was only a matter of time before Arik came home with another broken bone. Unlike the other Pinkcaps, the Dispensable were not protected under the law. While clients could be blocked for injuring Rags and Doms—or arrested for damaging Apps—Pences could be beaten and sometimes even murdered with little to no repercussions.

"Well, if you're not here about the supplies," Lock clasped his hands on his desk, "what can I do for you?"

"It's about Lydie," Grey said.

Lock hummed, and his expression turned serious. "I heard she broke her finger."

"Dislocated," Grey corrected.

The man nodded. "And how is it now?"

"She'll need to wear a splint for a few weeks—and ice it, if she can remember—but it should be fine," Grey assured him.

Lock ran his fingers through his black curls and leaned back with a frustrated sigh.

"I just wish I knew how it happened," he said. "If a client did it, I could block them and keep them from booking her again."

"Lydie couldn't remember how it happened." Grey shook her head. "I don't even think she knew it was injured before Roz noticed it. But it didn't look intentional. I think she probably just jammed it or fell on it."

Lock nodded, and a moment of silence hung between them before Grey spoke again.

"Isn't there something we can do for her?" she asked.

Shaking his head, Lock sighed. "Right now, I don't know."

"Come on," Grey persisted. "I mean, I couldn't even give her painkillers for her finger because I was afraid she'd go looking for more when I wasn't home."

"I understand." Lock's blue eyes were tired. "But Lydie would need twenty-four-hour surveillance to get clean, and we just don't have the resources."

"Why don't you send her to rehab?" Grey pushed, and her voice rose slightly. "I know the facilities exist. I've visited them."

"I can't."

"You're her Purplecap," Grey snapped. "You're responsible for her health. Why won't you help her?"

"If we send her in," Lock scrubbed at his forehead, "she might never come back."

"What?" Grey's eyes narrowed. "Why not?"

"The Whitecaps are uneasy about the lower caps right now," Lock hesitated. "There's been some unrest in the border territories."

"What kind of unrest?"

"Pieces—and a few Purplecaps—have started to rebel." His eyes locked on hers. "But even knowing that information is grounds for execution. Do you understand me?"

Grey's mouth went dry. "Then why are you telling me."

"You went with Jesse," Lock kept his voice low, almost urgent. "You tried to escape. I know where your loyalties lie."

"That had nothing to do with politics," Grey hissed. "It was about finding somewhere that we could be safe together."

"It's the same thing," Lock said sadly.

"It's not," Grey whispered between her clenched teeth. "Running away is not the same as rebelling. Anyone who tries is just lining up to get themselves killed."

"Is that so?" Lock raised his eyebrows. "Listen, people know High Chancellor Lachlan is dying. And that's an opportunity."

"How?" Grey glared at him.

"The Purplecaps are dividing," he explained. "Some are sucking up to any Whitecap with a chance at becoming the next High Chancellor. They want to protect their assets, their money. Others—like myself—are more interested in protecting their Pinkcaps."

Grey's palms grew clammy as she listened. He was right about one thing, she would keep this secret. But he would never convince her to join a rebellion. Not after what had happened to Jesse. She couldn't—wouldn't—watch people she loved die in front of her. Not again.

"And when Lachlan dies, and a new High Chancellor is instated—whether it's Huxley, or Shawcross, or someone else—one thing is certain: They'll want to reform the lower caps." His eyes grew dark. "But the Purplecaps who think they can keep their money and their power, they're wrong. The new order won't reform by integrating them into higher caps, they'll just eradicate them."

"How can you be sure?" Grey's voice was weak.

"We have eyes and ears everywhere." He stared at her pointedly.

Then realization struck. The Apicals. Whatever the Whitecaps said, the Apps brought it straight back to their Purplecaps.

"And we know there are only two ways a rebellion can end." Lock's frown deepened.

If what he said was true, and the rebellion succeed, it would still be a long journey to find peace. But if it failed, all Pinkcaps—whether they had participated or not—would be annihilated.

"Of course," Lock leaned forward. "If I were you, I'd pick the side with a fighting chance of survival."

"You don't honestly believe the rebels could win," Grey breathed, "do you?"

"I couldn't tell you," he shrugged. "I only know that for now, it's not safe to send Lydie away. Pieces are under scrutiny, and when Lachlan is gone, spending funds on rehabilitation for illegal drug use won't be permitted."

"What if we treat her here?" Grey asked. "What if she stays in until she's better, like Arik? What if we don't let her leave the Base?"

Lock shook his head. "Her tracker will show she's not working."

"But, Arik—"

"Had a legitimate medical injury sustained while working." Lock shook his head.

"And Lydie doesn't?" Grey demanded.

"A broken finger isn't a solid enough excuse to keep her out of work as long as she would need to get clean."

"I wasn't talking about her finger." Grey was incredulous. "She became an addict because of *this*." She motioned to the Base around her. "And where do you think she got drugs in the first place? I'd be willing to bet they were from a client. So even if you don't see it as a legitimate work injury, it's certainly a side-effect of her job."

"I don't disagree with you, Grey." Lock's eyebrows tilted up in sadness. "But the best thing—the safest thing—we can do for her is to help her keep a low profile."

Grey's shoulders sagged forward slightly as the truth of Lock's words sank in. Maybe he was right. They could try to come up with something better for Lydie, but even if she did get clean, she would still be a Piece, and there was nothing Grey could do to change that.

- ♦ -

The smell of the bleach-cleaned pod filled Grey's nostrils as she straightened out her skirt and adjusted the new headband in her hair. True to her word, Roz had taken her to a corner store that afternoon, and although it was cheap quality and pinched behind her ears, the headband got the job done.

Somewhere nearby, Arik and Roz were working as a team. And as uncomfortable as it was for Grey to face the fetishes of Roz's clients, she knew that for Pences like Arik and Megz, it was a small mercy that so many people with bizarre kinks existed. Without them, Roz and Nic would have no excuse to work with the Pences—no way to keep them safe.

Grey yawned deeply and leaned against the steel table. Only one more client to go, and she would be able to go home for the night. Though the metal table was heated from underneath, it still wasn't particularly comfortable to work on, and her knees and elbows were sore. But at least it kept clients from lingering after their sessions were over.

The pod beeped loudly, and Grey jolted and straightened up. She barely had a moment to glance at the screen before the door slid open, revealing a woman in a black cap. For a split second, terror spiked through Grey's body as the memory of Jesse's executioner flooded her mind. But as quickly as it had come, Grey forced the memory back and pasted an inviting smile across her raspberry-tinted lips.

She moved back a few steps, allowing enough space for the Blackcap to step inside.

"Take off that headband." The woman's face was hard and expressionless.

"But," Grey stuttered and tugged on the hem of her skirt, "isn't it illegal to remove your cap in public?"

Was this a test? Was the Blackcap trying to make her break the law? Was she just looking for an excuse to arrest her?

"You're not in public." The woman snapped. "You're in a pod."

Without hesitating, the Blackcap reached up, snatched the headband from Grey's hair, and tossed it on the ground.

At least the floor was clean.

"One rule," the woman growled as she stepped toward Grey. "You don't touch me."

Grey blinked.

"Understand?"

"Of course," Grey nodded.

In her limited experience, female clients were more comfortable to deal with. Just their knowledge of how a woman's body worked was enough to make a considerable difference. But this woman was a Blackcap. And like the majority of female Blackcaps that Grey had treated, there was something hard about this woman.

Most likely, the woman was just a product of her environment. Everything the Blackcaps did was on a schedule. When they ate, when they slept, when they took a shit. It was all worked out for them from the day they were born, and the only way to ease the rigidity was to climb the ranks and begin inflicting that same austerity on their subordinates.

Pieces of Pink

Wordlessly, the woman stepped forward and pushed up Grey's skirt. Her calloused hand raked up the inside of Grey's thigh, pausing only long enough to push Grey's panties aside before the woman slid her fingers inside of her. Then, using her free hand, the Blackcap unbuttoned her own pants and let them fall to her ankles.

It was control, Grey realized as she stood, arms hanging limply at her sides. The woman wanted to have control of something—anything—even if it was another person; because, like so many, she probably couldn't bear the restrictions of her own cap.

From the corner of her eye, Grey could see the pink headband on the floor, and as the Blackcap's fingers moved inside of her, she wished she could reach for it. Because even if it wasn't the color that she wanted it to be, that small band of pink was a reminder to anyone who saw it that she was not here by choice. And when clients took it from her, they took her control.

Grey gritted her teeth. She was done taking off the cap. Even if she had to weave it into her hair to keep it from being removed, Grey would never let a client take that strip of pink from her again.

Grey stood barefoot on the cold tile floor with her wet hair glistening against her ratty t-shirt as she watched herself in the mirror. Droplets of water beaded at the ends of the long strands and soaked into the shirt. As a Redcap, such a simple style had made for easy buns and braids. But she wasn't a Redcap anymore.

Leaning over the sink, Grey twisted out the excess water, patted it with a towel, and brushed it smooth. Thoughtfully, she pulled a section forward and folded it under, trying to imagine how she would look with shorter hair, but it was hard to tell.

Finally, with a sigh, Grey released the wet strand, wrapped her towel around her head, and yanked on a pair of clean socks before heading down to the third floor.

A light was on in Selene's room, its golden warmth spilling out from the crack under the closed door. Grey hesitated when she reached it, listening for any sound within, then knocked.

"Selene?" she whispered, not wanting to wake the Apical if she was sleeping. "Are you awake?"

Faster than she had expected, the door swung open, and Selene frowned down at her. The woman wasn't as tall as Roz, but she was taller than Grey, and even without makeup, she was gorgeous. Her jade eyes shone brightly against her dark skin, and the light bounced off the copper highlights in her curly, black hair.

"What?" Selene snapped.

"I was wondering if you could do something with this." Grey tugged off the towel and let the long strands fall free. "Can you cut it, or color it, or something?"

"It's 2:00 in the fucking morning," the woman growled.

"I know," Grey grimaced, "but it'll be a few hours before anyone else comes home. I just thought if we did it now, we wouldn't bother anyone trying to sleep."

Selene scoffed, and to Grey's surprise, she stepped aside so Grey could enter the room.

"Sit over there." She pointed to a chair beside a low vanity.

Obediently, Grey took a seat and watched as Selene pulled out her supplies and arranged them in front of her. With a large brush, Selene carefully began combing through the wet strands.

"What do you want me to do?" she asked as she smoothed Grey's hair down her back. "Just a trim?"

"I'm not really sure," Grey admitted. "I've always just kept it long, like this."

"Well, that's boring." Selene glanced at Grey's reflection in the mirror. "I can add some layers but keep the length, if you want. We can always go shorter later."

"That sounds good," Grey agreed.

"What about color?" Selene asked.

"I . . ." Grey paused. A thought had been growing in her mind over the past few days, but whether or not she wanted to try it, she still wasn't sure.

"Maybe some blonde highlights?" Selene suggested.

Still, Grey hesitated.

"Yes, or no?" Selene glared, losing her patience.

Grey's eyes locked on Selene's reflection as she took a sharp breath and let the words tumble out. "I want hot pink highlights."

Selene raised her eyebrows, and her mouth fell open slightly.

"My clients," Grey explained, "have been making me take off my headband. They like to pretend they're not paying for it, I guess."

Selene scowled. It was different for her, Grey already knew. The Whitecaps *wanted* others to know just how much purchasing power they had. For them, showing off a Pinkcap—especially an Apical— was a marker of their status, a part of the political game.

"I don't want them to be allowed to forget that they're buying us," Grey admitted, glancing away from Selene. "If we don't have a choice, they shouldn't either."

Behind her, Selene sucked in a slow breath.

"You're not wrong," she conceded. "But it is a pretty loud statement." She surveyed Grey carefully. "Are you sure that's what you want?"

Grey nodded, and with a shrug, Selene began to work.

- ♦ -

Slowly, Grey ran her fingers through her brown and pink hair.

"What do you think?" Selene asked with a smile.

Dried and carefully styled, the soft layers framed Grey's face in a cascade of loose curls.

"I love it." Grey turned to look at Selene, unable to hide her awe.

Selene's skill as a stylist easily matched any Bluecap Grey had ever visited. And since the App didn't accept payment, there was nothing illegal about it.

"It's perfect," Grey grinned, looking back in the mirror.

"Glad you like it." Selene rested a hand on her hip. "But I have to work tomorrow. So, if it's all right with you, I'm going to bed."

"Oh, of course." Grey climbed from the chair and stood, quickly heading for the door, but when she reached it, she stopped and turned back. "Thank you, Selene."

"Whatever." Selene brushed her off. "And not that you will, but if you decide to change it back, I can do that too."

"Thanks for letting me know," Grey smiled warmly as she stepped into the hall, but Selene only closed the door behind her with a thump.

Grey hesitated, mind still fixed on her decision, when a sudden voice snapped her out of her thoughts.

"Rougie!"

Roz stood at the end of the hall. A wild-eyed grin cut across her face as she stalked forward with her high-heeled boots clutched in her hand. Even barefoot, she towered over Grey.

"Look at you." the Dom grinned.

"What do you think?" Self-consciously Grey tucked her hair behind her ear.

As much as she loved what Selene had done, a part of her was still unsure of the new coloring.

"I think it's fierce." Roz gently tugged a curl, and her hand lingered for a moment by Grey's cheek.

"Yeah?"

Roz nodded, and her honey eyes sparkled.

"None of those fuckers can tell you to take off your cap now."

For an instant, something twisted in Grey's chest. She had barely mentioned it to Roz, but the Dom remembered.

"What's wrong?" Roz asked.

"You don't think it's too much?" Grey said.

Although she had grown to know Roz and Arik over the past month, she still felt separate somehow, as if no one really understood or listened to her frustrations. But she was wrong. They had listened, and they cared.

"What?" Roz laughed a little. "Are you disappointed that I'm not offended or something?"

"No," Grey smiled. "I'm just glad you like it."

"Me too," Roz grinned. "It's a bitch to dye hair twice in a row, so it's a good thing it looks so fabulous on you."

Grey blushed. "Thanks."

"And on that note, I need to get some beauty sleep of my own." Roz nodded to her door. "So, I think I'm gonna crash."

"Sounds good," Grey agreed. "Sleep tight."

"I always do." Roz winked, and with that, the Dom disappeared into her room.

SEVEN

A light in the back corner of the shop flickered as Grey tossed a chocolate bar into her basket. The store was small but close to the Base, and it had everything that a Pinkcap could purchase without having to go through Lock.

Behind the counter, the owner—with an orange fedora tipped sideways on his bald head—watched the Pinkcaps as they shopped. Most of the time, his eyes were fixed on Roz, whose sheer top was visible beneath her open coat. But sometimes, his gaze drifted to Grey and settled on the pink highlights in her uncovered hair.

It was strange to be in public without a headband or hat, and although Grey knew that they dye counted as an identifier, she felt oddly naked without it.

"Lock left again this morning," Arik said as he scanned the shelves with tired eyes. "He's visiting a unit out of town."

"Don't worry." Grey glanced at him. "He'll be back home soon."

Arik nodded, but the anxiety was still etched across his face. For the Pences especially, it was difficult to be without Lock for too long. If they had a problem or an injury, it was up to Jax to take care of it, and as an Apical, he could only do so much.

"If you want it," Roz's voice drifted over the aisle from where the Dom stood beside Lydie, "you have to put it in the basket first."

Lydie's mumbled response was inaudible.

"You're still working with Roz, though. Right?" Grey double-checked. Whether or not Lock was home, it was still too soon for Arik to be heading out on his own.

"Yeah," Arik nodded. "For now."

"Good."

With Lydie at her side, Roz rounded the corner carrying an already full shopping basket in the crook of her elbow.

"Ugh, you look amazing." The Dom winked at Grey as she approached, then turned toward the candy shelves. "It's too bad Lock left before he saw your hair. He would love it!"

"Maybe you'll start a new trend," Arik said.

"I doubt it." Grey blushed.

"Grey's right," Roz raised an eyebrow and glanced pointedly back at the shop owner. "Not everyone has hair to dye."

"Roz!" Grey hissed under her breath as the Orangecap scowled.

"What?" Roz shrugged. "I'm not the one who made him bald."

"You don't have to be rude about it," Arik suggested softly.

"I'm not being rude," Roz smirked. "I'm just pointing out facts."

With a mischievous grin dancing over her lips, Roz strode toward the register and plunked her basket on the counter. The Orangecap didn't greet her as he began scanning the items and dropping them unceremoniously into a brown paper bag.

"Card or chip?"

When he asked for the payment method—as if there was an option for Pinkcaps—Roz rolled her eyes and stuck out her wrist. And with a quick swipe, the man scanned her implant and passed her the paper bag.

"Have a nice day!" Roz crooned at the scowling Orangecap as she bumped open the front door with her hip and stepped into the sunlight with Lydie at her heels.

Shaking her head at Roz, Grey set her basket on the countertop alongside Arik's.

"Fucking Pinkcaps," the Orangecap muttered under his breath as he scanned their items and tossed them into a bag.

Blushing, Grey held out her arm for the scanner and quickly slipped out the door. She knew the man had waited to say the words until Roz was gone, and although the words had been hurtful, she was more embarrassed by her own unwillingness to stand up for herself and for Arik.

"What a dickhead," Roz huffed as they turned back toward the Base. "He probably makes most of his money off of Pieces, but he treats us like we're fucking criminals or something."

"Then, why go back?" Grey asked.

Roz rooted through her grocery bag as she walked. "It's convenient," she admitted as she pulled out a protein bar and handed it to Arik. "And they'd treat us the same in any other shop."

"To be fair," Lydie sighed, and a lazy smile slid over her cheeks, "they always have the best free samples."

"Free samples?" Grey asked.

"Yeah," Lydie nodded, reached up her sleeve with her uninjured hand, and pulled out two bars of chocolate.

"Holy shit," Roz's eyes bulged as she stared down at Lydie's haul.

"Did you steal those?" Grey gasped.

"Well, he spent so much time staring at your boobs and your hair," sleepily, she glanced between them, "I thought it was a fair trade of goods and services."

For a moment, there was silence. Then Roz began to laugh. It was contagious and deep, and before long, they had all joined in. As out of it as Lydie was, there was still a glimpse of her personality beneath all of the drugs. And it was a relief to know that in some small way, she was still hanging on—as long as she didn't get caught.

They were still giggling when they reached the entrance of the Base and stepped into the foyer.

"I hate to say he deserves it," Roz chuckled as she shimmied out of her coat and tossed it over her arm, "but Lydie has a point. People should have to pay to look at this." Sensually, she trailed her fingertips down her sheer top.

"What the fuck?" A voice broke through their laughter, and Grey spun to its source.

Jax stood in the doorframe of the dining room, holding his jacket in one hand and his pink cap in the other. He was still wearing the same outfit he had left the Base in over twenty-four hours ago, but his wrinkled dress shirt was unbuttoned at the collar, and his hair was disheveled.

"Have you lost your mind?" he demanded, and only then did Grey realize his eyes were locked on her.

"What?" she stammered.

In the dining room behind Jax, the Pinkcaps had fallen silent.

"Your hair," he spat.

"Jax." Roz's tone was warning.

"I'll assume it was a mistake," he growled, ignoring Roz, "and that you were going for a different color. Selene will fix it when she gets home."

Shoulders slumped with exhaustion, Jax turned away and trudged toward the stairwell.

"No." Grey took a step forward.

"What?" He twisted back to look at her.

"It wasn't a mistake." She stood up a little straighter. "I want it like this."

"Why?" Jax's lips curled back in disgust.

"I'm sick of clients telling me to take my cap off." Grey clenched her fists by her sides.

"What do you mean?" There were dark circles under his eyes, and his tone was ice-cold.

"I mean that people shouldn't be allowed to forget what they're doing and who they're doing it too," Grey said sharply. "They shouldn't be allowed to pretend that things are different, just because the truth makes them uncomfortable."

"And what if you want to forget?" Jax yelled, "What if you want to pretend that things are different? What if you want to come home at night and know that you'll be able to eat dinner with your friends without having to see a fucking cap on anyone's head?"

People were gathering in the doorway now.

"What if you just want to be human?" he roared.

Grey opened her mouth to speak but found no words. Then, Jax's voice went deadly calm as his eyes locked on hers.

"You're Dispensable tonight."

A shocked murmur rippled through the Base, but it was Arik who stepped forward on Grey's behalf.

"Come on, Jax," Arik pleaded. "You're just tired right now. You don't really mean that."

Jax shot Arik a glare.

"I do mean it," he said. "She's not even one of us. But she thinks she knows what it's like? How it feels?" He shook his head, disgust in his eyes. "No one would choose this for themselves, and that," he pointed at her hair, "is an insult to anyone who was born a Piece."

"That's not true!" Roz snarled back and stepped up beside Grey. "And you can't just make her a Pence. Lock won't let you."

"Lock isn't here," Jax snapped. And with that, he turned on his heel and strode up the stairs, leaving Grey standing in silence.

"Fucking prick!" Roz screamed after him, and when he didn't respond, she growled in frustration.

"Can't we stop him?" Arik asked. But from the defeat in his voice, Grey already knew they couldn't.

"He's the only one with clearance to change our tracker settings when Lock's away." Roz began pacing, like some caged animal. "Maybe he won't go through with it."

"I could try talking to him," Arik persisted.

Roz nodded. "It's worth a shot."

Without hesitation, Arik limped after Jax.

"I can't believe he would do this to one of us." Roz shook her head in disbelief.

"He wouldn't." Grey's voice almost broke on the words. "But I'm not one of you. Not to him, at least."

"Bullshit," Roz snarled. "He knows what it's like out there. He knows better than to punish someone like this. And you might be new, but you're still a Piece. You're family."

"Then why is he so upset?" Grey asked, an edge of desperation creeping into her words.

"We all have our masks," Roz frowned deeply. "You wear lipstick, Lydie uses drugs, and Jax takes off his cap. It's the only way he can feel at home. I just didn't know he cared so much about the rest of us wearing them."

Grey's heart sank in her chest. If he was truly projecting his emotions—whether from anger or exhaustion—he was unlikely to listen to Arik. She glanced at the clock on the wall. Only an hour left before it was time to head out for the night. She hoped that Arik could stall Jax long enough to stop him from changing the tracker settings, but in her gut, she knew talking wouldn't accomplish anything. Jax needed sleep to make any sort of rational decision, and by the time he had that, Grey would already be in the pods.

- ♦ -

The cobblestone sidewalk was slick with rain as Grey strode to keep pace with Roz. Without umbrellas, the water had already seeped into their clothes. Grey's hands shook; whether from the cold air or her impending assignment, she wasn't sure. Clenching her teeth, she shoved her fingers into her shallow pockets and tried to warm them into stillness.

At the sound of quick footsteps behind her, she paused and glanced over her shoulder. Limping up the street behind her, Arik rushed to catch up.

"Roz," Grey called ahead. "Wait a minute. Arik's coming."

The Dom whirled back, jogging the last few steps to close the distance between them.

"Did Jax say anything?" she asked.

"He wouldn't talk to me." Arik wheezed as he tried to catch his breath and cast his eyes to the ground. "He just went into his room and locked the door. I tried, Grey. I'm sorry."

"It's not your fault," Grey said. "Thanks for trying."

"That little shit," Roz grumbled. "He's all worked up over the fucking High Chancellor, but it doesn't give him the right to treat the rest of us like trash."

"I mean, really, how bad can it be?" Grey asked—although she already knew the truth—and Roz shot her a sharp glance out of the corner of her eye.

"Bad enough." The Dom frowned.

"Honestly," Arik countered, "some nights are okay."

"Come on, Arik." Roz frowned. "Have you ever even made it a full night without being hit?" She quickly amended, "When you weren't working with me?"

"Not everyone hits," Arik answered. "Sometimes, I just get the clients who can't afford to hire anything more than a Pence."

"And the rest of the time?" Roz raised her eyebrows.

Arik shrugged but didn't respond.

"Listen to me, Grey." Roz pivoted to face Grey and stopped dead in front of her. "You can take a sick day. Your pay will be docked, and you might get a light slap on the wrist, but there's paperwork you can fill out. And you're a Rougie. I'm sure you could come up with some medical excuse, something believable."

Grey shook her head.

"Food poisoning?" Roz suggested. "Uncontrollable vomiting and diarrhea? A twenty-four-hour plague?"

"No, Roz." Grey insisted.

"Is that a no, you can't think of a medical excuse?" Roz frowned deeply. "Or just, no?"

"Just, no."

Roz's eyes narrowed. "Why?"

"It's just," Grey hesitated, "it's not right."

"What do you mean, it's not right?" Roz threw her hands up, exasperated. "You're not a Pence. You're a Rag! You're training to be a Dom for fuck's sake. You shouldn't have to do this."

"Neither should Arik." Grey glanced at him, apologetically. It was unfair to drag him in like that, but it was also true. He returned a sad smile, but his dark eyes were understanding.

"I know." Roz's voice rose, bouncing through the empty street. "But how will things ever change for us—for Pinkcaps—if we don't even protect each other?"

"Roz," Arik warned softly. "Not here."

Sullen, she dropped her voice to a whisper. "Solidarity is one thing. But this," she crossed her arms over her chest, "is fucked up."

"If I don't go tonight," Grey said, "then Jax is right."

"How?" Roz glared at her incredulously.

"Then, I'm not a Pinkcap." She struggled for the words. "I can't just keep pretending I'm a Redcap. I can't just try to escape the truth all the time. I just end up screwing myself over whenever I try to take another path. So, for once in my life, I just need to accept that I've landed in a pile of crap and deal with it."

"That is the dumbest shit I have ever heard," Roz said slowly.

Finally, Grey snapped.

"Fuck, Roz!" she exclaimed, then dropped her voice to a harsh whisper. "This isn't a great time for us to be breaking any rules. So, if it's all right with you, I'm just going to do what I'm told for once in my life."

As soon as the words were out of her mouth, Grey regretted them. Somehow, admitting her fear had made it more real. But Roz's shoulders relaxed, and she uncrossed her arms. Gently, she placed her hands on either side of Grey's cheeks and looked her straight in the eyes. "What's going on with you?"

Grey pulled her face away from Roz's touch.

"Talk to us." There was a plea behind Roz's command.

"When you break the rules, bad things happen," Grey answered.

"Like what?" Roz insisted.

As much as her heart was screaming for her to tell Roz and Arik about Jesse and the border, and the uprisings in the South—just for the weight to be lifted from her chest—Grey couldn't bring herself to let the words out. Not yet.

"How do you think I became a Pinkcap?"

With a deep breath, Roz closed her eyes and nodded slowly.

"Fine. But if things start going south," she paused pointedly, "just get the hell out of here and run to the Base. Understand?"

Grey nodded—though she doubted her own ability to keep the promise—and Roz turned back to the road ahead.

- ♦ -

Pieces of Pink

In many ways, the night started like any other. Grey scanned herself into a pod, waited for a client, serviced him, and stepped outside while the pod was cleaned.

The only notable difference was that the client—a Bluecap—had been a little gruffer and dirtier than she was used to. His hands—the hands of a mechanic—were stained dark with grease and oil that would never really come clean, no matter how many times he washed, and a five o'clock shadow hung around his jaw.

The session had been quick and relatively painless, and when the man left, Grey had felt relieved. But now, standing outside the pod, waiting for the light to flash green, her hands were beginning to shake again. For every session that went well, the chance of a terrible client still lingered. And the memory of Arik crawling through the front door of the Base still clung fresh in her mind.

Grey pulled her jacket tighter around her shoulders, and when the pod light changed, she quickly provided a blood sample and slipped back inside. Protected from the elements, the heated pod felt safe, in a way. And even as a Dispensable, she was guarded from diseases by the mandatory blood tests.

Taking a deep breath, Grey combed her fingers through her damp hair—now free of any headpiece—and lightly shook the raindrops from her clothes.

A few minutes passed in silence, and she was just beginning to feel comfortable when the pod beeped, and anxiety bloomed in her chest. She glanced down at the screen to prepare herself, but unlike the pod formatting for Doms—and even the Rags—no additional information was given. Grey exhaled a shaking breath as the door slowly slid open, and a man—a Blackcap—stormed inside.

There was no hesitation, no cursory glance, or word of greeting as the man lunged across the pod while the door closed shut behind him. Grabbing a fistful of her hair, he yanked Grey's head toward the light, and she let out a sharp cry.

Staring down at her, he growled, "You don't look like a Pence."

"I—" she began to reply, but before she could get a second word out, he backhanded her across the face so hard that she fell, hitting her head on the steel table.

Lights swam before her eyes as the man yanked her arms and hauled her to her feet. With vision blurry from the impact of the strike, she struggled to fight back as he shoved her onto the table and ripped her shirt over her head.

"No deformities," he sneered, squeezing her breast too hard in his hand. "So, what are you? An idiot or something?"

"I'm a Rag!" she cried, but he only laughed in her face.

"That's not what your microchip says."

"It's a mistake." Her voice cracked as she tried to shove him off. Maybe the half-truth would work. "I'm a Rag, not a Pence!"

"That's between you and your Purplecap," he snarled. "It's not my problem."

"But, I—"

With a closed fist, the man punched her, and her head snapped sideways. A metallic taste flooded Grey's mouth, and she whimpered. She had bitten her tongue hard enough to make blood flow, and her cheekbone throbbed painfully. Dazed, she squirmed, trying to pull herself away, but he yanked open her pants and pulled them down around her knees.

"No!" she yelled and tried to stomp his foot, to knee him in the groin, to hit anything tender and unprotected. But when she tried to snap at him with her teeth, he pushed her away, bent her forward, and smashed her face into the table. Then, with his hand fisted tightly in her hair, the Blackcap entered her.

Grey screamed as he thrust, slamming her so hard that the steel fixtures on table legs clattered rhythmically against the floor. Fire burned between her legs as he forced himself in, over and over.

Pieces of Pink

Clenching every muscle in her body, she fought to keep him out, to get him off of her, but she was too weak. If only he tried to stick his dick in her mouth, she would bite it off. But he didn't, and she couldn't. He was too strong to beat.

The seconds dilated into eternity, and when the man came, Grey felt his semen exploding inside of her, hot and wet—an invasion. A broken sob cracked from her chest, and at the sound—sharp and hollow—the Blackcap finally released her.

Grey crumpled to the floor beside her discarded shirt, and staring through tears, she watched his booted feet recede from the pod and disappear into the night.

She didn't know how long she had been lying there, curled on the cold steel floor. But when the door opened again, and a pair of black boots appeared, Grey shrank back, whimpering.

"It's all right." The careful voice was not male.

Teeth chattering with cold and shock, Grey lifted her head and looked up at the woman.

She was a Blackcap, but there was something familiar in her face. Grey groaned as recognition sank in. The woman had been a client the night before, the client who didn't want to be touched.

A whine, like a cornered animal, cracked through Grey's lips. She couldn't take it, not again.

"I'm not going to hurt you." The Blackcap crouched beside her and reached out a hand, covered in an armored glove.

Grey recoiled, and the woman instantly pulled her hand back.

"Look." The Blackcap tapped the badge over her breast. "I'm on the clock, see?"

Scanning her up and down, Grey saw that the Blackcap was in full uniform: black cargo pants tucked into combat boots, a utility belt, a bullet-proof vest, a gun, and a black helmet. She was a part of the night patrol, and she wasn't here as a client, just here for work.

"Can you stand on your own?" The woman's voice wasn't gentle, but it wasn't hard either. It was professional. "Or do you need help getting up?"

Without answering, Grey slowly pushed herself to her knees. Her arms trembled as she clawed up the side of the steel table and into a standing position. Then, she began to pull up her pants. There was a trickle of blood running down her thigh, but she ignored it because to acknowledge it would be to admit that it was real.

Her fingertips shook against the button and zipper as the Blackcap scooped Grey's shirt off the floor and laid it on the table. Grey took it, pulled it over her head, and reached for her jacket.

"I know you're not a Pence," the woman stated matter-of-factly. "What happened?"

"There was . . ." Grey hesitated. It was uncomfortable to speak with her swollen tongue, and even if it weren't, she didn't entirely know how to answer. "A clerical error."

"All right, then." The woman nodded and pulled a scanner out of her belt. "Let's get you home so you can get this sorted out."

Without touching her, the woman aimed the device at Grey's wrist and picked up the signal of her tracker.

"What are you doing?" Grey's words slurred as she tried to speak.

"Just finding your unit," the woman answered calmly.

The scanner beeped, and the Blackcap glanced down at the screen as Grey slid her arms into her jacket.

"Can you walk there?" The woman's eyes traced over Grey—assessing her as any trained soldier would—but lingered a moment too long on the space between Grey's legs. "Do you need a Redcap?"

Grey shook her head. She didn't need a Redcap. There was no point. The only thing they could do was take samples to identify the rapist. But this wasn't rape.

Grey's breath hitched in her throat, and a sob took its place.

This had been completely legal.

Tears blurred her vision as the Blackcap shifted uncomfortably on her feet. "All right, let's head out."

Still crying, Grey followed the woman out of the pod and into the misting rain. But even with the Blackcap guarding her side, Grey was terrified. Every footstep, every voice, every movement of shadow, all of them clawed into her mind, whispering that the night wasn't over yet, sneering that she would never be safe, watching from behind every reflection.

"When you get home," the woman said, "make sure you tell your Purplecap what happened."

Grey glanced at her. "Why?"

"So, it can be fixed."

"It can never be *fixed*." Her voice sound detached, even to her own ears.

"I know that." The woman frowned. "But tell your Purplecap to make sure it never happens again."

Sucking in a shaking breath, Grey whispered, "Why are you trying to help me?"

The woman glanced sideways at her. "What do you mean?"

"I'm a Pinkcap." She broke on the last word. "Why are you helping a Pinkcap?"

"You are a citizen of Citoyen," the Blackcap answered without hesitation. "And you were injured while performing your duty to your country. *My* duty is to make sure you return home safely."

A part of Grey wanted to respond, but she didn't. Instead, she walked in silence until they reached the Base, and the Blackcap saw her inside.

Feet dragging like dead weights, Grey climbed the porch, pushed through the door, and closed it tightly behind her. She took the few steps toward the bottom of the stairs, but when she reached out for the rail, she realized that her hand was trembling, and it was not from cold or fear.

As she desperately tried to steady her breath, Grey's whole body began to quiver. Her heart beat faster and faster and she realized, she was in shock. Breath quickening, Grey sank to her knees and vomited.

- ♦ -

It was Roz who found her, curled under the stairs like an animal that had found a quiet place to die.

"Grey?" Roz whispered, dropping to her knees. When Grey didn't answer, she reached for her.

"Don't touch me," Grey hissed.

"Okay," Roz promised, quickly retracting her hand. "I won't."

Grey whimpered, and tears slid down her cheeks.

"Why don't you come upstairs with me?" Roz asked. "You can take a nice bath."

Grey didn't answer, but a movement above their heads made Roz look up.

"Roz?" It was Selene. "What's going on down there?"

"Your boyfriend fucked up," Roz snarled at Selene as she descended the stairs.

"How?" Selene asked.

"Jax didn't like the haircut," Roz glowered.

"What do you mean?" Selene demanded, but when she came into view of Grey, the Apical gasped.

Roz's golden eyes were glowing with hatred as she clenched her hands into tight fists. "I'm gonna strangle him."

"You'd be arrested, Roz." Selene's voice was stern. "He's the High Chancellor's Piece, and he's an App. You can't lay a hand on him. You of all people should know that."

Roz was not exaggerating, and Selene knew it.

"The fuck do I care if I get arrested?"

"If you get arrested," Selene said slowly, "you can't be here to help her . . . or Arik."

Roz huffed but didn't protest.

"Grey," Selene's voice was soft—warm, almost—as she dropped to her knees and crawled forward. "Roz and I are going to take you upstairs and give you a bath." Slowly, she reached out her hand. "Will you come with us?"

"No." Her teeth chattered together as she spoke. "I can't."

"Yes," Selene insisted. "You can. Now get up."

"Why?" the word was a broken plea.

"Because we've all been here," Selene answered. "And we've all gotten back up."

Grey's mind spun as she considered the implications of Selene's words. A part of her—the part that had been trained as a Redcap since birth—knew that she needed to stand and follow the women upstairs, but her entire body felt numb as if it had been detached from her in some intrinsic way.

"Selene's right," Roz whispered. "And if we've done it, you can do it too."

With every ounce of will that she had left, Grey reached for the piece of herself—that mask of calmness—that knew what needed to be done, and on trembling legs, she rose.

"That's it," Roz encouraged, and she took a step forward. "Lean on us."

Finally, Grey reached out and fell into their open arms, and one stair at a time, she let them lead her upstairs.

- ♦ -

"Sit here," Roz instructed as she pulled out the stool and draped two clean, dry towels around Grey's shoulders. "I'll fill the tub."

The Dom's eyes darted to Selene. "Could you find her some clean pajamas to wear?"

"Of course," Selene nodded and slipped from the bathroom, closing the door behind her.

Wordlessly, Roz plugged the drain, twisted the old brass taps, and watched as a stream of clear water shot from the spout. Splashing her hand through the cascade, she tested the heat, adjusted the temperature, and glanced over her shoulder.

"Can you undress yourself?" she asked. "Or do you need help?"

"I can do it myself." Grey's tongue felt thick and heavy as she formed the words.

"All right." Roz nodded.

Slowly, Grey stood, but as she moved to peel away the layers of her clothes, she caught a glimpse of herself in the mirror and froze. A tangle of pink and brown hair framed her face, and her lips and cheek were already puffy and swollen. It was clear that a black eye would bloom in the coming days.

"Grey?" Roz's voice cut through the echo of splashing water. "Are you all right?"

In silence, Grey nodded and turned away from the mirror. She let the towels fall to the floor, then slipped out of her jacket, and pulled her shirt over her head. She removed her pants last, and when she did, she saw Roz gazing at the lingering smear of dried blood streaked down her thighs.

Pieces of Pink

"Do you need to see a Redcap?" Roz's voice was calm and collected as she asked the question, but her eyes were full of rage.

"No." The bleeding had already stopped. Any tearing had been minimal—at least from a medical standpoint—and there was little anyone could do for her. "I'm fine."

Without questioning her, Roz simply nodded and held out a hand to help her into the tub. Hot steam curled from the water as Grey sank into its surface and drew her knees into her chest.

"Is it warm enough?"

She nodded.

There was a soft knock, and Selene entered, holding clean pajamas in her arms. She hesitated a moment in the doorway, face contorted in a nervous frown before she finally spoke.

"I told Jax what happened."

"What?" Roz's gaze was incredulous as she turned to stare down Selene. "How could you do that?"

"He woke up when I was getting these." She held up the pajamas.

Roz's eyes flashed behind Selene toward the sound of footsteps running up the stairs.

"He asked what was going on and—"

"You idiot!" Roz snapped. "Keep him out of here."

But it was too late. No sooner had Roz gotten the words out than Jax appeared in the doorway. His hair was disheveled from sleep, and he wore a plain, white t-shirt with dark sweatpants. As Grey's tired eyes fell over him, she couldn't help but think he'd never looked less threatening than he did now.

Why had she ever thought she needed to prove herself to him? What did it matter if he saw her as a Redcap, or a Pinkcap, or anything else?

"Grey." Jax's voice was low and tired as he tried to step around Selene. Mercifully, she held her ground and didn't let him pass.

"Jax," Selene warned. "Not now."

"I'm sorry." Jax's words sounded genuine, but it was hard for Grey to care. "I was tired, and I was angry, and I shouldn't have—"

"You need to leave," Roz whispered, and there was a deadliness in her gold eyes that sent a chill down Grey's exposed back. "Now."

But Jax ignored her. "It was unforgivable, and I'm—"

"Get out!" Roz roared, and her voice echoed off of the tile, drowning out the noise of the running water and the sound of Grey's broken sobs.

In the absence of Roz's voice, the bathroom plunged into silence, and Jax staggered back.

"Selene," he whispered, but she only shook her head and closed the door in his face. Grey heard it lock with a soft click, and finally, her shoulders began to relax.

"Let me get a new bar of soap," Roz said hoarsely as she pushed herself up and turned toward that cabinet.

Turning her back, she snatched a small box from the stash tucked beside the towels. But when she returned to the tub and knelt down, Grey saw silent tears streaming down The Dom's cheeks. Without another word, Roz dipped the fresh, white soap into the water and gently began to scrub Grey clean.

EIGHT

A golden shaft of sunlight streaked across the room. Grey had been staring at it for an hour, watching it slide toward the floor as the sun shifted across the sky. She had spent one whole day in bed, and then another.

Grey's eye had swollen, leaving only a narrow slit to see from, and her lips were puffy and sore. Her tongue still stung from where she had bitten it, but she knew it would be the first thing to heal.

In the hall, the sound of footsteps, then a soft tap on the door, drew her gaze away from the sunlit and toward the doorknob. She sighed but remained where she lay, tucked beneath the warm sheets.

"It's Arik."

Grey didn't respond.

"I was wondering if you'd like to come downstairs for breakfast."

She rolled over to face the wall, turning her back on the door. Roz had been bringing her meals for the past two days, but she'd barely touched them. She couldn't bring herself to feel hungry.

She couldn't bring herself to feel anything, really.

"Grey?"

When she didn't answer a second time, Arik's footsteps retreated down the stairwell and stopped on the third floor. A few minutes later, there was a second knock, and Grey pulled the covers up over her head.

"It's me," Roz said flatly. "I'm coming in."

Grey didn't move as Roz opened the door, crossed the room, and took a seat on the edge of the bed. Gently, the woman laid a hand on the blankets covering Grey's back.

"Well, you're warm," Roz said with a lightness in her voice that hinted at mirth. "So, I guess you're not dead, then."

Grey remained silent, and Roz paused for a moment, waiting. When there was no reaction, she gently folded down the blankets, so Grey couldn't hide from her.

"It's time," the Dom said, all teasing gone from her voice. "You're only as alone as you force yourself to be. There are two dozen Pieces down there who know what this feels like. Two dozen people who are there for you, if you'll allow it. And no one will think differently of you for what's happened."

In the silence that followed, Grey counted her breaths. She wanted to find the right words to explain her emotions, but there were none.

Finally, she mumbled, "I can't."

"Why not?" Roz demanded.

"I just can't."

"Is it because of Jax?" Roz growled slightly under her breath. "He isn't home right now."

Hesitant, Grey glanced up at Roz.

"He's with Lachlan," Roz said. "Lucky for him, or I'd have mounted his left nut on my wall by now."

The thought sent a shiver down the back of Grey's neck.

"How can you say things like that?" she asked.

"Like what?" Roz raised a dark eyebrow, her eyes serious.

Grey shook her head but didn't explain further.

"You didn't deserve to be punished." Roz's voice was icy. "But, Jax does."

Although a part of her wanted revenge, she didn't think taking it out on Jax would make a difference. Yes, he had been wrong, but she had seen his eyes when he'd tried to apologize. And there were things she wanted to tell Roz about guilt and regret, things that she was sure Jax felt. Then again, Grey couldn't bring herself to forgive him either.

Not yet.

Even if there was a part of her that had understood Jax's reaction—a part that didn't blame him—there was an equally strong part that hated him.

"But I guess karma's a bitch, right?" Roz asked with a dark chuckle. "He'll get his."

Grey frowned.

"So, what do you say?" Roz asked. "Breakfast?"

Reluctantly, Grey slipped from the bed. Then, grabbing a hair-tie from the dresser, she twisted her dyed hair into a sloppy bun and pulled up the hood of her black sweatshirt. She didn't want to be stared at, or waved at, or spoken to.

She just wanted to be invisible.

"By the way, Lock came home last night," Roz said. "He wants you to stop by his office when you're feeling up to it. Oh, and I changed the tape on Lydie's splint this morning."

Grey flinched. She had forgotten Lydie.

"Has she been icing it?" Grey asked.

Roz nodded. "I try to keep her on top of it—when I can—but honestly, it looks fine."

"Good."

When the pair reached the bottom of the stairs, and the sounds of breakfast met her, Grey froze. She was embarrassed somehow, though she didn't understand why. It felt like a black spot had been smeared on her face, marking her out as something unclean, something sub-human. Her breath rattled.

"You're all right." Roz patted her back, urging her forward. "And I'm hungry. So, let's get in there before Nic and eats everything."

Nodding, Grey dropped her gaze to the floor and allowed Roz to guide her into the room. When they reached their table, Grey slid into the seat beside Arik and peeked out from under her hood. No one seemed to notice her presence, and she wasn't sure if it was a relief or an insult.

"Here." Selene's tone was clipped as she set a glass in front of Grey's empty plate. "Drink some water. Your skin looks dry."

As Grey reached for the glass, Roz covertly slid a bowl of steaming scrambled eggs under Grey's nose.

Grey cleared her throat, trying not to dry-heave at the smell.

"You'll feel less nauseous if you eat something," Arik said, only loud enough for her to hear. "I know it can be hard at first, but things will get better."

Holding her breath, Grey reached for her fork and took a bite.

"Toast?" Across the table, Lydie offered her a waffle.

Grey was about to decline when a movement from the corner of her eye made her look up. In the small door that led to the kitchen, Lock was standing with his head bowed and his hands in his pockets. The Purplecap's black curls fell in his face, and his shoulders slumped forward, defeated, as he walked into the dining room.

When he reached the center, Lock looked up.

"Everyone?" His voice cut through the sounds of chatter and clinking silverware until one by one, the room settled into silence.

"I'm so sorry to interrupt your meal." His voice was shaking, and his face, paler than usual. "But I have an important announcement to make."

"Shit." Beside Grey, Roz muttered under her breath.

"The High Chancellor . . ." Lock's throat bobbed, and his voice cracked. "High Chancellor Lachlan is dead."

A collective hush descended, and as Lock turned back toward his office, Grey glimpsed a tear rolling down his cheek.

- ♦ -

A shadow moved behind the stairs as Grey walked toward Lock's office, and before she had time to think, her body reacted. Quickly, she shuffled to the side and put her hands in front of her face, prepared to defend herself.

"It's just me."

She knew the voice. It was Jax's, but it seemed so much smaller than it had before. Slowly, her shoulders relaxed, and Jax stepped into the light.

The man's hair was ruffled, and the collar of his white shirt was turned up on one side as if he'd hastily removed a tie. His pants were wrinkled, and dark circles hung under his eyes. Although she'd heard him called the most handsome Pinkcap in Citoyen, he did not look like it now.

"Grey." Jax took a step forward, but she stepped back.

Taking the hint, he stopped moving toward her and looked down at his hands.

"What I did was wrong," he said. "I shouldn't have made you a Dispensable, and I'm sorry."

When she didn't answer, he looked up.

"Grey?"

She had heard his words, understood the truth behind them, but she simply had no response. Accepting his apology would have required words like 'okay' and 'thank you,' but it wasn't okay, and she certainly wasn't about to thank him for feeling guilty, so there was nothing to say.

"Are you all right?" he asked.

Her swollen lips remained shut.

"Grey, I—"

With a soft exhale, Grey stepped around him, knocked twice on Lock's office door. She opened it before waiting for a response. And then, she stopped.

The room was so much smaller than she remembered—too small, like a pod—and if it weren't for the Apical standing at her back, she would have remained in the hall.

Hunched over his desk, Lock sat with his head in his hands.

"Lock?" she mumbled.

The man jumped as if he hadn't heard the door open and quickly wiped away his tears.

"Oh, Grey," he tried to smile but couldn't. "I'm sorry. Please, come in."

Silently, she stepped into the room, and as she turned to close the door behind herself, she saw Jax with his head bowed, retreating toward the dining room.

"I was just—" he shook his head, unable to finish his words.

Whatever had pushed Lock to tears, it had to be for something more than the death of a Whitecap. Grey watched him carefully as he spoke. Maybe something had gone wrong with the rebellion in the South.

"Listen." He was apologetic now. "I heard about what happened with Jax."

Grey frowned deeply.

"What he did was out of line," Lock said sternly. "He allowed his emotions to take control of his judgment, and he hurt another Pinkcap." The man's bright blue eyes met hers. "He hurt you."

She didn't respond.

Pieces of Pink

"And I don't mean to defend him, but—"

"Then don't."

Lock looked taken aback.

"If you don't mean to defend him," Grey said, "then don't."

"Fair enough," Lock said. "I'm sorry."

Grey sucked in a long breath, and her eyes fell to a spot on the floor as she spoke. A pattern had been worn in the dark finish by the passage of feet and time.

"Blame is just an excuse to ignore the truth." The words were quiet. "Everyone is blaming Jax for what happened the other night." She shook her head slowly. "I mean, I think Roz would try to hurt him if she had the chance."

Lock sat in silence, waiting for Grey to continue.

"And a part of me blames him too," she said. "But if I blame Jax, then I have to blame you."

Slowly, Grey lifted her tired eyes to meet Lock's.

To his credit, the man did not flinch.

"And if I blame you," she continued, "then I have to blame all Purplecaps. And if I blame all Purplecaps, I have to blame all Whitecaps, and before long, I'll be blaming all of Citoyen."

Grey's eyes fell back to the worn spot on the hardwood floor.

"And maybe all of Citoyen *is* to blame," she shrugged. "But I can't do anything about that. So, for now, I'm going to blame the man who did this to me," she pointed at her bruised face, "because human beings should know better than to treat other human beings this way, regardless of what their government allows."

"And if your government could be changed?" Lock's voice was barely above a whisper.

"Then, I would change it."

When Grey looked back up again, silent tears were sliding down Lock's pale cheeks.

Grey's eyes narrowed as she watched him. "Who was he to you?" she asked. "Who was the High Chancellor?"

Lock shook his head but didn't answer. After a moment of silence, Grey stood from her chair. But when she turned toward the door, the Purplecap's voice made her stop.

"He was . . ." Lock paused, "nothing."

Grey stood still, reaching for a response, but that sacred place where her emotions had once been held was void. Empathy, love, joy, even sadness, had abandoned her, and the only thing left to feel was the detached weakness of her own body.

"I'm sorry for your loss." The words were hollow, and with no kindness left to offer, she left the room.

-♦-

"At least we get a day off," Roz said as she reclined on Arik's bed with her head propped up in her palm. Her booted feet—crossed almost daintily at the ankles—dangled off the end of the mattress. On anyone else, the position would have looked prim and proper, but on Roz, it looked defiant.

"For what?" Grey asked. Not that it mattered. She would have the day off whether the others did or not. Lock had removed her from the rosters, at least until the swelling and bruising went down on her face . . . and between her legs.

"The funeral." Roz rolled her eyes. "Apparently, it's considered a national holiday when a High Chancellor dies."

"Oh." Grey's eyes drifted to the bedroom window, and to the dark gray clouds beginning to form outside. Lachlan was the first High Chancellor to die in her lifetime. Even so, as a Redcap, she had always been on call during national holidays.

"It's strange that we should mourn a Whitecap like this." An edge crept into Roz's voice. "I mean, the whole idea of a public procession is just so . . ."

She took a deep breath when she couldn't find the right word.

"I don't know," she continued, "It's like they're trying to make him into some noble hero who worked tirelessly for the good of Citoyen and its people."

"Well, he did try," Arik said softly.

"He was High Chancellor for decades." Roz scowled. "If he really cared, he would have done more."

"The pods were—" Arik began, but Roz quickly cut him off.

"The pods were literally the only thing he ever did for us."

"And the child labor laws," Grey pointed out.

"It doesn't matter," Roz growled. "He only did it because of—"

Roz stopped suddenly, golden eyes darting to the side.

"He did it for selfish reasons, not for the common good." She shook her head. "And I just don't think we should be worshiping him like some kind of deity."

Grey raised her eyebrows slightly. Though it wasn't from happiness, her swollen lips twitched up in a slight smile—a smile that she had learned from Roz—as she repeated the Dom's own words back to her: "But at least we get a day off."

Roz scoffed and chucked one of Arik's pillows at her. Grey caught it, and this time the grin that stretched her puffy lips was real.

"And without Lachlan," Roz smirked, "Jax will get knocked down a peg."

Arik frowned. "Don't be so nasty about it."

"I'm not being nasty." She shrugged. "Not if it's true."

"What do you mean?" Grey asked.

"I mean," her eyes narrowed, "without the High Chancellor as a client, Jax is fucked. The new High Chancellor—whoever he or she is—won't want Lachlan's Piece lying around," Roz explained.

"Actually, they probably won't let Jax into political functions at all anymore."

"Why not?" Grey frowned. "I thought he was supposed to be the best App in Citoyen."

"He is," Roz agreed. "But he knows too much about the other Whitecaps. Plus, he'll always be seen as sympathetic to the old High Chancellor. He's someone else's pet." She shook her head. "As long as Lachlan was alive, being the High Chancellor's Piece made Jax a commodity. He was the one Pinkcap no one else could have without explicit permission. But in the long run, it depreciated his value. Whitecaps don't want used goods."

"Well, what happens to Apicals when the Whitecaps don't want them anymore?" Grey asked. "Execution?"

If Jax truly knew as much about the Whitecaps as Roz had suggested, he might be seen as more than just a used toy; he might be seen as a threat.

"What?" Roz's face contorted in surprise. "No. Why would you think that?"

"Because he knows too much." Grey shrugged. "I thought maybe someone would try to get rid of him."

"Not a bad idea," Roz said thoughtfully. "But, no."

"Whitecaps will use him for private functions." Arik stepped in. "For a while, at least."

"But as he gets older," Roz explained, "if he can't find a new patron, eventually he'll stop being an App, and a younger Piece will take his place."

"What then?" Grey asked.

"And then he'll be a Dom." Roz grinned sardonically and winked. "We never get too old."

Grey wasn't entirely sure she agreed, but she didn't protest. She didn't have the energy.

"What about Selene and Arden?" she asked after a moment. "Now that the High Chancellor's gone, will the same thing happen to them?"

"No," Roz shook her head. "Not yet, anyway. They both have their own Whitecaps, so they'll be able to hold onto their positions for a while longer."

Grey sighed, and though she couldn't explain why, she felt relieved to know that at least some of the Apps were still safe.

- ♦ -

The next day and night passed by in a daze. While all citizens—excluding the Redcaps and Blackcaps who were on duty—were given the day off to watch the funeral rites, Lock barely enforced the policy. He projected the broadcast on a large, white screen in the lounge—per legal obligation—but turned the volume to its lowest setting, and for the most part, the political theater was ignored.

Instead of observing the occasion for somber mourning, the Pinkcaps took the rare opportunity for much-needed rest, and Lock disappeared into his office, only emerging at intervals to refill his coffee mug.

It wasn't until the following day that anyone began to watch the news with any real interest. Even Grey sat in the lounge, curled on a plush sofa while Arik read in the nearby window-seat. Between them, Roz sprawled in a wingback chair with her long legs slung over the arm and her head resting lazily against her fist. Bored, she stared up at the screen.

"Yesterday," a blonde reporter with a yellow headband spoke into the camera, "we mourned the loss of High Chancellor Lachlan. But today, the Whitecaps of Citoyen will announce the beginning of a new era, by inaugurating our newest officials."

She turned to acknowledge the guest—a Browncap—at her side. "It's been decades since a new High Chancellor was appointed. What can we expect to see this evening?"

"Well, Nancy," the Browncap's voice was annoyingly smooth, "policy is an important part of every High Chancellor's—"

"Blah, blah, blah," Roz growled, swung her feet down to the floor, and stood in front of the projector.

"'Well, Nancy,'" she mocked in a deep sultry tone, "'I'm honestly more worried about getting into your panties than telling the good people of Citoyen about this political charade. But if you insist: The Whitecaps are trying to decide who has the most money right now, and once they do, they'll send up a smoke signal from the Capitol, because some mythological priests used to do it, and the Whitecaps think it's a cute idea. But you know what's really cute, Nancy? That tight, sweet—'"

"Shut *up*, Roz." Nic, who had been reclining with Arden on the floor, chucked a pillow at her.

Without missing a beat, Roz caught it and whipped it back.

"Oh, come on, Nic." She rolled her eyes. "They've explained it a million times. You're not seriously listening to this shit, are you?"

Sighing, Grey rose from her chair. It was enough to hear the endless back-and-forth between the reporters. She couldn't stand to listen to Roz and Nic bickering too.

"Where are you going?" Roz asked.

Grey shrugged. "To get a glass of water."

"And miss all this?" Roz held her arms out at her sides like an actor on a stage.

A smiled tugged up the corner of Grey's lips. "Arik can fill me in when I get back."

"Suit yourself." Roz shrugged and turned back to Nic.

Pieces of Pink

Before things could escalate further, Grey slipped out of the lounge and veered toward the kitchen, but at the sound of footsteps, she paused and peaked into the dining room.

It was empty, except for Jax. The App was wearing a plain, navy sweater and a pair of jeans—a casual look for him—and he was pacing back and forth, nervously biting his thumbnail.

Jax didn't notice Grey as she watched him trace his path back and forth along the edge of the room. But there was a fragility to the man's movements that didn't match his typical, cold demeanor, a truth in his actions that begged to be witnessed. He was scared.

"They're making the announcement!" Nic yelled from the lounge, and Jax looked up at the sound.

For a moment, his eyes locked with hers, but before he could say anything, Grey quickly retreated into the crowded lounge and found her place beside Roz.

Jax followed her in and receded into a corner, where Selene stood with the light from the projector, reflecting in her jade eyes.

The screen cut away from the news reporter and her guest, replacing them with a shot of the Capitol building, where a lone podium stood in anticipation of the new High Chancellor.

As one, Citoyen held its breath.

Slowly, the doors of the Capitol swung outward, and a long line of Whitecaps filed out of the building. And at the very end of the line, the new High Chancellor—a woman whose name Grey couldn't remember—emerged, dressed in white from head to toe.

"No," Selene gasped from the corner, and when Grey turned to look at her, she saw Lock standing in the doorframe with his hands clenched into fists at his side.

"Fuck me," Roz whispered and slowly shook her head.

Grey ignored her, watching the screen as a short man approached the podium and stood on his tiptoes to speak into the mic.

"People of Citoyen," he began in a nasal voice, "I present to you, High Chancellor Mara Huxley."

As the camera panned in, the new High Chancellor took the podium and looked out over the large crowd of Blackcaps and Browncaps seated in the square. Mara Huxley was tall—beautiful in her own right—with glossy black hair that skimmed her shoulders. Her face was sharp and angular, and there was a hardness about her eyes and lips that hinted at ferocity. With glistening, black eyes, the High Chancellor stared directly into the camera.

"My fellow citizens," her voice was clear and steady, "yesterday, we mourned the loss of our High Chancellor. It is right to grieve, but we must also remember: Today is a day for new beginnings, and we must foster the promise of this new dawn!

"Although we will remember Chancellor Lachlan's legacy, we must also strive to move forward and build this once-great nation into a beacon of strength that shines from our borders, so that no person will ever question the might of our authority in this world."

The room hung in silence, waiting.

"Beyond our border live primitive peoples, prone to following their most base desires and urges. It is only through the sacrifices of Blackcaps serving at our perimeter that these murderers and rapists are kept from our country.

"We are not like them, but even so, this country has fallen prey to the carnal temptations of lesser beings by maintaining positions for those whose only purpose is to satisfy our animal impulses.

"It is with your money—money that could have been used for schools, housing, and defense—that the previous administration supported these sub-humans—these animals. And I will not stand for it!"

A cheer rose up from the crowd in the square, but the Pinkcaps watched on in horror.

Pieces of Pink

"Lachlan wanted to believe—wanted *you* to believe—that all caps serve a purpose, that all caps earn their place in this nation, but that is a *lie*. As a people, we cannot hope to maintain our supremacy if we allow filth to live alongside us. There is a blight in this country that must be eradicated, so that we—the people of Citoyen—may rise up in the glory of a new dawn!"

Suddenly, the screen cut to black, and Grey whirled to see Lock standing with the projector cord—yanked from the outlet—hanging in his hand.

"That's enough," he whispered, dropping the cord on the floor.

Slowly, he turned from the room, and a deafening silence consumed the Base.

NINE

An oval of frost clung to the window in the game room where Grey sat. There was a chill in the air, and even through her thick socks and sweater, Grey could feel it biting against her skin. Her fingertips were cold—almost numb—as she picked at the latch on her compact mirror, and it finally popped open.

In the days following Mara Huxley's inauguration, a thin blanket of snow had fallen over the capital of Citoyen, and with it, a bleak silence had settled over the Base.

For the other caps, little had changed. Few, if any, had noticed the new High Chancellor's political agenda. It didn't impact their lives in any meaningful way, so they ignored it. And if Grey was still a Redcap, she doubted she would have even cared about Huxley's speech. After all, before meeting Jesse, she had only visited the brothels to provide medical care.

But across the lower castes, subtle changes were already taking shape. The steady stream of medical supplies that Lock had been adding to Grey's inventory suddenly dried up. He had assured Grey that he would be able to find an alternate source with time, but there were no guarantees.

Pieces of Pink

A dart thumped into the wall, and Grey looked up. Roz stood in front of the dartboard, methodically working her aim toward the center of the bullseye. The task seemed oddly quiet for the Dom.

At the pool table, Nic and Arden practiced trick shots. And across the room, Megz and Arik sat chatting in the corner. Their words were too soft for anyone else to hear, but their eyes shimmered as they spoke.

Grey reached into her makeup bag and fished out a small tube of concealer. Dabbing the cream under her eye, she gently blended it with the tip of her finger. Though the bruising had gone down considerably, her cheekbone was still tender to the touch, and her lips felt puffy and stiff. Of course, with Roz's help and a little lipstick, she had mastered the art of disguising her bruised mouth in the form of a sultry pout.

"Meeting in the dining room!" Taryn called from the hall, and all activities in the game room paused.

"What now?" Roz growled.

"Who knows?" Nic shrugged and dropped his pool cue on the table. "Maybe someone put Huxley out of her misery."

"If only we were so lucky," Roz grumbled.

Clenching the remaining darts in her fist, Roz stabbed them into the corkboard and strode from the room. Like ducklings, the other Pieces followed her out.

In the dining room, Lock stood waiting with a stack of papers clutched in his hand. And as the Pinkcaps squeezed into the benches around him, Grey held back, watching from the far wall.

People chatted quietly as they found their places, but it wasn't the open, lighthearted discussions that normally filled the space, it was tight, anxious whispers.

Standing beside Lock, Jax flipped through his own set of papers. A grim frown lined his face as he turned to Lock and spoke. His words were too low for Grey to hear, but with a solemn nod, Lock looked up at the gathered Pinkcaps and took a deep breath.

"I apologize," Lock cleared his throat, "for calling this meeting during your free time, but I just received notification of a new mandate that's to be applied."

Lock's throat bobbed and his black curls fell against his forehead as he looked down at the paper and began to read.

"Effective immediately, section 16 of the labor laws, part C, is to be revoked."

Bile rose in Grey's throat as gasps and cries of disgust broke out across the room. Seated on the bench in front of her, Roz growled, and Selene went rigid.

Labor law 16 dealt with the appropriate working ages for children, and while parts A and B focused on Purplecaps, Bluecaps, and Greencaps, part C pertained exclusively to Pinkcaps.

"They can't do that!" Arden shouted out over the din.

"For the time being," Lock's eyes were glazed with worry, "it remains up to the discretion of Purplecaps to decide when Pinkcaps begin working. For those of you who have younger siblings and children under my care, rest assured, I will continue to use the parameters outlined when the labor laws were created."

A collective sigh of relief eased the tension of the room, but the fear was still palpable.

"But if any of you have children or siblings in the care of another Purplecap," he said, "give me their information, so I can find out their status and attempt to have them transferred if necessary. The rest of you are dismissed."

One by one, the Pieces began to stand. Some moved to the front of the room to form a line, and others wandered off into the Base. Together, Roz and Arik slowly walked toward the stairs, but Selene sat still, staring straight ahead—at Jax, whose eyes were on Lock—as if some invisible force had frozen her in time.

Pieces of Pink

Grey watched for a moment, waiting to see if Jax would look over; if he would see Selene waiting, but he never did. In silence, Grey stood, fell into step with Roz and Arik, and walked away.

- ♦ -

A fire crackled in the lounge where Grey sat reading in a wingback chair. The story was mundane, but it was a relief to escape into a world beyond her own.

The redaction of the child labor laws seemed like a useless, if not damaging, political move, but Huxley suffered no repercussions. It seemed impossible that a country could blindly follow a leader who supported such archaic and cruel policies. Yet, in the days that had passed since the announcement, the people of Citoyen had moved on, blissfully unaware—or unconcerned—with the revised mandate and the implications that it held for Pinkcaps and their children.

Outside, ice began to sprinkle against the window. A blizzard was coming—early for the season—and in a way, Grey was thankful for the still-healing bruises on her face. She hadn't started working again yet, and it was a relief to know she wouldn't have to brave the storm heading their way.

A voice in the foyer startled Grey from her thoughts. "You just seem out of it." It was Jax. "Are you sure you're okay?"

"Yes," Selene answered, but she sounded tired and drained as if some essential part of her had been ripped out. "It's just . . ." she paused, "I don't know. Never mind."

"Well, are you sick?" Jax pushed. "Do you need a Redcap?"

"No.

"Then, what's wrong?" Jax—only his true self around Selene—was gentle in a way that Grey had never heard before.

"Don't touch me right now!" Selene snapped.

Jax apologized, "I'm sorry, I—"

"Look, I know you're just trying to help," Selene sighed, "but I don't want comfort right now. I just—I just want to go upstairs and lie down, okay?"

"Okay," Jax said. "What about tea? Could I make you a cup of tea? Or—"

"Jax," Selene's voice was almost desperate, "I appreciate what you're trying to do, but everything with Mara just has me on edge. And the other Whitecaps . . ."

"Don't worry about that," Jax assured her. "Lock will make sure everything is all right."

"How?" Selene asked. "Lachlan's dead. Lock's power is *dead*. Don't you see that? Soon, even Lock won't be able to keep us safe. He may have had friends in high places, but they're gone, and Mara is a new kind of High Chancellor."

There was a moment of silence.

"Well, think of all the Pieces who have Whitecaps for fathers," Jax said. "Don't you think someone will try to stick up for their kid?"

"No," Selene exhaled sharply, "I don't."

"Why not?"

"Because they just don't *care*, Jax," she emphasized. "Nobody cares about any of us."

"Selene, things will settle again." He was doing his best to calm and reassure her, but even he didn't sound convinced by his own words. "This will pass."

"Be rational." There was a hopelessness in her plea. "Just a few weeks ago, you were the most valuable Piece in Citoyen. And we know Mara won't fill your place with a new Piece, so for all that it matters, you don't even exist anymore. You're just a sidepiece now, something for the Whitecaps to play with at orgies so they can have the satisfaction of fucking the old High Chancellor's favorite."

Jax heaved a defeated breath. "I know."

"I'm sorry," Selene whispered. "I'm not trying to be cruel. I just don't understand how you have such blind faith that things will turn around, or that Lock can do anything to help us."

"He does his best," Jax said.

"I know," Selene murmured. "But what will happen when that's not good enough?"

Jax didn't respond.

"I'll be in my room," Selene said and walked away.

Grey listened as the woman's footsteps ascended the stairs and vanished. There was a moment of stillness that followed, and she held her breath as Jax began to pace the foyer. Then, he walked straight into the lounge.

Frozen in her chair, Grey looked back down at the book in her lap, just as Jax turned toward the fireplace and spotted her. He paused for a moment, staring at her. But when she didn't look up, he retreated from the room and vanished into the heart of the Base.

"The bodega on the corner's closed," Megz lisped as Nic helped her into her coat.

For hours, the snow continued to fall. And across the city, shops and businesses began shutting down against the weather.

"The twins said the alley on 3rd Street has too much snow to cut through, too," Nic added.

"Not just that—" Arden, the Apical twin, stuck his head out of the dining room.

"—but they've banned all non-essential travel," Taryn finished his brother's sentence.

Grey felt a pang of guilt as she watched Roz and Arik bundle themselves in scarves and mittens.

"I don't understand how this is considered *essential*." Grey frowned as she spoke.

"I know," Megz agreed. "Even the grocery stores are closing up for the storm."

"Well," Roz shrugged it off with a playful smile, "you need three things to keep the species going: shelter, food, and sex. And since people can't get their groceries, they're gonna need sex instead."

Grey shivered when a Rag opened the door and stepped outside. A flurry of snowflakes sparkled for a moment under the foyer lights, then disappeared.

"Should I come?" Grey asked.

Roz stopped buttoning her coat and looked at Grey as if she were out of her mind. "Why the hell would you do that?" she demanded.

"It's just," she said, "I don't feel right staying here while you guys are all out there."

Roz shook her head. "Don't be an idiot. You're staying home for a reason, remember?"

The Dom bent down to tie up her winter boots. They were still four inches high, but with thick rubber soles for traction. How she would manage to walk in them through the blizzard, Grey had no idea. But if anyone could, it was Roz.

"Just use tonight to relax. Sit by the fire. Make yourself a cup of tea or something, and don't worry about us. We'll be safe together." She grinned as she straightened upright. "Though I can't say the same for our clients."

Roz winked, and Grey cracked a smile.

"Oh, and feel free to keep that fire burning." Roz reached for the door. "I'd love something warm to come home to."

"Will do," Grey said, and with a quick goodbye, Roz and Arik disappeared into the snow.

Pieces of Pink

- ♦ -

True to her word, Grey spent the last few hours of the evening sitting beside the fire with a warm cup of tea in her hand. With the snow dampening the sounds of the city around them, the Base felt warm and safe. She could almost imagine herself in a house in the country, with no one else for miles and miles. But that was a dangerous thing to dream about, because thoughts like those led her to Jesse.

Burying their wedding rings had helped her say goodbye, and she still thought of him every day, but a change had happened in her, and whether she wanted to or not, it forced her to move forward. Already, she was different than the woman who had spent the summer trying to escape Citoyen.

In moments like this, however—moments when she felt safe, secure, and protected—the need for him seeped into her chest. And that awful, wanting ache, came rushing back.

Heaving a deep sigh, Grey stood from her chair and stretched.

Live. She reminded herself. *Just live.*

After adding another log to the fire, she carefully closed the screen and grabbed her blanket from where it lay slung over the back of the chair. In a few hours, the others would begin to trickle home, and at least there would be enough embers burning for them to warm themselves before heading up for bed.

Wrapping the blanket around her shoulders, Grey trudged toward her bedroom. But when she reached the landing on the third floor, she heard a soft groan, and she stopped. The sound had come from Selene's room.

Cautiously, Grey made her way to the Apical's door and knocked.

There was no answer, just another low moan of pain.

"Are you awake?" Grey asked.

She hoped Selene was just dreaming, but when she heard the woman whimper again, Grey opened the door.

Selene lay curled on her bed, writhing in pain. Her brown and blonde curls were plastered around her face, and sweat shone on her forehead. The woman's dark brown skin was paler than usual, almost ashy, and she was clutching at her stomach.

Quickly, Grey crossed the room and laid a hand on Selene's shoulder. Her skin was burning.

"Help," Selene groaned.

When Grey pulled back the blankets, she saw why. Between her legs, Selene's pants and sheets were stained red with blood.

"Selene, what happened?" Grey tried to stay calm as she quickly pulled up her hair in a ponytail and knelt beside the bed.

"The b-, baby . . ." The woman could barely form the words as tears of pain slipped from her eyes.

"Are you pregnant?" Grey asked.

"Not anymore."

Grey scanned over the woman's body as her mind whirred. Selene was thin, not noticeably pregnant at all, but there was so much blood. Too much for it to be a miscarriage at this stage.

"Oh." The small gasp of realization slipped from Grey's lips before she could stop it.

"You had the abortion?" she asked as she carefully helped Selene roll onto her back. "When?"

"Two days . . ." Selene mumbled.

"Did you go to a Redcap?" Grey removed Selene's pants and threw them on the floor.

Selene shook her head. "A Purplecap."

"Okay." Grey glanced between Selene's legs.

In her training, she had heard of Purplecaps providing abortions to desperate Pinkcaps—for a price, of course—but without proper tools, they were notorious for going awry.

"I need to wash my hands," Grey said. "But I'll be right back."

Grey didn't wait for Selene's response as she turned from the room and ran to the bathroom, quickly scrubbing her hands clean.

Her thoughts raced with the possibilities of what exactly had gone wrong as the burning hot water flowed over her fingers, forearms, and elbows.

There were three main possibilities: infection, incomplete removal of the pregnancy, or some type of injury caused during the procedure itself. But regardless of the cause, Grey would need help. She was a Redcap, but obstetrics and gynecology had not been her primary field of study. And at the rate Selene was losing blood . . .

She forced the thought from her mind and ran back down the hall, past Selene's room, and into the stairwell.

"Lock!" Grey screamed his name as she bounded down the stairs. "I need help!"

Just as she hit the bottom step of the foyer, Lock swung around the corner from the dining room, nearly colliding with her.

"What is it? What's wrong?" he asked.

"Call a Redcap," she commanded. "Selene had an abortion two days ago. She's hemorrhaging. I don't know what's wrong yet, but I don't think I can help her on my own. She needs an ambulance!"

Lock's eyes grew wide. "The blizzard . . ."

"It doesn't matter." Grey said. "I'll do what I can for as long as I can. Just make the call!"

He nodded.

"When you've reached them," she gasped before disappearing into the stairwell to the third floor, "come up here and help me."

"I'll be right there!" he called and vanished back into his office.

Without wasting another moment, Grey turned and sprinted back up the stairs. When she reached Selene's room, she slowed and tried to calm her breathing, but there wasn't enough time to regain her composure entirely.

Still panting, she knelt on the end of Selene's bed and gently eased the woman's legs apart. Grey pressed on Selene's abdomen and, Selene whimpered.

"Can you tell me where it hurts?" Grey asked.

Selene only groaned.

In her studies, Grey remembered reading that low abdominal pain could be a sign of a perforated bowel. But there were hosts of complications that listed the same symptoms. Without diagnostic equipment, she had no way of knowing what was wrong. All she could do was try to keep Selene from bleeding out.

Sooner than she'd expected, heavy footsteps sounded in the hall, and Grey turned to look over her shoulder. Lock careened into the room and froze, staring down at Selene.

"They're on their way," he breathed. "But with the storm," he shook his head, "they could be delayed."

"All right," Grey said calmly. "That's okay."

The color had drained from Lock's face.

"If you don't mind," she said, pulling his focus away from the blood-covered sheets, "I have a box of medical supplies in my closet. Could you grab it for me, please?"

"Of course," he nodded, and Grey turned her attention back to Selene as Lock bounded for the fourth floor.

"Can you tell me when you started to bleed?" Grey asked.

Selene shook her head.

"And do you know how long you've had a fever?"

"No," Selene gasped in pain as she curled in on herself.

"You're okay," Grey said. The words were automatic, but it didn't make them true.

As she waited for Lock, she began a mental checklist of possibilities. Most likely, it was an incomplete abortion, and some portion of the fetus had remained trapped, causing infection and ultimately, the high fever. But that didn't account for the blood loss—not completely, at least. Uterine perforation was equally possible, considering the symptoms, but taking multiple days to present just didn't make sense.

Then again, with all of the birth control options—especially for and Apical, like Selene—pregnancy didn't entirely make sense either. And as the thought flashed through Grey's mind, another came with it, and her heart sank.

"Selene," Grey kept her tone steady, conversational, "Did you have your IUD removed?"

Selene shook her head.

"You mean, it's still in there?"

"I thought," Selene's voice cracked in pain, and she tried again, "I thought they would take it out."

"Did they know you had one?" Grey asked.

"I can't remember."

Just then, Lock burst into the room, clutching the medical supplies in his arms. Quickly, Grey stood and went to him. Reaching for a pair of gloves, she dropped her voice.

"I think," she spoke quietly, so Selene couldn't hear, "she has an infection. But," she shook her head, unsure of herself, "I also think the abortion dislodged the IUD."

Lock's face twisted with concern as he tried to understand what Grey was telling him.

"I think the IUD is still inside of her," she grimaced. "And it may have perforated her uterus."

"What does that mean?" he whispered.

"She needs surgery," Grey said. "But, I'll do what I can until the Redcaps come."

Lock nodded, and without another word, Grey turned back to Selene and got to work.

- ◆ -

Grey stripped the bloody sheets from Selene's bed.

It had felt strange to see the Redcaps loading Selene onto a stretcher. Mercifully, Grey hadn't recognized either of them. But even if she had, they were too focused on their patient to notice her standing there.

"Where is she?" Jax's voice roared down the hall.

"Jax!" Lock called up the stairs, chasing after him, but not before the App reached Grey first.

She turned toward the door and frowned, still clutching Selene's bloodied sheets in her arms as Jax rounded the corner.

"Where is she?" he demanded.

"At the hospital," Grey answered calmly.

"Jax," Lock panted as he came into view. "Just listen to me."

Frantic, Jax spun on the Purplecap. "I *did* listen. You said Selene had an abortion, and someone fucked it up. Who did it? *Her?*" He pointed an accusing finger at Grey.

"Of course not," Grey hissed.

"Then what happened?" There was fire in his eyes, both terrified and fierce as he took in the bloody sheets in Grey's arms.

"She wasn't very coherent," Grey admitted solemnly, "but from what I understood, she was pregnant, and two days ago—"

"How?" he interrupted. "I thought the IUD . . ."

"It's rare," Grey frowned sympathetically, "but it can happen."

Jax clenched his teeth.

"She said a Purplecap did the procedure," Grey said. "Their tools probably weren't sterilized, so I think she got an infection. And the IUD might have caused some internal damage."

"Will she be OK?" he asked.

"I don't know," Grey admitted. "We'll just have to wait and see."

"How long?" he demanded.

"Hopefully, they'll call Lock in a few hours." Grey turned back to the bed and pulled away the pillowcases.

Jax scanned the room, bright eyes tracing over everything that was Selene's. Then, he sat heavily in the chair beside her vanity, and his head fell into his hands.

"I should've known," he groaned. "I should've known something was wrong."

Grey stared, unmoving, as Lock crossed the room and knelt down beside Jax.

"There was nothing you could've done," he said.

"Do you think it was mine?" Jax whispered. "Did I do this?"

Grey blinked in surprise, and she felt a wave of hot color rise to her cheeks. As Lock muttered words of comfort, she suddenly felt as though she were encroaching on something too personal.

Selene's decision had seemed so obvious, so understandable—especially if the baby were a client's—that Grey had never even stopped to consider the implications it held for Jax. He'd had no choice in the matter.

Then again, even if the child was his, Grey wasn't entirely sure he deserved a choice.

Whether it had been Jax's or a Whitecap's, Selene was a Pinkcap, and that was all that mattered. As with all citizens, only the mother determined a child's cap, and Selene couldn't let her baby be a Piece.

A soft sob broke from Jax, and unwilling to dwell on the idea any longer, Grey gathered up the last of the bedding and left the room.

When Selene returned home a few days later, there was a stillness in the Base that had become too familiar. Word of the incident had spread quickly. And considering the new High Chancellor's stance on child labor, no one blamed Selene for her decision. Instead, they blamed the Whitecaps.

Seated on the end of Roz's bed, Grey pulled a blanket tightly around her shoulders as Roz looked between her and Arik.

"This is exactly what she wanted," Roz growled.

"Who?" Arik asked. "The High Chancellor?

Roz nodded. "She's an extremist, from what Jax has told me. I guess she's never taken a Piece to a single function. Apparently, she has some kind of moral hang-up about the whole thing. She hates that people like Selene and Jax are allowed to be a part of politics, even if they're just there for show."

"But she couldn't have possibly known Selene was pregnant," Grey said. "Revoking the labor laws wasn't a personal attack."

"No, I didn't mean she was targeting anyone in particular," Roz said impatiently. "I mean, she was trying to get Pieces to do exactly what Selene did."

"Don't you think that's a bit conspiratory?" Arik asked. "I mean, if she wants us to stop having children, she could just mandate vasectomies and . . ."

Arik hesitated, unsure of the term.

"Tubal ligation?" Grey asked.

He nodded.

"She won't mandate that," Roz answered, "because she's pushing the envelope. She's trying to see how much she can get away with first. After all, who in their right mind would want to have a baby if they knew—for a fact—that it wouldn't be safe? By revoking the law, Pieces will avoid having children. And if Pieces stop having children, she'll start to thin us out."

"Not everyone's born a Pinkcap," Arik reminded her. "Orphans and other people," he glanced at Grey, "end up being placed here."

"True," Roz agreed, "But most Pinkcaps are born, not made."

"Why does it even matter to her?" Grey asked quietly. "If she hates Pinkcaps, she doesn't have to hire them. Or better yet, she could redistribute us amongst the other caps."

Roz frowned skeptically. "Can you imagine the backlash she would get for that? If we got to move up, but no one else did? The Bluecaps would lose their minds."

Grey sighed. Roz was right.

Beside her, Arik yawned deeply. "Maybe she's just trying to prove that she's in control," he suggested. "She's new to her position, and there's a whole country looking up to her. Maybe she just thinks it's better to be feared than loved."

"How can you even defend her?" Roz scoffed.

"I'm not defending her," Arik responded quickly. "I'm just saying, maybe she'll realize she's been too extreme, and she'll back off a little."

"Extremists never realize they're too extreme," Roz frowned. "That's why they're extremists."

"I suppose that's true," Arik conceded quietly. "I'd just like to believe that people won't let things stay like this. They'll realize it's a mistake or see that she's a mistake."

"Maybe." Roz glanced over at Grey, "Or maybe this is just the way things are now."

Even if Roz was right, the thought of it was too heavy.

Grey stood up.

"Where are you going?" Roz demanded.

"I should probably check on Selene," she lied.

"Right." Roz frowned but didn't stop her.

Relieved to be away from the talk of politics, Grey stepped into the hall, and saw that Selene's door was closed. Gently she knocked, and Jax answered.

"Sorry," Grey mumbled, glancing around his shoulders to where Selene lay curled in the bed. "I just wanted to check in on Selene, and make sure everything's okay."

"She's sleeping," Jax said flatly. His eyes were rimmed red from dried tears. "I'll let you know if she needs anything."

Before Grey could even say goodnight, Jax turned away and closed the door.

She stared at the door handle for a moment, wishing there was something else she could do. Then, with a sigh, she took a step back and headed for her room. If nothing else, she would at least try to get a good night's sleep.

- ♦ -

A scream, broken and agonizing, ripped Grey from the safety of her dreams. Bolting upright in bed, she threw off the covers and ran into the hall.

"No!" The wail crashed up the stairs from the third floor, and Grey rushed down to meet it.

Along the corridor, bedroom doors were flying open, but she reached the bathroom first. And when she swung around the corner, she froze in her tracks, clutching the doorframe for support.

With eyes staring somewhere no one else could see, Selene lay dead in the bathtub. One arm had slipped beneath the surface of the water, but the other dangled limply over the lip of the tub. It had been slit from her palm all the way to her elbow, and the razorblade she had used lay bloody on the black and white tile floor.

"No, no, no, no . . ."

Jax crouched in the corner of the bathroom as if thrown there by some invisible force. He had pushed himself as far against the wall as he could and was clutching his hair in his fists.

His eyes didn't stray from the body as he rocked back and forth, repeating the same word over and over: "No, no, no . . ."

Ignoring him, Grey stepped toward the bath and reached for Selene's throat to feel for a pulse. She flinched when she touched the woman's cold, stiff skin. It was clear that she had been dead for at least an hour, maybe more.

A growing crowd packed around the doorframe, gasping as they craned their necks and caught a glimpse of the carnage within, but no one stepped beyond the threshold.

Slowly, Grey straightened.

"Someone, get Lock," she instructed, but her voice sounded hollow and cold. "Tell him to call the Redcaps."

No one moved.

"Now!" The word was a command, and in the back of the group, Arden and Taryn finally broke away and headed down the hall.

"If everyone could please just take a step back," she searched the growing crowd for Arik or Roz, "it would be really helpful."

Finally, Roz's blonde head appeared almost a foot above the others. The Dom's mouth dropped open as her gaze settled on Selene's corpse.

"Please," Grey repeated, louder this time. "Step back."

Her eyes locked with Roz's, who immediately took action.

"You heard her," Roz barked. "Everyone to the dining room!"

Pulling people left and right, Roz broke through the Pieces—some gawking, others crying—and blocked the doorway with her body. As they began to disperse, Roz quickly closed the door and turned back to face the body.

"Oh, Selene," Roz whispered to herself. "What did you do?"

"Roz," Grey kept her voice low and calm as she motioned to Jax, "I think he's in shock."

As if realizing he was there for the first time, Roz turned toward Jax and blinked.

In the corner, Jax's breathing was fast and uneven, and his eyes were glassy. A sheen of sweat shone on his face, and he was pulling at the neck of his shirt as if it would somehow help him breathe.

Without a word, Roz crossed the room and knelt in front of him, blocking the horror of Selene's death from his view. His eyes darted around her face, desperate to find something—anything—but his brain didn't even know it was looking for. Roz reached for him and gently laid her hands on his shoulders.

At first, he fought Roz's touch. But as Grey watched in silence, Jax crumpled against her like a child and began to sob. Grey had heard mourning before, but somehow the noises ripping from Jax's chest were foreign, and they were heartbreaking.

Gently rocking him back and forth, Roz crooned words of comfort—too soft for Grey to hear—into Jax's ear. As she watched, a lump formed in her throat, and she blinked, trying to will away the tears that brimmed around her eyelashes.

For minutes that seemed like hours, she waited until she heard the sound of heavy footsteps bounding down the hall, and Lock burst into the bathroom with a pair of Redcaps in tow. Grey made eye contact with the first—a young woman—and shook her head slightly, just enough to tell her that the patient was already gone.

With a brief nod, the woman and her companion laid their stretcher beside the tub and eased Selene from the water. At the sound, Jax bucked from Roz's arms and lunged across the room.

"Leave her alone!" Jax screamed. "Don't touch her!"

"Sir," the second Redcap caught Jax and held him back, "you need to stay back."

"Selene!" Jax cried and swung his arm out to grab her hand, but he only caught air.

"You need to step back," the Redcap warned, harsher this time, and Jax shoved against the man.

"For fuck's sake!" Roz roared, her sudden outburst deafening in the small space, and everyone but Jax froze.

Rage-filled breaths cut from Roz's throat as she spoke a second time, softer now.

"Let him say goodbye."

Finally, Jax caught Selene's hand in his own, and sobbing, he held it to his forehead. The Redcaps watched in silence for a moment, and when they began to stir, Roz moved toward Jax and laid her hand on his back.

"It's time," she whispered.

"No." Jax shook his head.

"Jax," Roz leaned in and rested her forehead against his hair. "Let her go."

Whimpering, Jax slowly released Selene's hand and curled against Roz as the Redcaps covered the body in a clean, white sheet. A tear rolled down Grey's cheek as the Redcaps lifted the stretcher, and she saw that the strands of Selene's curls, dangling from beneath the shroud, were stained pink with blood.

TEN

The smell of pine and spices greeted Grey as she opened the door and stepped into the foyer. Stomping her boots against the threshold, she shook the snow out of her hair and unzipped her coat.

Beside her, Megz inhaled deeply and released a happy sigh.

"Got to love Solstice." Nic grinned at the Pence as the pair dropped their coats on the floor and eagerly headed for the lounge.

Curious, Grey followed them and found an enormous evergreen tree—its vibrant, emerald boughs waiting to be covered in decorations—standing in the corner by the window.

Beside the tree, the twins sat in matching armchairs. When he saw Nic, Arden leapt to his feet, ran across the room, and swept the Dom into his arms.

"Happy Solstice," he grinned and kissed Nic on the lips.

Grey had known the holidays were coming, but after everything that had happened with Selene, she hadn't even considered the possibility of celebrating.

In the aftermath of Selene's suicide, Grey had felt numb at first. After all, she had barely known the woman, and the few interactions they shared had been detached. But as the days slipped by, and Grey returned to work, the proximity of death took its toll. Her sadness melted into exhaustion, and then the nightmares started.

At first, she dreamed of Selene's corpse walking slowly out of the third-floor bathroom, her bare feet leaving bloodied footprints. In every dream, the woman's dead, jade eyes stared ahead at nothing, and her mouth gaped open in a silent scream.

But that dream hadn't been the worst. No, the worst had come one morning just before dawn, when a noise in the hall had woken her. With her mind still trapped somewhere between sleep and reality, she had seen—or thought she had seen—Jesse standing in the center of her room with his face blown open, and a pool of dark blood slowly spreading out beneath him.

"Dibs on the star this year!" Arden flashed a grin and reached toward the top of the tree, but his reach fell short.

"No way," Taryn shook his head. "Lock would never give it up."

"Oh, come on. You don't think I could take him?"

Grey watched from the foyer as the group laughed and chatted about the upcoming celebrations. It hurt to see the joy they shared as they giggled and poked branches, testing for ornaments that Grey had never seen or known.

Solstice was supposed to be a holiday full of shared memories and traditions. But while the rest of the Base blissfully reminisced while anticipating the celebrations to come, Grey would be left with nothing but the memories of everything she had lost.

First, there were memories of her parents—hazy and golden in the glow of childhood—from before she'd left home for her education and training. Then, the memories and traditions she had made with other Redcaps in her boarding school.

But really, it was the nights of celebration with Jesse that she would miss the most. With blankets, candles, and baskets of food, they had made Solstice for themselves in the pods. And those years had been her favorite.

If everything had gone how she had dreamed it would, this would have been her first holiday of freedom with Jesse. They would have been together, safe and warm in some little cottage in the Pinelands.

Instead, she was a Pinkcap, and she would spend Solstice selling herself to the poor bastards who had nothing else to keep them warm on the longest night of the year.

- ♦ -

Grey stared at the ceiling as the Greencap spoke.

"Money, money, money," he muttered under his breath with each thrust. "Everything's about *money* with them."

"Mm-hmm," she feigned interest in his words even as his body crushed against hers.

"Solstice comes around, and it's all, 'buy me *this*, buy me *that*,'" he mimicked his wife. "The kids need new shoes and toys. Nothing's ever good enough for them. They're like tapeworms or something. Just guzzling it all down, drinking up every last penny I earn!"

Grey rolled her eyes. This man didn't need a Pinkcap, he needed a therapist.

"It's all about the fucking *money*!"

On the last word, he pulled out and came on the floor. That, in itself, was a small holiday miracle. It was bad enough when clients bitched and moaned for a whole session, and even worse when they left parts of themselves behind for her to try and clean out, especially after what had happened to Selene.

She had always known that failure rates existed with birth control, even with IUDs, but it didn't make what had happened any less traumatic. And it certainly didn't make Grey feel any safer about her already horrifying profession.

Pieces of Pink

After the man finished dressing and headed for the pod door, Grey smiled—not her real smile, but the one she had learned from Ama—and said, "Have a Happy Solstice."

Without returning the holiday wish, the Greencap grunted a mumbled response and stormed off into the snow.

Once he was out of sight, Grey gathered her clothes and initiated the pod's cleaning cycle. And just as she stepped through the door, Roz's bleached, blonde bun poked out of the pod beside hers.

"Jinx," Roz smirked, and a twinkle lit up her eyes. "I guess our clients finished at the same time."

Grey scoffed, but she was still glad to see the Dom.

"I feel like there's a joke there," Roz went on grinning, "about knocking on wood."

"No doubt," Grey half-smiled, then glanced around. "I thought Arik was working with you tonight."

Roz shook her head, "No, not tonight. He's one pod over."

"Oh."

"Yeah," Roz said and shoved her hands in her coat pockets. "All this holiday spirit really turns people into assholes. They want the cheapest deal they can get. They don't want to pay extra for a Dom *and* an assistant right now." She shrugged. "It's a seasonal thing."

Grey sighed deeply, and Roz nodded.

"It's just," Grey frowned. "these Blackcaps, and Orangecaps, and Redcaps, come to us. They pay to fuck us—"

She stopped abruptly and shook her head.

"And as a cherry on our shit sundaes," Roz finished for her, "they want to cry to us about how hard their lives are."

A dark chuckle slipped between the Dom's perfectly lined lips.

"It's kind of unbelievable when you stop and think about it," she said. "Just the other night, I had this Browncap—a lawyer for fuck's sake—who was sobbing in my lap because he was so stressed about having to make dinner for his mother-in-law on Solstice."

"Are you sure he wasn't sobbing over your riding crop?" Grey shot her a sidelong glance.

"Not a chance." Roz flashed an innocent smile, "Although it may have had something to do with the anal beads . . ."

Grey snorted, and a cloud of breath puffed from her mouth.

"Seriously, though," Roz stomped her feet in the snow to warm herself, "I can't wait for Solstice."

"To be over?" Grey asked.

"What?" Roz frowned. "No . . ."

"But it's the longest night of the year," Grey said, "and we'll be stuck in the pods."

Roz's eyebrows furrowed together, then her mouth opened in gleeful surprise.

"Oh, my gosh," she grinned, "you don't know?"

"Know what?" Grey raised an eyebrow.

"On Solstice," Roz explained, "Lock pays for us to have the night off. He books everyone at the Base!"

"Everyone?"

Roz nodded. "So, we get a night off, plus we're paid full wages."

"That's—"

"Amazing," Roz cut in before Grey could finish. "I know."

"Do you celebrate?" Grey glanced at the orange cleaning light above the pod. It would be green soon. "Or do we all just relax?"

"Well, during the day, people usually decorate the tree." Roz shrugged. "Then, at night, we have a party with plenty of punch."

Roz's nose wrinkled gleefully.

"Punch?" Grey asked.

"Oh, come on." The Dom rolled her eyes. "Do I have to spell it out for you? We all get shitfaced and sleep under the tree."

"Sounds kind of nice." Grey admitted.

"It is," Roz said, but before she could go on, the pod lights turned green again.

Pieces of Pink

The Dom huffed when she saw it. "Well, looks like it's back to work for us."

Grey grimaced.

"But from now on, if you need something to look forward to," Roz nudged her playfully, "just remember, I'm the one who came up with the punch recipe."

With that, the Dom blew Grey a parting kiss and disappeared into her pod.

- ♦ -

Rubbing her eyes, Grey yawned as she slid into her place between Roz and Arik. Across the table, Selene's seat remained empty.

"How'd you sleep?" Roz asked as she tossed a piece of toast onto Grey's plate and passed her the raspberry jam.

"Fine." Grey stifled a second yawn with the crook of her elbow. She hadn't told anyone about her nightmares—not in detail, at least—but she was sure she had cried out in her sleep.

Beside Selene's empty seat, Lydie sat with her elbows on the table and her face resting against her fists. Her finger had healed, and Grey had removed the splint, but Lydie remained as catatonic as ever.

In some ways, Grey was relieved to see that Lydie didn't appear to be going through any signs of withdrawal. At the very least, it meant the Rag's supplier was still operating under the new regime, and if that were true, Lock might still be able to find medical supplies she needed.

"Don't you want to know how *I* slept?" The Dom batted her eyelashes sarcastically.

"Sorry." Grey forced a smile. She didn't mean to be rude, but she still felt drained. "How did you sleep, Roz?"

"Naked." Roz ran the tip of her tongue over her lip and winked.

Grey snickered, and although it was weak, it felt good to laugh.

"Now that's what I like to see," Roz purred and flashed Grey a wide grin. "Especially with Solstice just around the corner."

But just as Grey's smile began to widen, her eyes caught a movement in the doorway that led into the kitchen.

"What's wrong?" Roz turned her head to follow Grey's gaze to where Jax stood in the shadows.

The Apical's mouth was set in a hard line, and dark circles hung under his eyes.

Immediately, Roz raised a hand to wave him over, inviting him to come and eat with them, but he didn't respond. Instead, he turned his back and walked away.

"I wish he would just sit with us." Roz's shoulders slumped forward slightly, and her eyes turned serious. "He needs to be around people, not lurking in the darkest corners he can find."

"People grieve differently," Arik said softly. "He'll come back to us when he's ready."

"He's not grieving," Roz countered. "He's just torturing himself. There's a difference."

Arik shrugged. "Maybe he just doesn't want to talk."

"It's not like he has to say anything." Roz motioned across the table to Lydie. "I mean, she barely says a word, and even she knows it's important to spend time with your people."

Grey raised her eyebrows and glanced at Lydie, but the redhead didn't seem to have heard Roz's comment. Or if she did, it didn't bother her.

"It's not healthy to bottle yourself up like that," Roz persisted.

Before Selene's death, Roz had been furious with Jax. Now, as if some switch had flipped, she was worried about his well-being. But one thing remained consistent: No matter what Jax did or said, Roz always disagreed.

"If he keeps doing it, eventually the pressure will just build up and he'll explode." Roz narrowed her eyes and glanced back at the empty doorframe where Jax had been standing. "I just hope we don't get hit with the shrapnel."

"Shock can make people numb," Grey suggested. "If he's traumatized enough, he might not be bottling anything up, because he might not be feeling anything at all."

"If that's true," Roz scowled, "then it's even worse."

"Why?" Arik asked.

"Just imagine what will happen when he starts to feel again. He'll be a wreck." She frowned deeply. "But whatever's going on, he's not right." Roz tapped her temple to show what she meant. "You can see it in his eyes. Seeing Selene in that tub, it broke him."

"Not broken." Lydie's voice startled them as she looked up from across the table, eyes glassy and slow. "Just changed."

Roz shrugged in consideration of the idea, not wholly writing off Lydie's words.

"I guess we'll have to wait and see."

Seated on the rickety chair under her window, Grey bent forward over her boots. Solstice morning had come, and the Base was already buzzing with sounds of clinking glasses and laughter.

"Are you heading out?"

Grey looked up to see Arik peaking around the corner.

"Yeah," she said. "I just thought I'd head to the store and grab a cup of coffee."

Arik knew as well as she did that there was plenty of coffee in the kitchen—much better than the burnt bargain brands in the bald, Orangecap's shop—but he didn't mention it.

"Do you mind if I join you?" he asked.

"Of course not." She said. "I could use some company."

"Great." Arik smiled sheepishly and ducked back into his own room. "Let me just grab my coat."

"Should we see if Roz wants to come too?" Grey called.

The walls were thin, and she could hear the hangers in Arik's closet clicking together as he pulled out his jacket.

"No," he answered. "She's getting things ready for the party. I think she's probably happier to stay here for now."

A moment later, Arik swung back around the corner and smiled.

"All set?" he asked.

She nodded, and together they slipped from the Base, unnoticed. In a way, it was a relief to leave Roz behind as they snuck into the crisp winter air. After all, Grey had planned to use her morning walk as a break from all of the Solstice enthusiasm, but still, she felt guilty for not wanting to share in the joy.

"Wow," Arik breathed as he looked up at the sky, "It's a perfect day, isn't it?"

Grey glanced overhead.

The sky was a brilliant blue. There were no clouds, apart from chimney smoke, and sunlight glinted off the snowy rooftops in flashes of pink and blue.

"It is," Grey agreed, turning her gaze back to the brown slush in front of her feet as they trudged to the mouth of the alley.

"Grey . . ." Arik hesitated a moment as if deciding whether or not he should speak.

"Yeah?"

"Are you feeling all right?"

"I just . . ." She forced a brighter smile, though she couldn't make it reach her eyes. "I just need to get some caffeine in my system."

Arik took a slow breath as he limped along beside her. "I don't want to upset you or anything, but . . ."

He paused, and Grey glanced over. There was concern behind his dark eyes.

"What is it?" she asked.

"You talk in your sleep," he answered.

"Oh," she grimaced. "Sorry if I've been keeping you up."

"It's not that," Arik shook his head, "I'm just worried for you."

Grey forced a laugh. "Why? What do I say?"

He shrugged, "Mostly you just whimper, but you've mentioned Selene . . . and someone named Jesse."

She stared ahead.

"And sometimes," his throat bobbed, "it's like your screaming, but not."

"What do you mean?"

"It's raspy, like a whisper almost." Arik looked down at his hands.

"Sorry," she apologized a second time. "I'll start sleeping in the lounge. I don't mind."

"No," Arik insisted. "You should stay in your room. I'm just telling you because I want you to know, if you need to talk, you can talk to me."

Grey frowned. There were so many things she wanted to talk about—so many things she wanted to scream—but she couldn't.

With the new High Chancellor in office, the world felt flimsy, as if her pardon could be revoked at any moment. And if people knew about Jesse—knew that she had made it all the way to the border with a Pinkcap—they might decide she was too dangerous to leave alive. Then again, the High Chancellor would have little reason to worry about one worthless Piece.

"Thank you," Grey said as they reached the doors of the shop. "I appreciate it."

Arik nodded, and relief washed through her. With him, she didn't need to explain that she didn't want to talk. He simply understood.

"Now, let's get that coffee." Grey smiled and pulled open the door for Arik to step through. "I have a feeling we'll need it."

- ♦ -

Grey shrank toward the fireplace as Pinkcaps bustled around the lounge. On a typical evening, the room felt spacious, but with the enormous tree—and every inhabitant of the Base packed around it—there was barely enough room to breathe.

The morning's coffee run had made the first half of the day easier, but the effects of the caffeine had long since worn off, and Grey was rapidly losing interest in celebrating. She had promised to stay until the arrival of the punch—for Roz—but once it made its debut, she would find a moment to slip away and take advantage of the long night off.

"It should be any minute now," Arik assured as if he could read her mind.

He was sitting on the arm of a wingback chair, where Lydie curled napping, and although he looked exhausted, there was a warm light in his deep, brown eyes. The Solstice celebrations were important to him—it was clear enough—and Grey ached to feel the same.

"Coming through!" Roz's unmistakable voice rang out from the foyer as she appeared with a bucket clutched between her arms. With a wild grin on her face, she marched her concoction to the snack table. Behind her, Lock followed with two tubs of sorbet, and Nic with an enormous punch bowl.

Even empty, the bowl was impressive. It was a massive crystal basin with intricate designs and patterns—clearly a relic from when the Base had hosted its clients—and it had probably come with the building when Lock purchased it.

Pieces of Pink

With a thump that rattled the glasses, Roz set the bucket on the table and moved out of the way so that Lock—beaming happily—could empty the sorbet into the bowl.

Pinkcaps gathered around, eager to help in any way that would get the alcohol served more quickly, but Roz staved them off with a silver ladle, waiting until Lock had scraped every last drop of the frozen dessert out of the containers before adding a few gallons of the bright red punch.

Vapor curled up from the bowl as the two ingredients met, but Roz didn't hesitate to admire it before she scooped a serving of punch into a small cup.

"Cheers!" Roz held up the glass in a toast, then downed it.

A buzz of silence hung as the Pinkcaps waited to see her reaction.

Careful not smudge her lipstick, Roz wiped the back of her hand across the corners of her mouth and grinned.

"What are you waiting for?" Roz's eyes gleamed as she addressed the room. "Drink!"

As soon as the words left her mouth, a clustered line took shape around the punch bowl, and one by one, Roz served each person in the lounge.

"It's like this every year." Arik smiled as he watched the Dom filling the cups. "She gets the first taste to make sure it's right, then we drink until everyone's . . ."

"Drunk?" Grey asked.

Arik grinned and nodded.

"What if she decides the punch isn't right?" Grey lifted an eyebrow. "Does she take it back to the kitchen?"

"No," Arik snorted. "She never gets the recipe wrong."

Grey grinned a little. It wasn't just the Solstice punch that Roz loved, it was the ritual. She had created a tradition—a way to show the others her love—that was quintessentially her, and as long as that was Roz's goal, the punch would never be wrong.

When Roz finished serving, and the line had broken off into clusters of conversation and laughter, the Dom filled three final cups and brought them over to where Grey and Arik stood, waiting.

"Punch?" Roz's honey eyes sparkled mischievously as she handed one glass to Arik and the second to Grey. Thanking her, they each took a sip.

Instantly, Grey coughed, and Roz cackled with delight.

"What the hell did you put in this?" Grey sputtered.

She had never been much of a drinker, but Roz's punch tasted like a recipe for disaster.

"Rubbing alcohol." Roz winked.

Grey's jaw dropped.

"I'm kidding." The woman laughed and pushed the bottom of Grey's cup with her long finger. "Now, drink up!"

Obediently, Grey gulped down the burning liquid, then slurped the melting clump of sorbet—a necessary relief—from the bottom of her glass. Instantly, she felt her cheeks flush.

"I'll get you another." Roz snatched Grey's empty glass from her hand and turned back toward the punch bowl.

"No, thanks." Grey shook her head.

"I've heard Rougies don't drink much," Roz teased, "but you're a Piece now. You can have as much as you want!"

As a Redcap, the rules surrounding alcohol had been strict. She had sipped cocktails a few times in the boarding house, but it was frowned upon to binge. After all, their duty was to be prepared for emergencies at all times, and whether she was on the clock or not, she had been trained that to be intoxicated was to go against her duty to Citoyen.

"Really," Grey shook her head. "I don't think I could—"

"Trust me," Roz laughed, "you need more."

"I—" Grey began to protest, but Roz was no longer listening. Her eyes were already focused on Jax, who had just emptied his first glass and was about to drain another.

"Jax!"

Holding the two glasses in one hand, Roz swept across the room and gave him a tight squeeze. "I was afraid you weren't coming."

"I'd hate to miss this," Jax scowled into the bottom of his now empty cup.

Roz grinned—either oblivious to Jax's mood, or too happy to care—and grabbed the ladle. With a practiced sweep, she refilled his cup, Grey's, and finally her own.

"Come celebrate with us?" Roz offered, nodding toward the fireplace where Arik and Grey stood.

With a shrug, he followed her.

"Look who I found!" Roz announced as Grey took her drink.

Beside Roz, Jax swayed slightly.

Arik was just opening his mouth to greet the man when Lock's voice cut through the chatter. Like Grey's, the Purplecap's cheeks were already flushed.

"Before things get too out of hand," Lock called, "I think we'd better put our last ornament on the tree. What do you think?"

As one, the Pinkcaps cheered.

"Roz? Nic?" Lock called out and glanced around the room, searching for their faces. "Where are you?"

Without hesitation, Roz pushed her cup into Grey's free hand and dashed toward the evergreen tree, which they had spent the afternoon covering with dazzling strings of lights and homemade ornaments.

One in particular—a creation of Roz's—cast sparkles across the branches whenever it moved. It was a simple orb, made from a burned-out lightbulb, which had been carefully painted with metallic eyeshadow.

"Now, you're not going to drop me this year, are you?" Lock laughed when the two Doms reached him.

"*I* won't," Nic promised then shot Roz a skeptical glance.

"Roz?" Lock raised his eyebrows.

"Not if we hurry up and get this done before the punch kicks in." She stuck out her tongue playfully.

"All right, then," he laughed. "I'm trusting you."

Together, Nic and Roz lifted Lock onto their shoulders, and Taryn handed him a massive, golden star. Clutching the top of Nic's head, the Purplecap carefully reached for the pinnacle of the tree and placed the decoration. It took a moment to fasten the ornament into place, but when it finally lit, drunken gasps of delight spread across the room.

Carefully, Nic and Roz eased Lock to the floor. When he was back on solid ground, Roz gave him a tight hug—and whispered something in his ear that made him smile—before weaving her way back through the buzzing crowd to Arik, Grey, and Jax.

When Roz reached them, she took her punch and finished it off before peering into Grey's now empty glass.

"Do you want another?" Roz asked.

"No, thanks." Grey shook her head. After two glasses, her cheeks were uncomfortably hot, and her head was swimming. "I don't think it's for me."

"That's all right," Roz shrugged. "More for me, then."

"What's that supposed to mean?" Jax growled at Grey.

Grey blinked. "What?"

"It's not for you?" He scowled. "What? Isn't it good enough for you? Aren't we good enough for you?"

"That's not what I meant," Grey shook her head in defense. "I just don't want to be—"

"What?" Jax cut in before she could finish. "You don't want to be a Piece? You don't want to lower yourself? I see how you look at us. You never talk to anyone who doesn't talk to you first. You just watch us and judge us."

People were beginning to stare.

"You don't give a shit what happens to Pieces, or what happened to Selene. You don't give a shit about any one of us! After all," he spat, "what's one more dead Pinkcap to a Rougie?"

As if moved by a force outside of her own body, Grey lifted her arm and slapped Jax across the face as hard as she could.

The room fell into stunned silence.

"If I'm such a fucking Rougie," Grey yelled in his face, "then how the hell do you think I ended up here?"

Jax slowly raised a hand to his cheek and stared at her, his green eyes wide. It was illegal to hit an App, but Grey didn't care.

"You've never stopped to think about that, have you?" she said as tears welled up in her eyes. "I'm here because . . ."

Grey took a shuddering breath, and before she could stop herself, the words came flooding out. "I'm here because I fell in love with a Pinkcap," she wailed. "We broke the Code and married in secret."

A dark, broken laugh slipped between her tears. "And we didn't want to hide anymore—didn't want to live the rest of our lives trapped by some bullshit law—so we tried to run."

She trembled as she spoke, never breaking eye-contact with Jax. "But Blackcaps caught us near the border, and they shot him in the back of the head. His face . . ."

Her voice cracked.

"They blew off his face." Grey reached a trembling hand toward Jax, who was too stunned to move, and touched his cheekbone, still red from her slap. "The bullet came right through here."

For a moment, she stood frozen by the memory of blood, bone, and pink mist. But even as the image faded, and she found reality once more, her voice was barely above a whisper.

"So, don't you fucking tell me," she hissed, "that I don't care about one dead Pinkcap."

Before Jax—or anyone—could respond, she turned away and left the room.

-◆-

Grey sat on her bedroom floor with her back against the bedframe, listening to footsteps on the stairs. Although it had been hours since she had stormed off, she could still hear the happy sounds of the Solstice party three floors below.

Lock had already checked on her once and admitted that he'd stopped Roz and Arik from coming up. He'd sworn it was to give her some space and privacy, but Grey suspected it had more to do with Roz being too drunk to climb the stairs.

Either way, she was glad they hadn't come. She had felt a pang of guilt for ruining the party, but it wasn't long before Roz's punch had everyone singing, and the Pinkcap's voices drifted up the stairwell in dissonant harmony.

A shadow of feet appeared in the gap of light under the door, and after a moment of hesitation, someone knocked.

"Come in," she answered, her voice still hoarse from yelling.

Slowly, the door opened. But it was not Lock standing in the hall; it was Jax.

If the man had been drunk earlier, he wasn't now. His eyes were dark and serious, and there was an expression on his face that Grey didn't quite recognize.

"Can I still come in?" he asked gently.

Grey looked down at the floor without answering.

Jax stood still for a moment as if waiting for her to shout at him a second time. When she didn't, he stepped into the room and sat down beside her.

"I'm sorry," Jax whispered.

Silence hung between them.

"The things I said to you earlier," he struggled to find the words. "I was wrong, and I'm sorry. I just, I just . . ."

Without warning, Jax began to sob.

"I don't know how to live without her."

Grey fought back the urge to flee the room and escape the onslaught of emotion spilling from Jax's lips.

"She was everything to me." The man's voice shook through his broken tears. "And I was—I thought I was—"

His voice splintered, and Grey bit down on her lip as she fought to keep herself from crying—yet again—but the tears won out.

"Why did she leave me?" Jax sobbed.

A heavy weight settled on Grey's chest as she considered his words. For Selene, death had been a choice. And in a way, that made it so much worse. Jesse had been taken from Grey, leaving no doubt as to how much he loved her. But Selene? She had left Jax behind.

Wordlessly, Grey reached out her hand and rested it on Jax's knee. There were no words for the kind of pain he felt—no pills, or salves, or bandages—nothing she could do to fix a broken heart.

"What am I supposed to do?" he whispered.

"Remember her," Grey croaked through her tight throat.

Together, they sat weeping for their own private losses: for the bodies that were never returned to them, the funerals that were never held, and the goodbyes that were never said.

Even through the tears, there was relief in their companionship. And when their breathing finally slowed, and their sobbing ended, Jax looked toward the window—gazing out at the clear night sky—and he smiled.

"Selene and I," he sniffled, "we had a Solstice tradition."

"What was it?" Grey asked as she wiped her eyes with the back of her sleeve.

"It was . . ." he paused and glanced up at the small clock on the nightstand. "Actually, it's better if I show you."

Jax pushed himself off the ground and held out his hand to pull Grey to her feet. When she was up, he snatched the blanket off the end of her bed.

"We'll need this," he said.

"Where are we going?" Her eyebrows pinched together as he led her from the room and toward the door at the far end of the hall.

"To the fire escape," he answered. "You're not afraid of heights, are you?"

"No," she shook her head, "but—"

"Good."

With his free hand, Jax pushed open the door, and as a burst of cold air swept inside, a sea of stars bloomed up in front of them.

"Come on," he urged her outside, and after a cursory glance at the black grate beneath his feet, Grey stepped into the darkness.

Behind them, the roof of the Base sloped upward—blotting out everything but the night sky—and in front of them, the lights of the capital sparkled in the crystal cold air.

"Here," he shook out the blanket, draped it around both of their shoulders, and squinted at the city lights. "Any minute now . . ."

"What?" she demanded.

But before Jax could answer, a loud whistle cut through the night, and an orb of light shot toward the sky. With a bang, the firecracker burst over the city in a shower of golden sparks, and Grey's mouth fell open in awe. From the ground, she had only ever caught glimpses of the Solstice fireworks, but from here, her view was unobstructed, and it was magnificent.

"Selene loved this," Jax murmured at her side.

Pieces of Pink

"I can see why," Grey said as she watched. "It's beautiful."

"What about you?" Jax asked, glassy eyes still fixed on the sky. "Did you and . . ." he paused, not knowing which name to use.

"Jesse," Grey whispered.

"Did you and Jesse have any traditions?" Jax's question was gentler this time as if knowing Jesse's name had finally made Grey's loss something real.

"It was hard to meet safely," she admitted, "so we usually just went to a pod and made our own Solstice there."

A lump formed in her throat at the memory of Jesse's laughter.

"It wasn't much," her voice quivered. "But we were together."

Unable to say any more, Grey turned her focus back to the fireworks, and together, they watched in silence until the last of the sparks blinked out into nothingness.

ELEVEN

Snow crunched under Grey's boots as she stepped from the entrance of the Base and into the alleyway. Beside her, Roz groaned and flipped up the collar of her jacket. Although the sky was overcast, the Dom wore a pair of oversized sunglasses, and her bleached hair was pulled into a rough bun with a pink scrunchie.

"Doing okay?" Jax raised a critical brow.

"Coffee," Roz grunted. "I need coffee."

"Don't worry." Arik's voice was unusually low as he rubbed his forehead. "It's not far."

Arik hadn't drunk nearly as much as Roz—or anyone, for that matter—but even he had a hangover. In the aftermath of the Solstice party, Grey understood why Roz's punch was a once-a-year event.

"You know," Roz frowned, "I just don't get it."

There was an edge to the woman's normally playful voice.

"What?" Grey asked.

"Why we even have laws like that."

Jax rolled his eyes. "Be more specific, Roz."

Pieces of Pink

"Not being able to have relationships across cap lines," Roz clarified. "I mean, when Pieces get knocked up, no one asks who the father is. It doesn't matter. If the mom's a Piece, the baby's a Piece."

"And?" Jax sighed.

"And, shit!" Roz threw her hands in the air. "There must be plenty of children in other caps whose fathers are Pieces too. But the Whitecaps don't care about that. Nope, as long as the baby's conceived in a business transaction, no one gives a fuck; but as soon as people fall in love, they send out the executioners."

Grey took a slow breath. Sharing the truth about her past had clearly impacted Roz. Instead of offering Grey sympathies or condolences—as most people had—Roz spiraled into a seething rage as soon as the Solstice punch wore off.

"Speaking of which," Roz lifted her sunglasses to look at Grey with bloodshot eyes, "how are you not dead?"

"What do you mean?" Grey asked.

"I mean, why didn't they execute you?"

"Luck?" Grey shrugged.

Roz raised a black eyebrow, "Luck, or Lock?"

"Both, I guess," Grey said.

The Dom huffed dropped her sunglasses back into place, unsatisfied with Grey's response.

"Lock came for Jesse," Grey explained, "but he was too late, so they let him take me instead."

"Yeah, but why would they let him take you?" Roz insisted. "You committed two capital offenses."

"For fuck's sake, Roz," Jax hissed. "He probably worked out a deal. Just leave it alone."

"But I'm surprised they allowed it," Roz pushed. "A story like hers could start a rebellion."

Grey licked her dry lips. "I don't see how."

It was a lie. She understood exactly what Roz was saying. It was easy to paint a picture of a star-crossed Redcap and a Pinkcap persecuted for the crime of love. It was also very convenient to leave out the detail that neither of them had actually been condemned until they tried to cross the border.

"All I'm saying," Roz lifted her hands defensively, "is that I can't be the only her there who thinks inter-cap relations shouldn't be an offense punishable by death!"

"I'm sure you're not the only one," Jax agreed as they emerged from the alley, "but this isn't the time to talk about it. So, shut up."

With a huff, Roz closed her mouth, shoved her hands in her pockets, and walked ahead. At the end of the block, she disappeared into the shop.

"She'll be better once she's had some coffee," Arik said softly. "She's just hungover."

"I know." Grey stared at the ground as they followed Roz's footprints down the sidewalk, "But, she isn't wrong."

When the trio reached the shop, and Grey pulled open the door, releasing a burst of warmth from within. But when she stepped over the threshold, she froze.

Roz stood at the counter with a cup of coffee in her hands and defiance in her eyes.

"What do you mean?" Roz's voice was deadly calm as she spoke to the smirking Orangecap behind the counter.

Instead of responding, he pointed a beefy finger at a sign—too far away for Grey to read—posted beside the register.

Red heat rushed through Roz's cheeks as her shoulders began to quiver with rage.

"Everything all right?" Casually, Jax stepped around Grey and strode up to Roz's side.

He flashed the Orangecap a bright smile, and in an instant, the serious and brooding man that Grey was used to vanished, giving way to a charming young App with a handsome face and a confident swagger. It was a side of Jax that Grey had never seen before—the face he wore while working—and the perfection of the act sent a shiver rippling down Grey's neck.

"We're don't accept chips for payment," the Orangecap sneered.

Jax's brows pinched together, but his smile didn't falter.

"Is the chip reader down?" he asked hopefully.

"No, the reader's fine," the man growled. "We're just not serving Pinkcaps anymore."

"Oh," the icy edge slipped back into Jax's words. He was himself again, "Come on, Roz."

The Dom didn't move.

"We can go to the shop on Baxter," he nudged.

"Good luck," the Orangecap laughed. "With the new mandate, no one will be taking chips anymore."

Jax's eyes narrowed on the Orangecap. And although he clearly didn't know about whatever new mandate the man was referencing, he hid it well.

"Same to you," Jax smirked. "Without taking chips, you'll need all the luck you can get—especially in this part of the city."

The man's shiny face twisted in a look of confusion, then anger.

Satisfied, Roz finally turned to follow Jax out of the shop.

"Once you Pinkcaps aren't in here all the time," he snarled after them, "decent people will come. You'll see!"

"No," Roz snorted and walked to the door with the coffee still in her hand, "we won't."

"Hey, you can't take that! You didn't pay for it!" The Orangecap charged out from behind the counter.

"Oh, I'm sorry." Roz held out the cup in her hand as if to hand it back. "Let me just . . ."

As the Orangecap reached her, Roz dropped the coffee in the entrance, and it splattered across the floor and walls.

"Oops," she simpered.

"Out!" The Orangecap roared. "Get out!"

Still smirking, Roz stepped into the sunlight and let the door slam shut behind her.

- ♦ -

"What the fuck is going on?" Roz demanded.

Grey stood with the small group of Pinkcaps that had formed around Lock, all of them with the same complaint.

"We stopped in three different shops," Roz hissed. "No one's taking chips anymore. How the hell are we supposed to buy things?"

"They wouldn't even let me and Taryn past the entrance of the diner on the Boulevard," Arden added.

"I hear you." Lock—still suffering from the after-effects of the Solstice punch—pinched the bridge of his nose. "Just give me a second to look into it, okay?" He turned to Jax. "You said someone mentioned a new mandate?"

Jax nodded. "The Orangecap at the corner store said no one would be taking chips anymore. I didn't think he was serious."

"All right," Lock said. "Let me just make a few calls."

He turned toward his office, and the Pinkcaps drifted into the dining room to wait.

Beside Grey, Megz perched on the corner of the table, watching Nic and Arden.

"Do you think they're switching us to cash?" Megz asked

Nic shook his head. "I doubt it."

"If that were true," Arden added, "they wouldn't have kicked us out this morning. They would have just told us we need cash."

"And it isn't just this," Nic's eyes were serious. "There's something else going on, too."

Pieces of Pink

"What do you mean?" Roz leaned into the conversation.

"Two nights ago, I was talking to a Rag from one of Ama's units," Nic explained. "She told me that people haven't been coming home after work."

"What's that supposed to mean?" Arden asked.

"It means they're disappearing," Nic frowned.

"Just vanishing?" Roz raised an eyebrow. "What about their tracker chips? Haven't the Beaks gotten any hits?"

Nic shook his head, tossing his dark hair. "From what she said, the Beaks aren't even trying to find them."

Grey bit the inside of her cheek. It was possible that some Pinkcaps had dug out their chips in an attempt to escape Citoyen—after all, she'd cut out Jesse's chip—but the fact that the Blackcaps weren't pursuing them was concerning.

"And they were all Pences." Nic glanced between Megz and Arik. "But not like you guys. They were all the kind that wouldn't be able to survive on their own."

Grey's heart sank. Arik and Megz had been made Dispensable for their physical appearance, but there were other Pieces in other brothels whose stories were different. Even as a Redcap, Grey had known about them—had seen them.

During her training, Grey had spent a summer shadowing on a maternity ward. Early one morning, a young Orangecap had given birth with complications. The baby survived the delivery but sustained brain damage due to a lack of oxygen.

When the doctors told the woman that her child would never have a mental capacity greater than a five-year-old's, the woman cried. She begged and pleaded for them to change the child's diagnosis—to give the baby a chance to prove itself—but there was nothing to be done. Unable to function as an Orangecap, the child was taken—and its guardianship reassigned to a Purplecap—to be raised as a Pence.

"What about bodies?" Arden pushed. "Did they find any?"

"Not that I know of," Nic said.

"Maybe not yet," Roz growled. "But they will. This wouldn't be the first time some sick bastard snatched a Pence off the street and cut out their tracker."

Grey's stomach lurched.

"Even if they don't kill them immediately," Roz's face twisted with disgust. "Someone always finds the body eventually."

"I don't think this was just some sicko," Nic countered. "She made it sound like dozens had gone missing."

"Well, let's hope she was exaggerating," Jax said as the door to Lock's office opened.

Immediately, all eyes turned to the Purplecap as he stepped into the dining room with a piece of paper in his hand and a deep frown carved across his pale face.

"That can't be good," Roz muttered under her breath.

"There was a notice in the mail," Lock said. His blue eyes fell to the paper in his hand, and he began to read: "Effective immediately, Pinkcaps are to be placed under curfew."

"When are we supposed to work?" Arden asked. Across the table, Taryn shushed him.

Slowly, Lock raised his eyes to look at them. "You're not permitted to leave the Base during daylight hours."

"Daylight hours?" Jax raised his eyebrows. "You mean, we can only go out at night?"

Lock nodded and looked back down at the paper.

"All Pinkcaps asked to perform work-related tasks during daylight hours will be required to carry appropriate documentation, which can be obtained from a Purplecap." He exhaled and took a long breath before reading the final sentence. "Any Pinkcap found in violation of the curfew will face appropriate legal action."

"What kind of legal action is appropriate?" Roz's lips curled back in a snarl.

"Is it a fine?" Megz asked.

"It doesn't specify," Lock admitted.

"Great," Roz scoffed. "So, it's up to the mood of whichever Beak you run into?"

Lock's didn't answer her.

"If anyone needs documentation to leave the Base," he said, "just come to my office."

He began to back away, but Roz thumped her fist on the table.

"No," she growled. "This isn't right!"

"I understand," Lock agreed, "but I can't change it."

"That's bullshit." Roz stood her ground. "If enough people stand up against it, there's no way they can enforce it."

"Roz . . ." Lock's eyes were tired as they found hers, pleading her to back down. "If any of you want to discuss this further, please stop by my office. In the meantime, I'll see what I can do about a petition for an appeal."

A soft murmur of approval spread through the small group as Lock turned to leave, and without hesitation, Roz followed him.

"Apparently," Roz grumbled as she pulled her scarf tight against the wind, "we're a blight to the public eye."

Grey clenched her teeth as a gust of snow blew into her face, and she shoved her hands in her pockets. Beside her, Arik pulled his pink cap down over his ears.

"And what about Jax and Arden?" Roz went on, "The Apps work all sorts of weird hours."

"Lock will give them passes, I guess," Grey shrugged.

"But what happens if some Beak decides the pass isn't valid?"
When Grey didn't answer, Arik chimed in.
"I'm sure they'll have some kind of regulation in place," he said.
"Hopefully," Roz agreed.
It was Grey's night to work with Roz, but she couldn't help feeling nervous for Arik, especially after everything Nic had said about the disappearances.
"At least when summer comes, working hours will be shorter." Arik flashed a hopeful smile.
"Summer Solstice is a long way off," Roz pointed out. "Last night was the longest night of the year. Remember?"
"Yeah, but at least every night will be a little shorter from here on out," Arik insisted.
It was true, but with the shorter nights, everyone would be trapped in the Base. They would still be permitted to use the gardens in the courtyard—since they were contained on the property—but beyond that, they would be cloistered in the old building during the hottest months of the year.
"The eternal optimist," Roz sighed heavily and draped an arm over Arik's shoulders.
"I try," he grinned.
Roz smiled down at him, but her golden eyes were still blazing.
"Listen, Arik," she said. "Don't let anyone book you too close to dawn, okay? The new mandate sounds shaky, and I don't want you to be the first one to find out the punishment for missing curfew."
"It's okay, Roz," Arik said. "I'll be home on time."
"Yeah, but if anyone gives you trouble, come and get me."
"Don't worry about me." he smiled and linked his small arm with Roz's. "I'll be fine."
Roz's lips pursed together, and although she clearly remained unconvinced, she gave him a curt nod, and arm-in-arm, they made their way to the pods.

Pieces of Pink

- ♦ -

Steam clouded the mirror as Grey slipped into her pajamas and dried her fading hair with a towel. Her feet still hurt from the long night spent in high-heeled boots, but standing in the shower for a few extra minutes had been worth it, just to feel clean again.

Yawning, she pulled open the bathroom door, but as she turned toward her room, a loud crash and cries of shock echoed up the stairwell. Without hesitation, she bolted down the stairs, taking two at a time, until she reached the second-floor balcony and froze.

In the foyer, a unit of Blackcaps stood with their weapons aimed and ready to fire. Behind them, Megz stood isolated from the other Pinkcaps, and a Blackcap held the woman's hands behind her back. On the ground, just beyond Megz's reach, Nic knelt sobbing.

"Please," he begged with his hands clasped together in front of his face. "Don't take her!"

Grey's stomach lurched. Panicked, she scanned the crowd for Arik—terrified that the Blackcaps had come for the Dispensable—but she found him safe between Roz and Jax.

"You can't just take them!" Lock's voice burst from the lounge as the commotion spilled into the foyer, and Grey's breath caught in her throat.

With a sharp yank, a Blackcap pulled Lydie around the corner. His hand was fisted in her bright red hair, and behind them, Lock snarled and reached for Lydie's arm.

"Sir, you need to step back," the Blackcap warned.

"I will not," Lock snapped. "Not until you tell me what they're being charged with."

"Possession of illegal substances," the man answered.

Still holding Lydie's arm, Lock followed them toward the door. "You can't prove that!"

"We can." The Blackcap was losing his patience. He yanked Lydie with a firm tug, and she whimpered.

"How?" Lock shot back, but there was desperation growing in his voice.

"The blood samples in the pods," the Blackcap answered.

Lock's face paled. There was no denying that kind of evidence.

"Where are you taking them?"

"To a rehab facility," the Blackcap said calmly. "They'll decide who gets to come back here."

"Lock," Lydie cried. "Help!"

When the Blackcap tried to pull her away, Lock slammed his hand against the man's chest. Faster than anyone could react, a second Blackcap clubbed Lock's temple with the butt of his gun, and Lock crumpled to the floor.

"Lock!" Lydie was sobbing now, but as they dragged her toward the door, a blur of blonde fury shot across the foyer and dove for the weeping Rag.

"Don't touch her!" Roz roared, but as soon as her fingertips found Lydie's arm, a Blackcap pressed the barrel of his rifle directly between her perfect eyebrows.

Roz froze but didn't let go.

"Ma'am. You need to step back." The man holding the gun snarled at Roz. "*Now*."

"No." The Dom held her ground.

The Blackcap cocked his gun, and in the terrified silence that followed, even Nic stopped sobbing. All eyes were locked on Roz.

"This is your last warning," the Blackcap sneered. "Three . . ."

Still, Roz held on.

"Two . . ."

"Let them go," she hissed.

Pieces of Pink

"One . . ."

"Wait!" Lydie cried, "Don't shoot her. I'll come with you."

The Blackcap paused.

"I'll come with you," Lydie repeated.

"No," Roz pleaded.

"Roz," Lydie whispered up at her friend. "Let me go."

Eyes as fierce as any wild animal, Roz shook her head. "No."

Tears streamed down Lydie's cheeks as she spoke. "I never belonged here anyway."

"Lydie," Roz whispered, and Grey could hear the woman's heart breaking. "Please, no."

"Let me go," Lydie repeated, and finally, Roz let go.

In stunned silence, the Pinkcaps watched as the Blackcaps dragged Lydie and Megz from the Base and loaded them into a transport van idling outside.

There was nothing left to do—no way to help—as the women were shoved into the back of the vehicle. And when the last Blackcap finally slammed the front door shut, chaos erupted.

"Where are they taking them?" Arden called out to his brother as he crouched on the floor beside Nic.

"I don't know," Taryn yelled from the door. "They turned right!"

A group of Pinkcaps rushed to look out the windows, but it was already too late. The van was gone.

"Lock!" Arik's cry broke through the noise, and Grey rushed down the stairs.

"Grey, help!" Jax called for her, but she was already there, dropping to her knees and reaching for Lock.

He was unconscious, and blood oozed from a deep gash on his temple, where the rifle had left its mark.

"Is he dead?" Roz asked, frantically.

All around them, people sobbed as Grey pressed her fingers under Lock's jaw.

"Lock?" she asked, "Can you hear me?"

There was no response, but there was a definite pulse. Quickly, she made a fist and rubbed her knuckles against his sternum, trying to stimulate a response. And after an agonizing moment, he groaned and tried to sit up.

"Just stay down." Gently, Grey pressed her fingertips against his shoulders. "Don't try to get up yet. I think you have a concussion."

"Lydie?" Lock croaked. "Megz?"

"They're gone." Roz's voice cracked. "I'm sorry, I couldn't . . ."

Blinking through the blood streaming from his forehead, Lock reached for Roz.

"It's not your fault," he mumbled.

"Let me see your eyes," Grey said, ignoring the moment passing between the pair.

Gently, she lifted his lids and examined his pupils. They weren't dilated. And apart from needing stitches, he seemed to be okay.

"Jax?" Grey looked over her shoulder, and the Apical crouched down, ready to hear her command.

"How can I help?"

"Can you and Roz get him to his room?" Grey asked.

"Of course." Jax nodded.

"All right. I'll meet you there in a minute," she said. "I just need to grab some supplies."

Jax nodded, and together, he and Roz eased Lock to his feet. But as Grey turned toward the staircase, her eyes fell back on Nic, still quivering in Arden's arms. She took a step toward him, but Arik stopped her with a gentle hand.

"It's okay," Arik said. "I'll take care of Nic. Just help Lock."

- ♦ -

Pieces of Pink

Gripping the needle driver between her thumb and middle finger, Grey pierced through the wound on Lock's temple and smoothly pulled the surgical thread through his skin. The man winced but did not cry out.

"Just two more," Grey assured him. "Are you okay?"

"Yes," he mumbled, still delirious from the concussion.

Behind her, Jax stood pressed up against the wall. Lock's bedroom—barely more than a converted utility closet—was only large enough for a bed and a simple side table. Squeezing three adults inside was a tight fit.

Grey had never noticed the room through the back door of his office. Or if she had, she had taken it for a closet. With all of the rooms the Base had to offer, why he had chosen this particular one was a mystery. It seemed so modest for one of the wealthiest Purplecaps in Citoyen.

"Almost finished," Grey assured as she looped the last knot and pulled it taught.

Lock grunted.

One delicate snip later, and the stitches were done. Grey sat back, set her tools in an empty bowl, and reached for a bandage.

"This is it," Lock whispered as Grey covered the stitches.

"Yes," she said, "That's it."

"No." Lock frowned. "This is it."

Grey paused. "What do you mean?"

"I can't keep you safe anymore." He shook his head. "I can't keep any of you safe."

There was a long pause before Jax spoke: "Don't admit that."

"I've been trying not to." Lock looked up at them with tears in his eyes. "But ever since Huxley took over, I've been losing my grip. Whitecaps who supported Lachlan," he shook his head sadly, "they're switching sides. They want to stay in her good graces."

Grey glanced at Jax.

"I'm losing support," Lock said. "And I'm not the only one. Huxley isn't just cracking down on us, she's trying to eliminate us."

"It can't be that bad, can it?" Jax asked. "Not yet."

"I don't know." Lock drew a tired breath. "I don't know."

- ♦ -

Grey closed Lock's door with a soft click.

"We'll need to wake him up every few hours," she whispered to Jax as they stepped into the hallway beyond Lock's office. "Just to make sure everything's okay."

"I'll take care of it," Jax murmured, then held up the surgical supplies he was carrying. "What should I do with these?"

"Take them to the kitchen," Grey answered. "I'll clean them."

Jax nodded and followed Grey toward the swinging door. But when they pushed inside, she paused. There, on the steel prep-table, was a plate of half-eaten waffles.

Grey's throat grew tight as she veered toward the sink and turned on the hot water. It was all too much. First Jesse, then Selene, and now, Blackcaps were storming units to drag off drug-users, turned in by the very pods that had been promised to protect them. It was more than she could take.

Swallowing down the tears, she focused her attention on washing her tools. When she was finished, she turned back to the table where Lydie's half-eaten meal still sat.

There was something too final about throwing away the food, as if leaving it there might somehow make Lydie come home. But she knew the truth. Lydie and Megz were gone.

A sob ripped from Grey's chest, and for a moment, Jax stared at her in startled silence. But as realization struck, his expression sank, and he took a slow breath.

"There's no rehab facility," he whispered. "Is there?"

"If there were," Grey's voice trembled, "Redcaps would've come, not Blackcaps."

Defeated, Jax exhaled heavily, and with his mouth set in a grim line, he picked up Lydie's plate and carried it to the garbage. No matter how badly they wished for it, Lydie was gone, and she was never coming home.

TWELVE

Roz sighed deeply and flopped down in her chair. Beside her, Arik sat curled on the edge of the bed.

"He really said he can't protect us anymore?" Roz frowned. "He said that?"

Leaning against the wall with his hands tucked in his pockets, Jax nodded. Though solemn, his face had regained its usual mask of composure, and even in the wake of everything that had happened, he was still handsome.

"We all knew Lachlan would die eventually," Roz said. "Why wasn't Lock prepared for this? It's not like he didn't see it coming."

"I don't know," Jax hesitated. "But I think Huxley was a shock for him."

"Why?" Roz shook her head in frustration. "Both you and Selene warned him. He shouldn't have had such blind faith in Lachlan's sycophants. They're all just power-hungry parasites. Without him around, it's no surprise they just followed the money."

"Lock knew that," Jax insisted. "But he never thought they'd go for such an extremist. Half of them have a Perp in their pocket, so it doesn't make sense for them to support her. If she eliminates

Pinkcaps, it'll take out part of their income, too. And he never believed they would actually go against their own best interest."

"Speaking of the Perps . . ." Roz leaned forward in her chair. "Is Huxley after all of them? Or just Lock?"

Jax shook his head. "I don't know."

"Why would she just target Lock?" Grey cut in. "Because he owns the most units?"

"Not exactly." Roz exchanged an uncomfortable with Jax.

"But not everyone knows this," Jax said after a slight pause, "So keep it to yourself, okay?"

"Of course." Grey nodded.

"Lock wasn't born a Purplecap," he said slowly.

For a moment, the words didn't make sense. And as Grey's mind scrambled through the memories of their conversations, realization struck. He had tried to help her and Jesse escape Citoyen, he'd taken her from the wall, spared her from execution, had even told her that he understood how hard it was to love someone across the Color Code, and through it all, she had never even considered the possibility that he hadn't been born into his cap.

"What was he?" Grey whispered.

Had he done what she had done? Had he tried to escape and been punished for it?

"What was he before?" she repeated.

Jax answered, "Lock was born a Piece."

"What?" Grey was taken aback. "He moved *up*?"

"He was born a Pinkcap," Roz confirmed.

"That's not possible," Grey shook her head. "No one has *ever* moved up. You can't do that."

"Before Lock was born," Jax explained, "his mother was the High Chancellor's—Lachlan's—favorite Pinkcap."

Grey stared at him in disbelief.

"Lock," Jax said, "is Lachlan's son."

"No," Grey shook her head. "No. It doesn't matter how powerful you are. You can't just move up. You can't."

Jax didn't respond.

"How can Whitecaps expect us to stay in line if they're willing to make exceptions for themselves and for their families?" Anger rose in Grey's voice. "You are your mother's cap, not your father's, and you sure as hell aren't some random cap in the middle."

"We know it looks bad," Roz nodded in agreement. "But that's exactly why Huxley might be targeting him."

Grey clenched her teeth together and listened.

"Lock's been breaking the Code his whole life," Jax said. "But most of the time, he does it to keep us safe. And with Lachlan, he could get away with it. How else do you think he got all of those medical supplies you asked for?"

In all honesty, it was something she hadn't spent much time considering. She had just assumed he was rich enough to buy them for himself.

"So, for Huxley," Jax went on when Grey didn't answer, "Lock is a threat. And if word spreads about what he really is, no one will trust the Whitecaps anymore. No one will want to hear about how the Code is the law and all that bullshit. It'll be over."

"Huxley's afraid of him," Roz said. "She's afraid of what he could do if he set his mind to it."

"Then why doesn't he do it?" Grey demanded. "Why doesn't he just do something?"

"He *is* doing something," Roz shot back. "And you of all people should know that."

Grey's cheeks flushed.

"For as long as I've known him," Roz continued, "Lock has done everything he can for the people around him. He doesn't care if it breaks the Code or not. No other Perp would've taken you in. And it wasn't just because he knew your husband, or because you were a Redcap. Lock saved you because it was just the right thing to do."

Roz was right. Lock had tried to give her a better life without ever having met her. And even though it hadn't worked out for her and Jesse, she knew he had saved countless others.

"What do you think, Jax?" Arik broke his silence.

Jax looked up. "About what?"

"Could Huxley be targeting Lock?" he asked. "Have you heard anything during your shifts? What do the Whitecaps talk about?"

"Honestly," Jax shook his head, "not much. Now that Lachlan's gone—and no one's trying to suck up to him—they treat me like any other Pinkcap." His eyes shifted to the floor. "They're only keeping me around because they couldn't have me before. And without Selene, I'm just . . ."

His voice drifted away.

"They probably don't want you to say anything to Lock," Roz said quietly. "If Huxley's going after him, she wouldn't want her plans to make it back to the Base."

Jax shrugged.

"But if that's true," Grey's heart sank, "if Huxley really is going after Lock, and she gets rid of him, what will happen to us?"

There was a moment of silence before Roz answered.

"Hopefully," she said, "we never find out."

- ♦ -

Lock leaned back on the edge of his desk as Grey peeled away the square of gauze covering his wound. She had made it back to the Base just before dawn, but Lock had caught her at the bottom of the stairs, hoping she might remove his stitches. And even though she was exhausted, she followed him to his office.

It had been nearly five days since the Blackcaps invaded the Base, taking Megz and Lydie. And with no word or updates about the women, the awful truth of the situation was beginning to sink in. If they weren't in rehab, they were imprisoned. But more likely, they were dead.

All around, Pinkcaps were disappearing without a trace. But even if the Blackcaps tried to sweep away the truth of what had happened at the Base, Lock would always wear the evidence on his temple.

"What's wrong?" Lock glanced up at Grey, and she realized she was frowning. "Aren't they ready to come out yet?"

"No, they're ready." Grey forced a smile, but it felt more like a grimace. "But you're going to have a scar."

"There are worse things than scars," Lock sighed.

He wasn't wrong.

Grey pushed Lock's hair out of the way with her wrist and carefully cleaned the area.

"I'm just glad I won't have to travel with them," Lock said.

"Why?" Grey asked, "Where are you going?"

He paused a moment, choosing his words carefully, then finally answered, "I'm going to one of my southern units."

Grey stopped cleaning the stitches and looked up.

"The South?" she raised her eyebrows, trying to ask the question she didn't dare say out loud: Was the rebellion still alive?

As if he had read her thoughts, Lock gave her a subtle nod.

"When are you leaving?"

"My driver will be here to pick me up in an hour or two."

"Oh." Grey bit the inside of her cheek. If it was true, and the rebellion was still clinging onto life, Huxley could be targeting Lock for more than just his patronage. But if Lock was heading to the South to join forces with the rebels, the Pieces left at the Base would be defenseless.

"How long will you be gone?"

He shrugged. "Maybe a week."

She nodded and reached for her tools.

"You might feel a tug," she warned.

"Mm-hmm."

Using a pair of tweezers, she gently lifted each knot, snipped the loop, and pulled the loose thread from his skin. It was a short procedure, and within minutes, she had removed each stitch, replaced the bandage, and let his black curls fall back into place.

"Keep it covered for now," she advised as she packed up her medical supplies. "And when you come home, I'll take another look just to make sure everything's okay."

"Sounds good." Lock nodded.

"Okay, then."

She took a step toward the door and paused. She wanted to say something, tell him not to leave the North behind, tell him to come home when his business was finished, tell him that people here depended on him, but she couldn't.

"Have a safe trip."

"Thank you," Lock said, and the sincerity in his voice was a small reassurance, as if he recognized her apprehension and understood her fear of being abandoned to the Blackcaps.

"I'll be home as soon as I can," he said. "I promise."

A soft noise pulled Grey from her dreamless sleep. Still exhausted, she rolled over and blinked. The room was dark apart from a sliver of light, which pierced through the gap in her curtains and cast a thin golden line along the ceiling. Her eyes followed it, trailing to the top of the doorframe. But when she realized her bedroom door was wide open, Grey jolted upright. In the darkness, she could just make out the form of a man—his face shining with blood—kneeling in the center of her room.

A scream rose in her throat, only to be strangled off by her own terror, as Grey fumbled in the darkness to escape the nightmare before her. She wanted to cry out, wanted to leap off the bed and turn on the lights, but she was frozen, trapped in the memory of Jesse's execution.

"Help me," the man whimpered.

Grey blinked. The voice was not Jesse's.

"Please . . ."

It was Jax.

In an instant, the terror vanished, only to be replaced by new horror as she threw back her covers and switched on the light.

Crumpled on her bedroom floor with his head in his hands, Jax knelt, covered in blood. It had soaked through his torn shirt, matted his hair, and masked his swollen face. In places, it had dried to a rusty brown, but too much of it was still bright red, still fresh.

"Shit," Grey hissed under her breath as she dropped to the floor beside him. "What happened?"

Jax didn't answer.

"Were you shot?" she asked. "Or stabbed?"

His shoulders began to tremble, and his teeth clacked together as his body slipped into shock. Without waiting for a response, Grey reached for the collar of his shirt and peeled it down, but as the fabric separated from his skin, Jax cried out in pain. Immediately, she understood why.

Jax hadn't been shot or stabbed, he'd been whipped. Stretching from his shoulders past his beltline, rivulets of blood oozed down his butchered back. In too many places, the skin had been split, and small ribbons of flesh dangled where the wounds intersected.

Pieces of Pink

"Oh!" A small voice gasped from the hallway, and Grey whirled around to see Arik standing in the doorframe with his black eyes transfixed on Jax.

"Get me Roz," Grey said, trying to retain the calm, practiced tone of a Redcap, but she was beginning to lose her grip.

Arik hesitated.

"Now!"

Snapped from his trance, Arik bolted down the hall, and Grey turned to her closet. Shelf by shelf, she tore through her supplies, tossing what she would need into a spare box: thread and needles, iodine, gauze, and antibiotics. It was illegal to beat an Apical, and whoever had done this to Jax clearly had no fear of repercussion.

"Fuck!" Roz gasped as she flew into the room and came to a dead stop. "What the hell happened?"

"I don't know," Grey answered and pushed the supply box into Arik's arms and spun on Roz. "Help me get him into the bathroom. Third floor," she added. "It's cleaner."

Without hesitating, Roz crouched beside Jax.

"And try not to touch his back," Grey warned as she knelt on the other side and took hold of Jax's arm. "One, two, three . . ."

On the last count, the two women hoisted Jax to his feet.

"Come on, Jax," Roz grunted under his weight as they turned toward the stairs. "Use your feet."

Jax stumbled as he tried to find his footing, but his legs were too shaky to stand.

"Just a little further," Grey urged. "We're almost there."

When they reached the bathroom, Arik set the supply box on the counter. "Should I get Lock?" he asked.

Grey shook her head. "He left this morning to visit another unit."

"Damn it," Roz growled. "What do we do?"

"Help me strip him," Grey said. "And get him in the tub."

"Should we call an ambulance?" Arik asked, biting his lip.

"No!" Roz and Grey said in unison.

After what had happened to Lydie, Megz, and even Selene, she didn't dare call other Redcaps for assistance. Even if she did, she wasn't entirely sure they would be permitted to treat a Piece who had been whipped for missing curfew—if that was even what had happened—and if they let an ambulance take Jax, they might never see him again. There was no choice. Grey could only do the best with what she had.

"Arik," Grey glanced over her shoulder, "I need clean sheets on Jax's bed. Can you do that?"

"Of course," Arik nodded and slipped into the hall.

For his stitches, Jax would need a place to lie down, but first, his wounds would need to be cleaned. And after Selene's suicide, the bathtub had been replaced, making it the safest bet.

As Roz began to peel away Jax's blood-soaked clothes, Grey quickly pulled her hair into a bun and washed her hands.

"Was he out after curfew?" Roz asked. "Did the Beaks do this?"

"I don't know," Grey admitted and took Roz's place. "He hasn't told me anything."

Roz turned to wash her hands, and Grey assessed the injuries, now much more visible under the bright, bathroom lights. Jax had two black eyes—one worse than the other—and his nose was broken. A deep gash, probably from a knife, stretched diagonally from the top corner of his forehead, over the bridge of his nose, to the base of his cheek, narrowly missing the corner of his lips.

When Jax was stripped and kneeling in the front of the tub, Grey turned on a steady stream of cool water, snatched up one of the few surgical towels she had, and took the fresh bar of soap from Roz. Then, she began to wash his wounds.

Jax sobbed through gritted teeth as Grey painstakingly worked her way down his back. As important as it was to clear away any debris that may have entered the deep gashes, there were some places so damaged she didn't touch them, for fear that the skin would fall off.

"Hang in there, Jax," Roz squeezed both of the man's hands. "Grey will have you fixed up in no time. This is what she's good at."

The Dom shot Grey an anxious look, but they both knew the truth. Even under the best possible circumstances, Jax was no longer an Apical.

Grey had seen floggings before. And while corporal punishment was unpopular in the capital city, it wasn't unheard of. She had even witnessed it once or twice. But this was so much worse than the public displays the Blackcaps usually carried out. While those whippings had been focused between the shoulders and carefully administered to avoid drawing blood, this beating had been done with random, unchecked violence.

For Jax, there had been no crowd to watch, no Yellowcaps to object, no Whitecaps to feign horror, and no school children walking by. There was nothing at all to stop them from tearing Jax to pieces, and so they had.

"How long?" Roz asked over Jax's head. Her face was smooth and calm, but there was worry in her eyes.

"Hours," Grey answered honestly. "He needs a lot of stitches."

Roz grimaced, and beneath Grey's hands, Jax groaned.

"It's okay," Roz murmured. "I'll stay right here with you."

Grey snipped the final thread and took a step back. Without any anesthetic to dull the pain, Jax had lost consciousness midway through the procedure. But Roz—true to her word—had remained by his side through all of it.

The days when Roz had wanted to murder Jax for making Grey a Pence felt distant, like a half-forgotten dream. But considering the circumstances of the past few weeks, it wasn't surprising.

"Is it over?" Roz yawned deeply.

Grey nodded. "I just have to bandage him, then it's done."

With a grunt, Roz leaned back in her chair and closed her eyes.

Outside, the sky was already glowing pink with the setting sun. In less than an hour, they would have to leave for the pods. It had taken all day to piece Jax's flesh back together, and now, as Grey stared down at the latticework of dried blood, she felt exhausted to the point of tears.

"Coffee?" Arik stepped into the room with two mugs of steaming liquid clutched between his small hands.

"Thank you." Grey sighed in relief at the sight of the coffee. But there was still more to finish before she could take it. "If you just put it on the nightstand, I'll drink it as soon as I set these bandages."

In the hours that Grey had worked on Jax's back, Arik had kept the onlookers at bay. Most of the Base had been asleep when Jax first appeared on Grey's floor, but as the day wore on, news had traveled, and a steady stream of Pinkcaps passed by Jax's room, anxious to see the truth.

Grey could hardly blame them for wanting to witness it for themselves. After all, if Jax—an Apical—could be whipped, no one was safe anymore.

Beside her, Arik nudged Roz and passed her the second cup of coffee. Gratefully, the Dom took the mug and drank.

"Well, he's obviously not an Apical anymore," Roz frowned as she leaned forward to watch Grey place the last of the bandages.

Grey glanced up. "What will happen to him?"

"He'll probably be a Dom," Roz shrugged. "I think he'd prefer it to being a Rag, no offense. Then again, if the Beaks are allowed to maim Apps like this, I guess it doesn't really matter what we call ourselves anymore. We're all Pences now."

A small frown curved on Arik's lips.

"Sorry," Roz said.

"No, it's not that." Arik shook his head. "It's just, are you sure Beaks did this?"

Roz's eyes narrowed. "Why?"

"Blackcaps are usually more . . ." he hesitated.

"Precise?" Grey asked.

Arik nodded. "I mean, I understand that he was out past curfew, but this just seems excessive. No one else has been flogged like this. Why start with an Apical?"

"Who knows?" Roz took a deep sip of her coffee. "Probably just to scare us."

"Maybe," Arik agreed.

"But right now, I'm not going to worry about who did it." Roz drained the mug and stood up. "I'm just going to go to a pod and hope my ass doesn't get murdered."

Grey scoffed. It would be a feat to take down Roz.

"Arik, you're coming with me," Roz said. "And Grey, you're staying here."

"What?" Grey looked up. "What about my tracker? I don't have an excuse to miss tonight."

"We'll log it as the stomach flu or something," Roz shrugged. "And Beaks don't hunt down people for missing one night of work—not yet, at least. Either way, you look exhausted, and you're no good to anybody if you're too tired to see straight."

A wave of relief flooded through Grey's chest. She hadn't even had time to use the bathroom since Jax had woken her that morning, let alone sleep.

"And since you're going to bed," Roz reached for Grey's coffee, still sitting on the nightstand, "you won't mind if I take this, right?"

"No," Grey smiled. "It's all yours."

"Excellent." Roz gulped it down and glanced at Arik. "Well, we better get ready to go."

With the two empty mugs in her hands, the Dom took a few steps, then paused in the doorway and looked back.

"Take care of him," Roz said, and though there was still a smile on the woman's face, her true request was clear in her eyes: *Don't let him die.*

"I'll do my best," Grey promised.

With a nod, Roz turned and followed Arik from the room.

- ♦ -

Grey's eyelids drooped from exhaustion as she set a glass of water on the nightstand and tossed her pillow on the floor beside Jax's bed. Roz was right, she needed sleep, but she couldn't find it in her own room. With the rest of the Base empty, she was too anxious to leave Jax alone, and so she resolved to sleep on his floor.

Jax—who had only regained consciousness briefly after Roz and Arik had left—was lying on his stomach with the sheets folded down and tucked around his hips. The weight of the fabric had been too painful to bear, so Grey had left his bandaged back uncovered.

As lightly as she could, Grey pressed two fingers to his wrist and checked his pulse. Jax's heartbeat was steady, but his skin was too warm. Trying not to disturb him, she reached for his forehead. A thin layer of sweat glistened above his eyebrows. Even with all of the iodine and ointments she had used, there was a fever on the way.

"Selene," Jax sighed.

Grey flinched.

"No," she whispered. "It's Grey."

He groaned and drifted back into sleep.

Pieces of Pink

Beneath his eyelids, Grey could see eye movement as his mind darted through dreams. She only hoped he could sleep off the fever. There weren't enough antibiotics for a serious infection, and with Lock out of town, there was no telling when she would get more medical supplies.

Grey glanced at the clock. It was still early to change his bandages, but in the places where there had been too little flesh to stitch back together, the blood had already soaked through.

For the sake of tempering any infection, she decided it was worth it to add more ointment to the most severe wounds. And with a frown, she pulled on one of the last pairs of medical gloves and carefully lifted the bandages.

Clenching her jaw, Grey stared down at the raw welts and open cuts on Jax's back. A few of the wounds—which she had luckily been able to stitch closed—had been split nearly down to the bone. But even with the hours of careful work she had spent piecing him back together, the scars would be brutal.

Although some might fade with time, the majority would twist into knotted white streaks, no matter how well she treated them. With a piece of gauze, she began to dab the wounds with ointment, and Jax went rigid.

"It's okay," she murmured. "I'm just changing some bandages."

He groaned in discomfort—still trapped somewhere in the delirium between sleep and consciousness—and gripped the sheets under his hands.

"You're all right," she repeated the phrase as she worked, but Jax didn't relax until the last bandage had been resealed. And blinking back the exhausting in her eyes, Grey stumbled to the bathroom to wash her hands.

- ♦ -

Grey stifled a yawn with her arm, reached for the cool cloth draped over the back of Jax's neck, and tossed it in the bowl of water beside the bed. His fever had risen throughout the night, but she was reluctant to interfere too much in bringing it down. Without many resources at her disposal, it was rational to let the heat serve its purpose and kill off any infection trying to take hold, but logic did little to dispel her fear.

Jax was barely two degrees away from hyperpyrexia, and soon intervention would be necessary. Allowing the body to fight for itself would only be worth it if Jax's brain wasn't injured in the process, and as his fever continued to rise, Grey began to consider her options. Soon, she would have no choice but to force it down.

"Can you open your mouth?" she asked softly.

Jax groaned, and his lips parted just far enough for Grey to slip the thermometer under his tongue. She held it there, waiting as it took a reading. But when the device beeped, and Grey read the numbers flashing across the screen, her heart sank.

Immediately, she tossed the thermometer on the nightstand and bolted from the room. In a medical facility, she could have soaked him in an ice bath or spritzed him with water, but with the wounds on his back and face, she didn't want to risk further contamination, so she went to the kitchen.

When she reached the freezer, Grey yanked open the doors, searching for icepacks, but all she found were vegetables. Snatching a large bowl from under a prep table, she filled it with bags of frozen peas and dashed back upstairs.

Still winded from the climb, she quickly wrung out the soaking rags and wrapped them around each frozen bag. The first, she wedged against the top of Jax's head, then she draped the second over his neck, tucked two under his armpits, and finally stuffed the last between his legs.

Pieces of Pink

Jax gasped and flinched against the cold, but Grey didn't falter as she yanked away the remaining covers and methodically checked every wound, dabbing antibiotic cream wherever it could be spared.

The Base had lost too many people already, and Grey had made a promise. She wouldn't let him die.

- ♦ -

An hour before dawn, Jax opened his eyes, and Grey exhaled a sharp sigh of relief.

"How are you feeling?" she asked as she tested his forehead with the back of her hand. He was still a little warm, but it was no longer a cause for concern.

Slowly, Jax licked his dry lips.

"Thirsty," he croaked.

"Can you sit up a little?" Grey asked as she reached for the glass on the nightstand.

On shaking arms, Jax eased himself onto his elbows and took the water. He sipped just enough to wet his mouth. Too exhausted to hold the glass any longer, he handed it back to Grey.

"More?" she asked.

Jax shook his head, lowered himself back onto his stomach, and turned his head to stare at the wall.

Grey watched him in silence for a moment, then she glanced out the window. Soon, the other Pinkcaps would trickle home from work, and once again, the Base would be crawling with activity and questions. She only hoped that they all made it back before sunrise. Another set of injuries like these would require more medical supplies than Grey had.

"They didn't pay." Jax's voice was cold and hollow as it cut through Grey's thoughts.

"What?" she asked.

He didn't answer.

"Jax," she prodded. "What happened?"

His throat bobbed.

"The Whitecaps who booked me last night . . ." his voice cracked. "They didn't pay for it."

Grey's eyes widened as realization sank in.

"Whitecaps did this to you?"

Slowly, Jax nodded.

"The one who booked me invited friends, and they tied me up," he whispered. "There were too many of them. I couldn't fight back. I tried to fight, but they . . ."

The words trailed away.

Nausea rolled through Grey's stomach as she listened.

"When they were finished with me, they whipped me and broke my nose." His words were barely audible. "Then, they cut my face so I couldn't be an App."

A tear rolled from the corner of his eye and disappeared into the gauze taped over his nose.

"At sunrise, they threw me in the snow and called the Blackcaps."

Grey bit down on the insides of her cheeks.

"They took me to the back of the van, and they—"

Jax stopped, unable to repeat what had happened.

"When they were finished, they threw me on the steps of the Base." His voice shook through the tears. "I thought I was going to die. I *wanted* to die. But I didn't."

There was a heavy moment of silence, and fighting back the tears in her eyes, Grey gathered up the damp washcloths and melted bags of frozen vegetables, desperate to keep herself from falling apart.

"I'm just going to throw these in the laundry—"

Her voice broke with the effort of keeping her tears at bay.

"And I'll grab some dry sheets for your bed." Her voice trembled. "I'll be right back, okay?"

Jax nodded, and Grey slipped into the hall.

She managed to hold her breath all the way down to the second floor, but when she finally reached the laundry room, she crumbled.

Sinking to her hands and knees, Grey sobbed. But the tears weren't all for Jax. No, she cried for Lydie and Megz. She cried for Selene. She cried for Jesse, and she even cried for herself. But most of all, Grey cried for the future, and for the terror of not knowing what tomorrow would bring.

THIRTEEN

Jax lifted his chin to the light as Grey eased up his stitches with a pair of tweezers. The wound on his face—though deep—had healed nicely over the past week, and the sutures were ready to come out. One by one, Grey snipped the small black knots and pulled away the thread.

Across the room, Lock stood by the window with his arms crossed over his chest. There was still a stark, pink line where the Purplecap's own stitches had been, but it was easily hidden under his hair. For Jax, however, the scar would be unconcealable.

In a few places—along his brow bone and across the bridge of his nose—the skin hadn't quite scabbed over yet, so Grey replaced the stitches with small strips of medical tape. When it was finished, she finally stepped back.

"Do you want to take a look?" she asked, motioning to the mirror that hung over the dresser.

Jax nodded, and with a grunt of pain, he pushed himself off the bed. As Jax walked across the room, Lock stared at his ruined back. It was hard not to gape at the tapestry of shredded flesh and scabs twisting over the once enviable skin, and although Lock's eyes flashed with shock at the full sight of it, his expression remained smooth and calm.

Staring in the mirror, Jax slowly reached toward his face and trailed his shaking fingers along the scab.

"Will it fade?" he mumbled.

"A little." Grey shrugged. "Even after it heals, it will be pink for a while. With time it should turn white. But it will always be visible."

With a curt nod, Jax turned away from the mirror and sat down heavily on the edge of his bed. His face was lax, and even through the bruises, Grey could see dullness in his eyes. He was exhausted, and it would take time for the full reality of his injuries to sink in.

"And his back?" Lock frowned, "How long before those stitches come out?"

The flood of relief Grey had felt when Lock returned to the Base that morning had been visceral. Even though he had promised to come home, a part of Grey hadn't believed him. Then again, if Lock had chosen to stay in the South—far away from Huxley and her mandates—she could hardly have blamed him.

"Probably another week," Grey answered. "But it will be at least two weeks before he can start working again."

Lock nodded, but Jax frowned.

"Do you think they'll let me miss that many days?" Jax asked.

"Why not?" Grey glanced between the two men. "You have a valid reason. And if your Purplecap signs off on it, you're not breaking any laws."

But even as she spoke, Grey could hear the uncertainty in her voice. According to law, it was illegal to hit an Apical, yet the Whitecaps had done it with no repercussions. And there was nothing to stop Huxley from changing the labor laws again. After all, she had already forced children into the brothels. It was only a matter of time before Blackcaps began rounding up those who were no longer deemed productive members of society.

"Plus, we can't risk another infection before you're completely healed." She glanced pointedly at Lock, "The Base doesn't have enough resources left to handle it."

"Grey is right," Lock said smoothly. "And right now, the most important thing is that you rest and heal."

"But what if the Whitecaps—"

"And if it really comes down to it," Lock cut him off, "I will personally cover your shifts."

Jax frowned but didn't protest.

"Now, Grey," Lock turned to face her, "you said we're running low on medical supplies?"

She nodded.

"Well, if you make another list for me," he exhaled sharply, "I'll do everything I can to find what you need."

"Thank you," Grey answered. "I will."

"Excellent," Lock said. "There are still some things I need to take care of today, so I'll be in and out of the Base, but if you leave it on my desk, I'll make it a priority."

Grey nodded.

"And if it's all right with you," he turned to Jax. "I'd like you to remain my second."

"But, I'm not an Apical." Jax's words were hollow.

"That's not important," Locks said. "You know the Base better than anyone else. And if a time ever comes when I'm not here, it'll be easier knowing that everything's in your hands."

Before Jax or Grey could respond, Lock slipped from the room and disappeared down the hall.

- ♦ -

Pieces of Pink

"Damn, Jax." Roz's deep burgundy lips quirked up in a smile as she leaned on the doorframe. "How are you still so hot?"

Jax grunted and pulled his shirt back over his head in a stiff sweep as Grey replaced the medical supplies in her box. The scabs on his back were tight and drier than Grey would have liked, but she had already used up the few small tubes of ointment she'd had; and while Lock was aware of the shortages, it would be days—maybe weeks—before he could find more.

"Now that you're on your feet," Roz remained in the doorway with her eyes fixed on Jax, "I thought you might like to come downstairs. Maybe grab some lunch?"

He didn't respond.

"Jax?" Roz pushed.

"No, thanks," he grumbled. "I'm not hungry."

"Well, I know everyone would be happy to see you," she took a step into the room. "We've all been missing your sunny disposition."

"Roz," Jax said without cracking so much as a smile. "I said no."

The Dom's eyes flashed with irritation, but she didn't fight him. Instead, she turned her attention to Grey.

"What about you?" she asked. "Lunch?"

"Sure." Grey shrugged and glanced at Jax before following Roz out the door. He didn't look up.

When they were out of earshot, Roz glanced back toward Jax's bedroom door and lowered her voice.

"Has he eaten anything?" Roz asked. "He looks like shit."

Roz was right. In barely seven days, Jax had transformed from an exceptionally handsome man into a gaunt shell of his former self. His eyes were sunken and tired, and his warm complexion had faded to a pasty gray. Where he had once been straightforward and efficient, Jax had become withdrawn. Only leaving his room to use the toilet, he kept his door closed to everyone but Grey and Lock.

"Not nearly enough," Grey admitted. "But I'll bring food up to him later."

"Try bell peppers," Roz frowned. "He's always loved those. And oranges, too."

Grey nodded. "Thanks for the advice."

When they reached the second-floor landing, Roz paused and glanced over the balcony. Below, chattering voices drifted from the dining room and up the stairs.

"Come with me." Roz nodded toward the end of the hall. "I want to talk to you about something in private."

Without questioning, Grey followed her to the window alcove that looked out over the street, and together they sat. For a moment, Roz was silent as she glared over the pedestrians below. Then she turned to Grey.

"Two things." Roz kept her voice low. "First, when Jax starts working again, I want him to switch places with me. I want him to start acting as your mentor."

Grey blinked in surprise. "Why?"

"For starters, I think you could learn from each other," she said. "But really, we need more Doms to protect the Pences," her eyes grew serious, "and the kids."

There was a gravity to Roz's tone that made Grey uncomfortable.

"Now that Megz is gone, Nic and Taryn have been working with a few Pences from another unit, and you know I stick with Arik. And eventually, I'm sure Jax will be a Dom, but it will take time before he's ready to let someone touch him again."

Grey swallowed. It was something all Pieces understood too well.

"And you're so close to being ready to make the switch," Roz continued. "Once you're a Dom, you can take on a Pence or a kid whose Purplecap is forcing them into the pods. So, if you and Jax work together—just to get started—it will free me up to keep an eye on Arik."

Pieces of Pink

It was hard to argue with Roz's logic, but the thought of permanently becoming a Dom still didn't sit well with Grey.

"But I understand if you don't want to work with Jax after what happened . . ." Roz hesitated, "when he made you a Pence."

"I thought you forgot about that." Grey glanced out the window and fidgeted, still uncomfortable with the memories of that night.

"No," Roz said, and her eyes flashed. "I don't forget things like that. But if we start in-fighting, then there really is no hope for us to come out of this alive."

It was true. Grey exhaled a shaking breath.

"And between Selene and . . ." Roz's voice trailed off. "Jax has been punished enough."

Grey stared out the window a moment longer. It felt foolish to care whether or not she worked with Jax, but she did. And although they had taken strides to form an amicable relationship, there was a degree of trust that Grey knew he could never earn.

"I . . ." Grey hesitated. There was no real choice. "I'll work with him," she agreed.

With a sober nod, Roz thanked her.

"So, what was the second thing you wanted to talk about?" Grey asked, anxious to change the subject.

"I want to know how you and your husband tried to escape."

The words hit Grey's chest like a cinderblock, and her mouth fell open as she gasped, "What?"

"Hear me out." Roz held up her hands defensively. "I know you almost made it. And if you just told me how, maybe we could create a new plan—a better plan."

Slowly, Grey shook her head.

"We could learn from the mistakes you made—"

"Roz," Grey choked out the word. "No."

"But, we could do it!" Roz's eyes were pleading now. "We could make it out. Just a few of us at a time. Couldn't we?"

"No," Grey whispered again.

"Why?" Roz's voice almost broke.

"Trying to run," Grey said slowly, "was the worst decision I ever made in my life. It cost me everything, Roz."

The Dom's face sank into a deep frown, and the light blinked from her eyes.

"And what will it cost you to stay?" There was an edge in Roz's words, designed to cut, but there was a truth in them, too. "How long before they come and drag another one of us off?"

Grey didn't answer.

"Maybe you're right," Roz's lips curled back in disdain. "Maybe we'll get caught, and they'll kill us. Or maybe we'll finally make it out of this shithole. Either way, Huxley doesn't follow the Code. It's only a matter of time before she decides to eliminate us all."

"Roz!" Grey pleaded, but the Dom shook her head.

"At least if we run, we can die on our own terms," she spat. "So, think about that."

Before Grey had a chance to respond, Roz stood up and stormed down the hall.

- ♦ -

As Roz had predicted, it was only a matter of days before Huxley made her next move. First, all Bluecaps working in the employ of a Purplecap were reassigned to new positions. Then, three days later, food rations were put into place.

"I bet she ditched the Bluecaps, so there'd be no one to witness these rations," Roz scowled at the gritty porridge and dropped her spoon into the bowl with a loud clatter. "I mean, I can handle oatmeal every once in a while, but what's this shit even made of?"

Beside her, Arik continued eating his meal without complaint.

Pieces of Pink

"What's your professional opinion?" Roz turned to Grey with one eyebrow raised.

"Professional?" Grey asked. "I was a Redcap, not a chef."

"Yeah," Roz rolled her eyes. "But you know what it takes to keep someone alive. Do you think this will cut it?"

"Honestly," Grey grimaced and poked the mealy liquid with the tip of her spoon. "It looks kind of synthetic. It probably has protein, maybe a few vitamins."

She took a nibble, then quickly sipped a mouthful of water. Over the past few days, it was the only useful method she had found for getting the meals past her gag reflex.

"And if there's not any protein or vitamins?" Roz asked.

"Then we'll all be malnourished." Jax scowled at her across the table. "Just eat it."

No matter how disgusting the food was, it was a relief to see Jax eating, especially in the dining room. Even after Grey had removed the stitches in his back, it had taken days before Jax was willing to come downstairs.

It was only when the bruising and swelling receded from his face, that he finally began to socialize again. But still, the angry, pink scar cut across his face in a jagged line, and his once-perfect nose was now crooked.

"No." Roz pushed herself back from the table. "Fuck this."

"What?" Arik looked up in surprise.

"Just come with me." Roz scoffed. "And bring your slop if you have to."

After a moment of hesitation, they abandoned their lunch and followed Roz to her bedroom. When they were all gathered safely inside, Roz shut the door and pressed a long finger to her lips.

"Keep your mouths shut about this, all right?" she warned.

Together, they nodded as Roz turned to her closet and dropped to her knees. Clearing aside a few pairs of boots, she exposed the wooden floor, and with the broken heel from an old pair of stilettos, she pried up a floorboard, pulled out a large sack, and dumped its contents onto the bed.

Grey gasped as a stash of candy bars, crackers, and snacks spilled out over the bedspread.

"Where did you get all of this?" Jax eyed the food suspiciously.

"Here and there," Roz shrugged. "I started hoarding it the day the shops stopped reading our chips for payment."

"How did you know?" Arik breathed in awe.

"I didn't," Roz admitted. "I was just saving it for—"

She stopped and glanced at Grey.

"I was just saving it for a rainy day."

The rainy day was not in preparation for a food shortage, but for an escape. And as Grey stood staring down at the bedspread, covered in treats, a hollow pit formed in her stomach.

It was clear that Roz had begun forming her plan well before Jax's injury—possibly as soon as she'd learned of Grey and Jesse's attempt—but now, she was sharing her supplies, as if she had finally realized it was too late to escape.

"Go on." Roz grinned. "Take your pick."

Jax acted first, rifling through the snacks until he found a protein bar and peeled back the wrapper.

"I don't know how long this will last us," Roz admitted as she fished out a chocolate bar and handed it to Grey, "But for as long as I have it, my stash is yours."

Gratefully, Grey took the chocolate, and together they ate their last hope of escape.

- ♦ -

"I'm still working on the list." Lock patted his breast pocket. "And some things might take longer than others, but this is what I've been able to find so far."

Grey peered into the box, balanced on the corner of Lock's desk, and exhaled a sigh of relief. A case of disinfecting ointment—slightly crushed and discolored, as though it had fallen off the back of a truck—rested under a layer of gauze and bandages. Beside them were three bottles: ibuprofen, aspirin, and iodine.

"This is perfect." Grey smiled.

Even for Jax, the supplies Lock had tracked down would have a huge impact.

"I'm surprised you were able to get this much," she said, "considering all of the shortages and rations."

"There's always a way." Lock shrugged and lowered his voice. "Plus, I had a feeling the rations would be coming, so I established some new trade lines."

Grey's eyes narrowed. "What do you mean?"

Lock glanced at the open door, and Grey quickly stepped over to shut it.

"Did something happen in the South?" she whispered.

"The rebels have cut off major supply lines to the capital," Lock said solemnly. "But it will still take time for them to reach us."

Grey's chest tightened as the Purplecap's words sank in. For a while, the rationing would only get worse. But if the rebels could make it to the north—the heart of Citoyen—there was still hope that Huxley and all of the Whitecaps could be deposed.

"But more and more Blackcaps are sent south every day," a slight grin twitched up the corners of Lock's lips. "Which means . . ."

"Less Blackcaps here," Grey breathed, and her eyes locked with his. "Does that mean we're going to join them? Are we going to revolt too?"

"I don't know," Lock answered honestly. "But I hope so."

"What do you mean?" Grey frowned. The question had been simple enough. "What's the plan?"

"There isn't one," Lock said. "Not yet, at least."

"Well, what about Huxley?" Grey pressed. "How far do you think she's willing to go to end this?"

"I wouldn't put anything past her," he said. "But, if history is any indication, things will only get worse before they get better."

Grey clenched her jaw and stared down at the box of medical supplies. There was a chance—a very real and terrifying chance—that if things grew too serious in the South, Huxley might retaliate by eradicating the threat in the north. In some ways, she had already begun. Snatching Pieces who took drugs, forcing children into the pods, implementing a curfew; they were all methods for the Whitecaps to instill fear. And it was working.

"How many Pinkcaps know?" Grey asked.

"Not all," Lock answered. "But enough have heard."

"And where do they stand?"

"For the most part, they agree that there's no point in inciting a revolution before everyone's ready," Lock answered. "It's better to wait until we actually have a way to win."

Grey swallowed as Roz's words came back to her. On one hand, a revolution could bring about a new world, but on the other, it could lead to mass extermination. Then again, if Huxley's new policies were any indication of the future she envisioned for Citoyen, Pinkcaps were already in serious danger of being eliminated.

"What about escape?" Grey asked. "Have you worked anything out for people who want to leave?"

Lock pursed his lips in consideration before responding. "We're working on something for the kids," he answered. "But that's all I can say for now."

Grey nodded. The less people knew, the better.

"When it's time," she said, lifting the box of supplies off of the corner of the desk, "let me know. I'd like to help if I can."

"Of course," Lock agreed. "I'm sure we could use a Redcap."

- ♦ -

Jax flinched as Grey dabbed ointment over his healing back. At the end of his bed, Roz sprawled, her legs crisscrossed with Arik's as she absentmindedly clicked dirt from under her fingernails.

"I think I have a few clients who would be willing to bring food for our sessions." Roz looked up from her nails with a wicked glint in her eye. "There's this one woman who has a thing for peanut butter. If I make it part of the fun, I bet I could get a new jar every time she sees me."

"Nobody wants to eat your sex butter," Jax sighed, but from where Grey stood, she could see a gleam of amusement in his deep, green eyes.

Although Grey had been able to remove the stitches a few days prior, some of the larger scabs still tended to split slightly when Jax moved around. And while the majority were fading into superficial scratches, it was worth it to keep them lubricated, especially to help reduce the scarring.

"You say that now," Roz smirked and dropped her voice into a sultry purr, "but there will come a day when you'll beg me for my butter. Just you wait."

Jax snorted and smiled despite himself.

As much as she hated to admit it, Grey had no reservations about eating any peanut butter that Roz managed to bring home, no matter how it was obtained.

"Well, if Jax doesn't want any," with a quick twist, she screwed the cap back on the ointment and tossed it in her supply box, "it'll mean more for the rest of us."

"Oh, scandal!" Roz gasped in mock surprise and clutched Arik's shoulder. "Did you hear that? Grey *already* wants my butter!"

"I'll take some too," Arik laughed beside her.

"Well, Jax," Roz grinned, "I hate to say this, but I think you've missed your chance."

"I'm sure I'll survive." Jax rolled his eyes, and Roz's smile softened into something more serious.

"I hope so," she said.

A silence settled over the room in the wake of Roz's words, and she glanced between Jax and Arik.

"I know why they've started rationing," she said as her gaze settled on Grey. "Jax and Arik know too." Roz raised a black eyebrow. "Do you?"

Slowly, Grey nodded.

"Lock told you?" Jax turned toward her.

"Yes," she answered, "but I knew before I came here."

"How?" Roz's eyes narrowed slightly.

"Because, Lock . . ." Grey paused, unsure if she should share the information. "Lock's the one who helped me and Jesse escape."

Roz's frowned and clenched her jaw in frustration. The answer she had been looking for had never been with Grey, but with her own Purplecap.

"Does anyone else know?" Grey whispered, glancing between the three of them.

"A few people in each of Lock's units have been told," Jax answered. "And the rest have only heard rumors."

"But I've been trying to get him to spread the word," Roz sighed heavily and leaned her head against the wall. "If people knew how hard he was fighting for them, maybe they wouldn't be so afraid."

"They should be afraid, Roz." There was an urgency in Jax's words as he turned to look at her. "We can't assume anything about what's happening in the South. The longer they fight, the more Blackcaps Huxley will send. And even if that clears the way for the northern brothels, it could crush the southern rebellion."

"But this is where the power is," Roz insisted. "There are over six thousand Pieces in this city, and when our time comes, we might actually have shot at this."

"Our time?" Jax looked at her pointedly. "What do you think we'll do when our time comes? Fight them with kitchen knives? We need the South for supplies."

"I know," Roz huffed. "But I'm sure someone has guns. Or at least smoke bombs."

"Smoke bombs?" Jax raised his eyebrows cynically.

"Or real bombs!" Roz rolled her eyes, but after a moment of frustration, her scowl softened into a smirk. "I don't know about you, but I think a bottle of my Solstice punch would knock a few Beaks on their asses."

They all chuckled at the moment of much needed levity, but there was still a heaviness to the conversation.

"I'm sure it could." Jax smiled sadly. "But we can't even get the ingredients for that anymore. How could we possibly smuggle the weapons we'd need?"

To Grey's surprise, the answer didn't come from Roz, but from Arik. With a dark frown, his eyes met Jax's.

"There's always a way."

FOURTEEN

Grey's knees dug into the cold tile as she scrubbed around the base of the fourth-floor toilet. With the dismissal of the Bluecaps, Lock had posted a cleaning schedule for all inhabitants of the Base—including himself—and for the first time, it was Grey's turn to take care of the bathrooms. Although the basics had been maintained for the past few weeks, whoever had last cleaned it was not nearly as thorough as they should have been.

"So, let me get this straight," Roz said slowly. "You're willing to bust your ass, scrubbing someone else's piss out of the grout, but you're still grossed out by your own piss when clients ask for it?"

"Why do you not see how different those two things are?" Grey scowled at Roz, who was sitting on the lip of the bathtub with a pair of rubber gloves pulled up to her elbows.

The Dom was wearing one of her signature fishnet shirts with a burgundy bra underneath—loungewear, as she considered it—but the black gloves looked oddly professional.

"Oh, I do see how different they are." Roz held up her two hands as if weighing the options. "One is someone else's piss, and one is your own. Personally, I'd rather deal with my own."

"Is that why you're not helping?" Grey asked.

"Not at all." Roz's eyes gleamed as they lingered on Grey's rear end. "I was just waiting until the show was over."

Grey snorted but couldn't help the smile that crept up the corner of her lips as Roz finally turned her attention to the spout of the tub and began to rub it clean with a coy wink.

"Really, though," Roz said as she buffed the faucet. "Why are you so anxious about becoming a Dom? You work alone as a Rag all the time. What's so different about tying up your clients?"

"I just . . ." Grey sighed. "I feel like I wouldn't know what to do without you there."

"Oh, that's bullshit," Roz rolled her eyes. "The last three times we went out, you barely needed my help with anything."

As much as Grey appreciated the support, she knew Roz was wrong. So much of their weekly sessions still depended on Roz's careful planning and rapport with the clients. But Grey knew she would freeze at some point, and without Roz, there would be no one to fall back on.

"I guess," Grey shook her head. "I'm just not like you."

Pursing her lips in dissatisfaction, Roz raised a dark brow. "What's that supposed to mean?"

"It means I'm not as creative as you." Exasperated, Grey tossed down her scrub brush and pushed away a loose strand of hair with her forearm. "Just look at yourself. For you, being a Dom is like an art form or something. I'm not like that."

Roz's dark lips twitched into a frown.

"As a Rag, I can just tune it out and wait for the clients to get it over with." Grey shrugged. "But as a Dom, I feel like I'm acting the whole time. And I'm just not that good at putting on a show."

"Yes, but as a Dom, you have so much more control," Roz persisted. "More freedom."

"The control isn't worth it if I have to spend every ounce of energy to get it."

"Weird." Roz's brows pinched together. "It always makes me feel more energized."

"Case in point," Grey reiterated. "We're different."

"I guess," Roz said. "But once Jax is healed, it will be such a help when you're ready to work alone. There are so many Pieces—so many kids—who could use a Dom to keep them safe.

"You're right," she agreed. "It's a good idea, but . . . ."

Grey bit her lip and frowned down at her hands.

"But what?" Roz asked.

"Will I even make a difference?"

"Of course," Roz's eyes softened. "What do you mean?"

"I mean," Grey scoffed, "how could I possibly make someone feel safe? I couldn't do shit for Selene or Lydie . . ."

Grey shook her head and rocked back on her heels.

"People get hurt, and I just clean them up and send them back out." She threw her hands in the air. "And then, it happens again."

Roz listened in silence.

"And what could I possibly do," Grey asked, "if a client attacked me or someone else in a pod? I'd be completely useless."

"No," Roz insisted, "as a Dom, you would have control."

"You keep saying that," Grey rolled her eyes, "but *how*? How would I have any more control? It's not like putting on a corset and stiletto boots will give me superpowers. It won't make any difference if I'm a Dom or a Rag."

"Seriously?" Roz stared at her in disbelief. "You think your stupid little corset and boots won't help you?"

Before Grey could respond, Roz yanked off her rubber gloves and pulled a knife from the waistband of her pants. With a soft click, the blade sprung free.

"The difference," Roz's eyes settled on the sharp edge, "is that Doms carry weapons."

Grey had seen the knife before—when Roz used it with clients who liked the danger of a blade dragging over their most vulnerable places—but she had thought it was only a prop.

"And I know you might not like it," Roz's lips quirked up in a dangerous smile, "but you should probably learn how to use one."

- ♦ -

"Roz is right," Grey frowned as she plucked a case of eyeshadow off the dresser. "There are Pinkcaps who need Doms."

Behind Grey, Arik sat hunched on the end of the bed, listening.

"And I feel bad," she admitted, "because I'm just not ready yet."

"It's okay," Arik assured her. "Things like that take time. And Roz knows that."

"Does she?" Normally, Grey would have agreed with Arik, but there was a growing uneasiness in the Base, and around Roz, the feeling was palpable.

"She's just anxious about leaving me alone," Arik said.

"Leaving you alone?" Grey glanced at him in the mirror. "Why?"

"She's booked for a few private house-calls this week," Arik explained. "And there's no one else to take me, so she's upset."

"What about Nic?" Grey asked, "Or Taryn?"

"They already have assistants lined up," he shrugged. "But this won't be the first time I've worked on my own, and I'm sure it won't be the last."

"Oh," Grey frowned. "I can try moving things around with Jax."

"No," Arik shook his head. "Jax needs some time to adjust to the pods, and you need to get comfortable with your own routine. Plus, after a few nights with him," a mischievous smile curled up the corners of Arik's lips, "you might be glad to work alone."

"He's not that bad." Abandoning her makeup, Grey turned to face Arik. "Is he?"

"No, I'm just teasing," Arik laughed. "I mean, he definitely has his own way of doing things, but he's not terrible to work with."

"So, you've worked with him before?" she asked.

"Not exactly," Arik answered. "But we were raised together, so we trained together."

As different as they were, it was easy to forget that Jax, Arik, Roz, and Selene had all grown up in the same boarding house. As a Redcap, Grey and her classmates had constantly been tested and moved based on their aptitudes. By the time she was ten, the friends she had made were long gone.

"So, Lock doesn't separate the Apicals?" Grey asked, taking a seat beside Arik on the bed. "I thought their training was different."

"It is." Arik nodded. "And usually, he does. But when Lock found me, he knew he would bring me back to the Base someday, so he just decided it was easiest to place me with them."

"Why?" Grey asked. "Why the Base."

"Because this is where my mother left me."

"Oh," Grey blinked in surprise.

"When I was born, my mother—whoever she was—wrapped me up in a blanket and left me on the steps outside," Arik said. "It happens more often in the other units, but Lock says I'm the only one who ever showed up here."

"Do you know where you came from?" Grey asked.

It was possible that he had been abandoned for his physical deformities. Grey had certainly seen mothers leave their babies to a Purplecap for less, but they didn't usually leave them on doorsteps.

"I don't," Arik shook his head. "But we think my mother was probably a Piece."

"Then why leave you at the Base?"

"Not all Purplecaps are like Lock," lost in thought, Arik's dark eyes turned toward the window. "For some Dispensable, life is much worse. We assume she gave me away to protect me from whoever she worked for. With Lock, she knew I would be safer."

Arik was silent for a moment as he gazed outside. Pale blue and pink slivers of sunset were beginning to creep over the horizon. Dusk was coming, but there was still time before they had to head out for the night.

"I guess she was right." He smiled a little.

Considering Arik's circumstances, his words were a cold reminder. The luxuries Grey had seen at the Base were not the reality for all Pinkcaps. For some, the new reign of Mara Huxley was no worse than what their own Purplecaps forced them to endure.

"After all," Arik turned to Grey, and his eyes brightened, "if she hadn't left me here, I would never have met Roz. And she's the best family I could ever ask for."

- ♦ -

Grey tightened the thin cords, binding the naked man's wrists and ankles to the steel table. She had turned off the heating mechanism that normally kept the surface warm—per the client's instructions—stripped the man and strapped him down.

It was too easy to stare at the client in disgust, but trying to look sexy while doing so was a challenge of its own. Luckily, the man had indicated a preference for being blindfolded, which Grey planned to take full advantage of, just as Roz had taught her. She only wished she could blindfold Jax as well.

Standing in the corner with his arms crossed over his chest, Jax watched—his face, a mask of boredom—as Grey reached down the front of her corset with two fingers and pulled out a black, silk scarf. Slowly, she walked along the table, trailing the tip of the scarf up the client's body until she reached his throat. There, she stopped and carefully folded the scarf into a neat strip. The man groaned as Grey slipped the silk over his eyes and tied it firmly behind his bare head.

Free from the man's gaze, Grey fidgeted against the tightness of her black corset as she silently patted it down. Roz had taken care to provide her with any props she might need—along with a knife—but their positioning was awkward, and Grey couldn't free the props with the ease that Roz had demonstrated.

Rolling her eyes at the Dom's methods, Grey fumbled with the binding at the base of the corset, clawing for the pinwheel hidden just beneath the fabric. Grey had used a similar tool as a Redcap—primarily to test nerve reactions in patients—but this one was much sharper. At least it would be; if she could free it from its hiding place.

Exasperated, Grey gritted her teeth and was about to give up on the client's request, when she caught Jax's movement out of the corner of her eye. Wordlessly, he stepped toward her, slipped his hand under the lip of her corset, and easily pulled the pinwheel free.

Mouthing a silent, 'Thank you,' Grey took the device from his hand and turned back to her client, who was already beginning to squirm with anticipation.

Without warning him, Grey pressed the pinwheel into the base of the man's bare foot, and he shuddered. Careful not to apply too much pressure, she rolled it between his toes, over his foot, and up his leg. But when she reached the base of his hip, she stopped and drew back.

Not knowing where she had gone or what she would do next, the man shivered against the restraints. It was all part of the game for him—these long pauses of blindness—and the more she toyed with his other senses, the better.

Pieces of Pink

Biting the pinwheel between her teeth, Grey unleashed a small cable tie from her wrist with a loud zip, and the man on the table trembled. Holding the tie in her free hand, she rolled the pinwheel over the base of the man's other foot. Again, she traced a line up his leg, but this time, when she reached his hip and paused, she used the cable tie to bind his balls.

A part of her wanted to laugh at the man as she watched him turn purple, but remembering the expression on Roz's face when she had performed the same task had a sobering effect. When Roz worked, there was no laughter in her eyes. Every move she made was cold and calculated as if torture were her true calling.

If Grey had never seen the Roz who had carried Arik when he was hurt, the Roz who had charged a Blackcap when Lydie was taken, and who had forgiven Jax—even when she was still angry with him—Grey would have feared her. But as much as Roz seemed to enjoy what she did in the pods, Grey knew it was not sex that the Dom loved, but retribution.

- ◆ -

Slush seeped into Grey's boots as she trudged back toward the Base with Jax at her side.

"You know," he said after a long silence. "You're not bad."

Grey's cheeks flushed. Working with the ex-App had been humiliating, though she couldn't place why. After all, she had worked in front of Roz plenty of times. But Jax had only ever seen her as a Rougie. Revealing herself in front of him had eliminated the last wall that separated them. And she wished she could build it back up again.

"But you could stand to work on your improvisation."

She huffed, "What do you mean?"

"What would you have done if you were alone?" Jax asked. "What if you couldn't get the pinwheel free?"

"I don't know." she shrugged. "I would've gotten it out eventually, I guess."

"Or you could have used another tool," Jax suggested.

Grey scowled, "But the client requested it."

"It doesn't matter." Jax shook his head. "As long as you get it done, they don't care what you use. Some of them even like to have their requests ignored. They like to feel out of control."

"But *I* don't like to feel out of control," Grey shot back.

Jax was silent for a moment, and when he finally spoke, his voice was small.

"Neither do I," he admitted. "But trust me when I say, you're safest when you're a Dom."

As much as she hated to admit it, Grey knew Jax was right. In her time at the Base, there had been significant injuries and fatalities in every group except for the Doms. But it was only a matter of time before the violence found them too. And when it did, there would be no one left to protect.

-♦-

It was after dawn when Grey awoke in a beam of sunlight on the couch. She had not meant to fall asleep in the lounge, but the fourth floor had been empty when she had returned home, and the eerie silence had urged her downstairs.

Yawning heavily, she stood and stumbled her way upstairs. But when she reached the fourth-floor landing, she paused outside her bedroom. Beside it, Arik's door was still ajar, as it had been when she had first come home.

Pieces of Pink

A tight pressure formed in Grey's chest as she nudged open the door and peered inside. The room was empty. Arik's bed was still made, and there was no sign that he had ever even made it back to the Base.

Without wasting a moment, Grey bolted down the stairs and burst into Roz's room.

"What the hell?" Roz sat upright as Grey launched toward her.

"Is Arik with you?" Grey demanded, glancing over Roz, only to find the rest of the bed unoccupied.

"No." Roz rubbed her eyes. "Why?"

"He's not in his room," Grey said. "I don't think he came home last night. And with curfew—"

She shuddered at the memory of Jax's injuries. If the same thing were done to Arik, she doubted he would survive.

"He probably fell asleep in the lounge." Roz yawned. "Have you checked downstairs?"

"I was just down there." Grey shook her head. "I didn't see him."

"Shit!" Roz growled and threw off her covers.

Quickly, the Dom pulled on her clothes and pushed past Grey into the hallway.

"Where are you going?" Grey asked.

"To wake up Lock," Roz answered. "I'll have him call around. If Arik knew he couldn't make it home before dawn, maybe he decided to crash at one of the other units."

"Okay." Grey nodded, and Roz stopped.

"But you should check every room," Roz said. "Make sure he's not sleeping in here somewhere."

"Got it." Grey agreed, and as Roz headed for Lock, Grey beelined across the hall to Jax's room.

It was dark when Grey pushed open the door, and with the blackout curtains tightly closed, she could barely make out Jax's form in the bed.

"Jax?" she said. "Are you awake?"

"Who's there?" he grumbled.

"It's Grey," she answered. "Arik didn't come home last night."

Slowly, Jax clicked on the lamp beside his bed.

"When did you last see him?" Jax squinted in the bright light as he stumbled out of bed and reached for a pair of jeans flung over the back of a chair. The scars on his bare back rippled tightly as he bent to pull on his pants.

"Before we went out last night," Grey said.

"Did you tell Lock?" Jax asked, yanking a clean shirt over his head. "Maybe he was booked somewhere last night."

"I'm pretty sure he was in the pods last night." Grey shook her head. "But Roz went to wake Lock, and she wants us to check the Base to make sure he's not here somewhere."

"Good plan," he agreed. "You take the first and fourth floor. I'll take the second and third. Ask *everyone*. Maybe someone knows where he ended up."

With a nod, Grey turned away, but even as she headed upstairs to begin her search, the cold knowledge of truth gripped her gut. Arik wasn't home. She only hoped that he had found somewhere safe to hide when the sun rose.

- ♦ -

With each room that Grey checked, another Piece joined the search for Arik. But even so, Lock hadn't waited for them to finish before he pulled on his coat and ran out into the sunshine, promising that he wouldn't come home until Arik was found. But hours had passed, and there was still no sign of them.

"We should be out there looking for him," Roz growled as she paced back and forth in front of the door, "not just standing here with our thumbs up our asses, waiting for Lock to comb the whole city by himself."

"He's not by himself," Nic said. "I'm sure he has other Perps with him. Just stop pacing. You're making me anxious."

Spinning to face him, Roz threw her hands in the air.

"You *should* be anxious," she snapped. "Look what they did to Jax! Do you think Arik could even survive that?"

"Arik's survived worse," Nic retorted. "And Grey will heal him."

Grey frowned. As much as she appreciated the man's trust and confidence, with limited resources and no access to a hospital, nothing was guaranteed. It had been a miracle that Jax had survived. And if Arik came home in the same condition, she would need all the help she could get.

"Until Lock brings him home," Jax stepped between the two Doms, "there's nothing we can do about it. So just—"

"We could help!" Roz yelled.

"No, we can't," Jax said. "It would only endanger more people."

"I don't care!" Roz roared.

For a moment, Jax only glared at her, his own rage a quiet, seething thing, just beneath the surface of his skin.

"Well, you should," he hissed.

In the silence that followed, the other Pieces scattered into the lounge and dining room, unwilling to be caught in the crosshairs of a fight between Roz and Jax.

Grey didn't move. She watched in silence as Roz's lip curled back in snarl, but as the woman opened her mouth to speak, Arden ran into the foyer with Taryn on his heels.

"They're back!" he yelled.

All at once, the Pinkcaps rushed to the windows, peering into the alley as Lock trudged toward the Base, and he wasn't alone. From where she stood, Grey could just make out Arik's form, cradled in Lock's arms.

"Shit," Jax breathed, and Grey slowly turned to Roz.

Before anyone could stop her, the Dom threw open the door and leapt down the front steps. As one, the Pinkcaps followed, hovering under the portico as Roz ran toward Lock and Arik.

Grey's eyes narrowed. Lock had removed his coat and wrapped it around Arik, but there was something strange about the way Arik's legs swung, the way his neck was bent toward Lock at an impossible angle, and the thin trail of blood that followed them both through the snow.

"Roz!" Grey pushed through the cluster of Pieces. "Don't!"

But it was too late.

When she reached Lock, Roz froze. Then, she began to scream. And as the noise—more animal than human—ripped from her throat, Roz sank to her knees. Turning her face to the gray sky, she howled in anguish, clutching at her chest as tears spilled down her cheeks. Still wailing, Roz reached for the body in Lock's arms, like a mother, grasping for her baby.

For a moment, Lock hesitated. Then reluctantly, he passed Arik's broken body into Roz's arms and slowly made his way to the group of Pinkcaps waiting at the door. When he reached Grey, he stopped. He opened his mouth, but when no words came out, he shut it. And his blue eyes—exhausted and broken—trailed back toward Roz.

Grey simply nodded, stepped into the snow, and slowly made her way toward Roz and the body. When she reached them, her stomach heaved, and a gasp of horror slipped from her throat. Beneath Lock's coat, Arik was naked, and he was covered in blood.

"Help me," Roz sobbed as Grey crouched down beside them.

Arik's face was swollen almost beyond recognition. If it weren't for the dark crop of hair, the crooked back, and small arms, she almost wouldn't have known it was him.

Pieces of Pink

White blisters, the size of pennies, were seared around his face and torso. Someone had burned him—branded him—over and over, and they'd done it while he was still alive.

"Help me!" Roz cried.

Inch by agonizing inch, Grey's eyes scanned his body, absorbing everything that had been done to him. Both of Arik's arms and legs were broken, and the side of his neck bulged out as though it had been snapped by a rope. And between his legs, there was nothing but blood.

"Help me!" Roz wailed over and over, a lullaby of death as she rocked Arik back and forth in her arms.

In silence, Grey wrapped her arms around the woman's shoulders. There was nothing else to be done.

Arik was dead.

"He's gone," Grey whispered.

"No," Roz whimpered. "No."

"I'm sorry."

Roz's glassy eyes turned toward her, and Grey shook her head. And when the realization finally sank in, Roz buried her face in Grey's chest and wept.

Still holding her, Grey glanced back to the front steps. One by one, the Pinkcaps began to withdraw into the house until only Jax remained watching.

They had seen enough death.

FIFTEEN

Roz lifted Arik from the snow and slowly walked back to the Base. Following behind them, Grey choked back her tears. Terrible things had been done to Arik—too many of them while he was still alive—and if she started crying, she was afraid she might never stop.

When they reached the stoop, Jax held open the door and bowed his head. It was too much to look at the mutilated body dangling in Roz's arms, and Grey understood.

The Pieces waiting in the foyer parted as Roz carried Arik to the lounge and laid him on the couch. Without looking up, she knelt beside him, stroking his frozen, black hair with trembling fingers. For a few moments, Roz remained on her knees, whispering a eulogy too softly for anyone else to hear. Until finally, she pushed herself to her feet.

"Lock," she rasped, still staring down at Arik's body. "Someone, get me Lock."

Grey turned to search for the man, but he was already there, moving across the room like a ghost, covered in Arik's blood.

"What can I do?" he whispered when he reached Roz's side.

"Make the calls you have to make," she said. "I'm done with this place. I'm done with everything."

"Roz . . ." Lock hesitated, but when Roz turned to face him, there was fire in her eyes.

"How many more Pinkcaps have to die while we sit here waiting for the southern rebellion to reach us?" she asked.

Lock's mouth was set in a grim line.

"How many kids will have to go to the pods? How many will be dragged off by Blackcaps?" She looked around the room. "When it comes to Pinkcaps, Huxley doesn't discriminate. Beautiful, hideous, old, young, strong, weak; it doesn't matter. We're all animals to her. We're all pests that need to be exterminated. So, if she thinks we're infecting this perfect world of hers, why don't we just leave it? All of us, together."

The Pinkcaps stood in silence.

"Lock," Roz gazed at him, pleading, "I know you can get people out of Citoyen. You've done it before."

"Yes, but it hasn't always been successful." He glanced pointedly at Grey. "With the number of Pinkcaps in this city, there's no way we could slip out unnoticed. And we can't just storm the streets. The Blackcaps would kill us all."

"Can't we?" she asked. "What if we could create a diversion?"

"What do you mean?" Lock's eyes narrowed.

"I know who did this," Roz answered simply. "And I'm going to kill him."

"Shit," Jax hissed under his breath.

"If I go alone, it's a suicide mission," Roz swallowed hard. "But I'm not the only person in this room—in this city—who wants revenge for someone. And with enough people, maybe we can create a distraction."

Around her, the Pinkcaps began to whisper amongst themselves, and Roz pushed on.

"If killing a few Whitecaps is enough to save everyone else," Roz's voice grew stronger, and the flame in her eyes flared brighter, "then I'm willing to die for it. Are you?"

For an agonizing moment, no one said a word. In stunned silence, the Pieces only stared at Roz, waiting. Until finally, a movement in the back of the group caught Grey's eye. With his jaw tightly clenched, Nic slowly approached Roz and stopped.

"For Megz," he said, "I'll go with you."

Beside Nic, Jax stepped forward.

"For Selene," he said, "and Lydie."

Grey stared at the three Pinkcaps before her, then her eyes fell to the couch—to Arik's body—and she took a shaking breath.

"I'm coming, too," she said. "For Jesse."

Roz blinked in surprise, then her throat bobbed as she gave Grey a nod of appreciation and turned to the rest of the group.

"If you want to escape," she said, "follow Lock."

Then, her voice turned deadly.

"But if you have something to settle, follow me."

- ♦ -

Grey sat in the dining room with a scalpel in her hand and a bottle of iodine by her side. Even though the Pinkcaps had divided evenly between Roz and Lock, it was safest to remove everyone's chips. At least without trackers, anyone who survived the diversion would have a chance to rejoin those trying to escape.

Taryn held out his wrist. He had willingly decided to join Lock, but only Nic's pleading had convinced Arden not to go with Roz. With a practiced hand, Grey cut a small incision just above the man's chip and popped it free with a gentle push. As she had with each Pinkcap before, she quickly dabbed antibiotics on the wound, covered it with a small adhesive bandage, and dropped her scalpel in the cleaning solution beside her.

"All set," she said.

Nodding in appreciation, Taryn stood. And as Grey cleaned her tools, the next Pinkcap took his place.

Across the room, Pieces were gathering supplies, laying them out on the long tables, and carefully separating them between backpacks. The only resources which had not been deemed communal were Grey's medical supplies. Those had been carefully divided between two packs. One, to go with Lock, and the other—Grey's pack—to follow the diversion team.

A pale wrist appeared in front of Grey, and she looked up. Seated across the table, Roz leaned forward with fierce determination sketched over her face. The Dom had swapped her fishnet shirt for a plain, black turtleneck and a pair of pants. Her thigh-high heels had been replaced with combat boots, and her blonde hair was pulled into a tight bun. But the most striking change was the lack of makeup. Roz's face had been scrubbed clean, and no trace of color remained on her pale, cracked lips.

"I think you should go with Lock," Roz said as Grey reached for the iodine.

"No." Grey shook her head and wiped down the Dom's wrist. "I'm the only other person here who knows the way out of the city. You'll need me to get away when everything's—"

Grey stopped and peered down at Roz's wrist. A faded scar—about the size of a penny—stood out against the iodine.

"What's that?" Grey asked.

Roz's lips curved in a vicious frown. "I didn't do it to myself, if that's what you're asking."

Pale as it was, the scar—a brand—had been easily hidden under Roz's makeup and jewelry; but exposed in the bright lights of the dining room, the small circle was sickeningly familiar.

"Arik's body . . ." Grey's voice trailed away into nothing as Roz slowly nodded.

The Dom had more than one score to settle.

"So, as much as I appreciate your willingness to come with us," Roz's eyes—still red-rimmed with tears—grew hard, "I don't expect to make it out."

"Roz!" Lock's voice echoed across the dining room, and Grey glanced up to see the Purplecap striding toward them.

With her pale lips set in a stoic line, Roz turned to face him.

"Did you reach anyone?" she asked.

He nodded. "More Pieces are planning to join you in the streets. And the rest will find me in the sewers."

"How many for the diversion?" Roz frowned.

"With you? Two, maybe three . . ."

"Hundred?"

Lock shook his head. "Thousand."

Roz sucked in a sharp breath, and Grey's mouth fell open as the gravity of what was about to happen sank in. A revolution was coming, and she was caught dead in its center.

"Three thousand?" Roz repeated in awe.

Lock nodded.

"Well, that should hold off the Beaks for a while," Roz said. "We'll try to give you as much time as we can."

"Thank you." Lock's bright eyes were earnest. "But when the time comes, promise me you'll get out of there. Don't be a martyr."

"I—" Roz looked away. "I'll do what needs to be done."

Worry flashed across Lock's face, but before he was reduced to begging, Grey spoke up.

"Don't worry." She met his gaze. "I won't leave without her."

With a shuddering breath, Lock nodded in gratitude and turned back to the supply tables.

Pieces of Pink

- ♦ -

Standing in the dining room with her medical pack strapped snugly against her shoulders, Grey looked around the room. It was beautiful in its own way, with dark wainscoting and ornately carved beams, arcing overhead. To Grey, it had never really been a home, but it hadn't been a prison either.

"Where's Jax?" Roz nudged Grey's shoulder, drawing her out of her thoughts.

"Lock's office," Grey said. "He went in a few minutes ago to help Lock get the last of the supplies."

Roz glanced at the clock, then toward Lock's office door.

"Let's see if we can move this along," she said, her expression grim. "It's time to go."

Obediently, Grey followed Roz into the office and around the corner of the desk; but when they reached his open bedroom door, they froze.

Lock's bed was pushed across the tiny space, and the wall it had once rested against gaped open as if pulled on invisible hinges. In the space beyond it, Jax and Lock stood in a dusty arsenal. Rows of pistols hung mounted on the walls, and clusters of rifles leaned in each corner.

"Holy shit," Grey breathed. For anyone but a Blackcap or Whitecap, possessing a weapon was beyond illegal. It was grounds for immediate execution.

Jax looked up at the sound of her voice, and in the dim light, his scar cast a jagged shadow over his face.

"Where the hell did you get all of these?" She asked Lock as she gaped at the hidden room.

"Different places," Lock answered. "I've been gathering them together for years, waiting for today."

"There are rifles for the diversion team," Jax pointed to the corners. "Roz, you can take those and start passing them out."

Without question or hesitation, Roz collected the rifles and marched them out of the office. Even from Lock's bedroom, Grey could hear the collective gasp that rose from the Pinkcaps gathered in the dining room.

"And the pistols will go with those who are trying to escape," Jax said. "It'll be easier to keep them dry in the sewers."

"This one is for you." Jax pressed a pistol into Grey's trembling hands and gave her two magazines. "Put these in your pack."

She shook her head. "I'm going with you and Roz."

"We know," Jax said. "But you're the only Rougie we've got. So, when it's time, get to the sewers as fast as you can."

Grey fought the tightness in her throat.

"I will."

- ♦ -

There was no speech as Roz strode into the swirling snow with a dozen friends at her back. Each of them followed her without question or dispute, because she was right. If they stayed, the Whitecaps would pick them off one by one. But if they stood up and fought for everything they had lost, maybe they could buy some time for those trying to flee. And it was better to die in the sunlight than to spend any more nights in a pod.

As they marched in blatant defiance of the curfew, Pinkcaps began spilling out of brothels. Some slipped unnoticed into the sewers, but the others fell into step behind Roz. Whatever calls Lock had made, the Pieces—and even a few of their Purplecaps—had answered. And not a single person was wearing a cap.

Beside Grey, Jax sucked in a steady breath.

Pieces of Pink

"I guess this is it," he murmured.

Unable to find the words to respond, Grey simply nodded. Whether they lived or died, Jax was right. This was the end. She only hoped that whatever new beginning followed in their wake, it would be better than the world they were leaving behind.

When they reached the river, Roz turned back.

"Blackcaps on the bank," she pointed over the bridge, where two black helmets glinted in the sun. "Get ready."

At first, the men didn't notice the Pinkcaps, and by the time they did, Roz had already lifted her rifle and taken aim. Immediately, the two men dropped their weapons and ran.

When they were out of sight, Roz lowered the gun, and a smug sneer curled up the corners of her lips. If everything went according to plan, the Blackcaps would gather forces to crush the Pieces marching through the streets. And hopefully, they wouldn't even notice the Pinkcaps slipping into the sewers.

"It's not far, now." Roz growled, and as the fire in her eyes began to burn, her face twisted into a mask of rage.

Whatever Roz had planned, Grey was sure the Dom's retribution would be brutal. And as Grey glanced to the army of Pieces at her back, a sinking fear settled in the pit of her stomach.

On the other side of the bridge, Roz veered sharply to the right, following an invisible path as if she had practiced it over and over in her mind. With her head held high in defiance, Roz marched the Pinkcaps down a wide street—a Whitecap district—lined on either side with richly decorated homes. And in front of a white, stone townhouse, Roz halted.

For a moment, she stared up at the building. It was an opulent home with high windows, elegant ironwork, and a small balcony with double, glass doors that hung out over the entryway.

"We're here," Roz said, her voice like sandpaper, as she turned to the mass of Pieces that had gathered behind her.

Some Pinkcaps, unable to fit completely in the street, began climbing light posts for a better view. Others stood on the roofs of cars and windowsills. But all of them watched Roz as she stared in silence, and for a moment, Grey thought she glimpsed regret in the Dom's eyes.

In a flash, it vanished as Roz straightened her back, turned to the white house, and roared, "Shawcross!"

"Oh, hell," Jax whispered.

"What?" Grey asked, "Who's Shawcross?"

Before Jax could answer, Roz screamed the name a second time.

"Roz was an Apical once." The color drained from Jax's face, and his pink scar stood out in stark contrast.

"I thought she quit," Grey whispered. "I thought she chose to be a Dom instead."

"Only after she spent a night with him." Jax's throat bobbed. "Her first night."

"What happened?" Grey's heart sank at the memory of the brand on Roz's wrist and the small circular burns covering Arik's body.

"She never told." Jax's green eyes were fixed on Roz. "But Shawcross had to pay an enormous fine, and Roz became a Dom."

Grey bit down on the inside of her cheek as Roz yelled up at the house, "Come out, come out, wherever you are!"

When no one answered her, Roz climbed the three marble steps that led to the front door, held onto the iron railings, and kicked. The wood shuddered. Again, Roz slammed her booted foot into the door, and it cracked. On the third blow, the door flew inward.

"Roz, wait!" Grey took a few steps forward, but Roz held up a hand to stop her.

"Stay there," she commanded. "I'm doing this alone."

"Don't," Grey pressed, but Roz looked past her, toward Jax.

There was a moment's hesitation before Jax laid his hand on Grey's shoulder.

Pieces of Pink

"Let her go," he said, but Grey didn't back down.

"Not alone," Grey pleaded. "Don't go alone."

"I know this house," Roz said, her icy voice calm. "Trust me."

Before Grey could protest further, Roz disappeared into the darkness beyond the splintered doorframe.

For a few agonizing seconds, there was only silence. Then, the screaming started. Stunned Bluecaps spilled from the house and fled through the neighbors' yards as a guttural cry ripped from an upstairs window. A moment later, the balcony door exploded outward, and Roz emerged, dragging a short man by the wisps of his thin, gray hair.

"Please," he begged, but Roz's face remained a mask of death.

Somewhere in the back of the crowd, a voice—maybe Nic's—cheered for Roz's small victory. And as the mob of Pinkcaps joined in, Shawcross looked out over the streets and began to tremble.

Snarling in irritation, Roz held up her free hand, and the commotion died away. When silence reigned once more, the Dom began to speak.

"This man," Roz yelled, voice echoing over the cobblestones, "murdered my best friend."

"He was a Dispensable." Shawcross was sobbing now. "I swear! He was a Dispensable."

"It doesn't matter *what* he was," Roz spat. "It's *who* he was. His name was Arik, and he was not dispensable, not to me."

Roz turned her gaze back to the Pinkcaps.

"To those of you who knew him, Arik was kind and gentle. And he never hurt anyone." Tears of rage bloomed in Roz's eyes. "But I would." She threw Shawcross to his knees. "And you? You hurt everyone you touch."

"I didn't mean to," he insisted. "I didn't—"

Roz backhanded the Whitecap across the face, and he careened sideways, catching himself against the bars on the balcony.

"When I was sixteen, I was an Apical," Roz roared. "And this pathetic excuse for a man won the bid on my first night."

She yanked the man's head back, and he screeched.

"Please don't hurt me," he stammered. "Please . . ."

"I am *talking*!" Roz screamed, and the man's pleas turned into whimpers as she reached down and began to unbuckle his belt. With a harsh yank, she pulled the leather free and used it to bind his arms behind his back.

"It's supposed to be illegal to harm an Apical," Roz said to the crowd. "But he tied me up with belts, just like this one. He branded my wrists. And when he was done with me, he, he . . ." Roz's voice trailed away, dragged off by some horrific memory. "He took the brand, and he mutilated me."

Grey's stomach heaved.

"But I lived with it," Roz growled. "I became a Dom so that I wouldn't have to fuck every client who bought me. I became a Dom because after that night, it hurt to sit. It hurt to piss, and I lived with it. I lived with it," she spat, "because what he did was only punishable with a fine. And what's a little money to a man born with a white hat on his head? He destroyed me, and our government—our perfect Code—let him do it!"

As she spoke, Roz tore open Shawcross's button, then his zipper, and finally, she yanked his beige pants down around his knees, revealing his genitals to the now horrified crowd.

"But you know what I can't live with?" Roz snarled.

From the street, Grey saw the flash of a knife as Roz slipped it from its hiding place.

"I can't live with the knowledge that this man will never be punished for torturing and murdering Arik."

She stared down at the shaking man with nothing but disgust in her golden eyes.

"So, I'll do it myself."

Pieces of Pink

With the knife clutched in her hand, Roz raised her fist in the air.

"For Arik, and for all of the Pinkcaps who have ever been abused or murdered at the hands of this government," Roz's voice rose up above the crowd, "I say we take justice into our own hands!"

The crowd erupted into cheers, and before anyone really knew what happened, Roz reached between the man's legs and severed his cock. Shawcross's mouth gaped open in a scream, but it was drowned out by the wild roar of Pinkcaps.

With every beat of the man's heart, blood spurted from the wound. Jax doubled over and vomited, but Grey's eyes remained fixed in horror as Roz yanked back the screaming man's head and dragged her blade in a slow sweep across his throat.

Twitching, the man dropped to the ground, and the mob exploded outward, washing over the capital city in a wave of vengeance. And with the bloody knife still clutched in her hand, Roz turned her back and withdrew into the darkness of the house.

- ♦ -

Grey threw her arms over her head as glass shattered from a second-story window. One instant, the Pinkcaps were watching Roz, and the next, they were breaking into the homes of every Whitecap on the street, throwing furniture—and sometimes people—to the ground below.

"Where's Roz?" Grey screamed, clinging to Jax as the sea of Pinkcaps swelled around them.

"Still inside!" Jax yelled over the chaos.

A Whitecap shouldered past Grey, knocking her sideways, and she stumbled. Before she could fall under the feet of the mob, Jax grabbed her arm and pulled her toward Shawcross's broken front door. Together, they burst through the splintered doorframe and into the gilded foyer.

"Roz!" Grey called.

Blinded from the bright snowy street, Grey blinked as her eyes adjusted to the dim light. When they did, she saw Roz sobbing in the stairwell with her face buried in her hands.

"Roz?" Slowly, Grey climbed up the stairs and sat beside her.

"He's dead." Roz's shoulders shook as she gasped between the words. "He's dead."

"He deserved it," Jax said from the bottom of the stairs. "For what he did to you, he deserved it."

"Not *him*," Roz finally looked up.

Tears and freckles of blood were splattered across her face, twisted in agony.

"Arik—" Her voice broke. "Arik's dead."

Grey squeezed Roz's shoulder.

"It won't feel this way forever," she said softly.

"Well, it should," Roz groaned and leaned into Grey's arms.

Across the city, sirens wailed. The Blackcaps were coming.

"I know it hurts," Jax said, and though his voice was calm, his eyes were wide with fear. "But we can't sit here forever. We'll hold out for Lock and the others as long as we can. And if we can't, we have to get to the sewers."

"You're right," Roz sniffled and wiped the blood and tears from her face with the edge of her sleeve. "What should we do?"

Jax glanced toward the window.

"It's mayhem out there," he said. "People are building barricades. If we can hold a few, maybe we can help get people out."

Roz sucked in a shaking breath, and regaining her determination, she stood. But as she and Grey descended the stairs, a burst of gunfire blasted through the street outside. Reflexively, the trio dropped to the floor and crept to the windows.

Pieces of Pink

In the streets, Pinkcaps—some with little more than knives and bats—rushed a group of Blackcaps. And although there weren't enough firearms for everyone, it was clear that Lock hadn't been the only Purplecap hoarding weapons.

But it wasn't the gunfire that terrified Grey; it was the low rumble that shook the very foundation of the building where they stood.

"Oh," Grey gasped. "Please tell me that's not—"

"A tank," Jax finished before she could. "They have a tank."

"We'll never be able to fight that," Grey whispered frantically.

Panic was rising in her chest, closing her throat with each breath she took.

"This way." With her tenacity awoken by the imminent danger, Roz snatched them both by the backs of their shirts. "We'll go out the back."

Following the Dom's lead, Jax and Grey snuck through the empty townhouse. With the Pinkcaps rioting in the streets, the Bluecap servants had abandoned their posts and left their employer to the mercy of Roz's retribution. Now, an eerie silence hung over the marble-floored hallways. But as Grey crept toward the back door, the opulence was impossible to ignore.

"Come on." Roz motioned them into the kitchen.

A luxurious spread of meat and cheese lay uncovered on the counter. Even after weeks of rationing, it appeared that Shawcross had been untouched by the food shortages.

For a moment, Grey paused, wondering if they should take some food from the Whitecap's cupboards, but when Roz pushed open the kitchen door, all thoughts of escape vanished. The street was washed in chaos. But at least the barricades were holding.

"Lay down your weapons now," an earsplitting voice crackled from a megaphone, "and you will be spared."

"Don't do it!" a Pinkcap screamed.

Then another, "They're liars! They'll kill us anyway!"

"We have you surrounded. Lay down your weapons," the Blackcaps repeated their warning.

"There's Nic." Roz pointed to a car that had been tipped over on its side. And with a carbine nestled against his shoulder, Nic peaked over the barricade and released a spray of bullets into the rows of oncoming Blackcaps.

Grey spun around, searching in vain for a place to run, or hide, or fight, but the noise around her was deafening. Plumes of black smoke billowed from a burning car on the other side of the barricade. Bullets ricocheted off the walls. Pinkcaps screamed. Blackcaps barked orders. Blood sprayed from a woman's skull as she tumbled off the barricade beside Nic. And then, a low whistle ripped through the air.

"Get down!" Roz roared.

Throwing her arms around Jax and Grey, Roz tackled them back through the door of Shawcross's kitchen, just as a grenade sailed over the barricade and exploded in the middle of the street. One moment, a small cluster of Pieces stood reloading their weapons. The next, they were scattered in chunks of bone and flesh, showering onto the cobblestones.

Grey lurched forward—ears ringing from the blast—but Roz held her down.

"People are wounded!" Grey screamed, "I have to help them!"

"You're too valuable." Roz pinned her against the cold marble floor. "More people will need you later."

"Look!" Jax shouted, and together, Roz and Grey looked up.

The barricade opposite Nic was shuddering. In a frenzy, Pinkcaps leapt from their positions, struggling to get away; but for some, it was too late. A tank burst through their only defense, crushing everything and everyone in its wake.

Without hesitating, Roz dashed from their hiding place, sprinting toward Nic with Jax and Grey at her heels.

Pieces of Pink

"It's time to go," Roz yelled and pulled Nic down off the car.

On the opposite end of the street, a swarm of Blackcaps spilled through the gap in the barricade, torn open by the tank.

"This way!" Jax urged them toward the broken window of an abandoned storefront and crawled through.

Rushing past aisles of neatly organized trinkets and clothes, the group stormed through the back room of the shop, and burst into an alley, hidden behind a pair of dumpsters. And there, in the center of the narrow lane, was a manhole cover.

"Quick!" Grey pointed. "We have to open it."

In an instant, Roz was on her knees, clawing at the rim of the iron plate.

"We need a crowbar." Jax turned back to the shop, but as he did, gunshots rang out inside the building.

"No time." Nic shook his head. "Barricade the door!"

Frantically, Grey looked around, searching for anything they could use, and her eyes fell on the dumpsters.

"Help me move this!" She ran forward and grabbed the heavier of the two. "We'll use it to block the door!"

With Jax and Nic at her sides, Grey dragged the dumpster backward and wedged it into place just as Roz found her purchase on the manhole cover. Groaning against the weight, Roz hauled it upright and braced a foot on the edge of the hole.

"Go, go, go!" Roz gritted her teeth. "I can't hold it long."

"You first!" Jax pointed to Nic, who quickly lowered himself through the opening. When he was down, Jax held out his hand for Grey. "Come on!"

"Take this." She pushed her backpack, full of medicals supplies, into his open hand. "Go. I'll be right behind you."

Jax hesitated.

"Faster!" Roz growled, her face turning red with exertion.

With a nod, Jax took the pack and followed Nic down the hole. But when the space was clear for Grey, she froze.

"Hurry!" Roz insisted.

"Grey!" Jax peered up from below. "Come on!"

Slowly, Grey's eyes turned up to Roz. If she followed Jax, there would be no way for Roz to get down.

"Go!" Roz grunted under the strain of the cover's weight.

"Not without you." Grey shook her head.

"Don't be stupid." sweat streamed down Roz's forehead. "I can't hold it. Hurry, before I drop it."

In the mouth of the alley, brakes screeched, and a transport van swung to a halt.

"Let go!" Grey insisted.

"No!" Jax shouted from the manhole and frantically began to climb upwards, but before he had even made it halfway up the ladder, the cover slipped from Roz's fingertips and slammed shut.

"You idiot," Roz panted, but when she spun on Grey, there were tears in the Dom's eyes. "What were you thinking? We're dead up here. There's nowhere to run."

"I made a promise." Grey dropped to her knees beside Roz as the van doors flew open and a Blackcap leapt to the ground. "We'll find another way out—together."

"On the ground!" The woman barked as she ran toward them with her weapon raised. "Hands on your head!"

Immediately, Grey dropped. But as the Blackcap drew closer, their eyes locked, and the woman paused. They had met before; once in the pods and again when the Blackcap had walked Grey home after her night as a Pence.

"You . . ." Grey whispered, but the woman tore her gaze away.

The Blackcap's eyes fell on the rifle beside Roz, and before the Dom had a chance to react, the woman kicked the weapon under the dumpster and reached for the radio on her uniform.

Pieces of Pink

"Two females," she said. "Unarmed."

"Let's load them up," a voice crackled back.

"You can come quietly," the woman said as a second Blackcap appeared in the mouth of the alley, "or you can die here."

Grey glanced at Roz, but she was exhausted. Weaponless and with nowhere to run, they had no choice but to obey.

"Stand up and face the wall."

Almost imperceptibly, Roz nodded, and with her arms still trembling from the strain of lifting the manhole cover, she stood, and Grey followed.

"On your knees," the Blackcap instructed as her partner came to a halt beside her. "Hands behind your back."

A shock of nausea rolled through Grey's stomach as the cold gravel bit into her knees.

She had been here before.

From the corner of her vision, Grey could see the barrel of the second Blackcap's rifle pressed into the back of Roz's skull. Tears welled in her eyes as she waited for the bang—the spray of blood—but it never came. Instead, she only heard the familiar click of a zip tie snapping into place.

A wave of relief washed over Grey as the Blackcap stepped away from Roz, and with practiced efficiency, she zip-tied Grey's hands behind her back, reached a hand under Grey's armpit and hauled her to her feet.

"Walk to the van," the woman ordered.

At gunpoint, Roz and Grey stumbled toward the armored vehicle. But when they reached the mouth of the alley, they froze. The street had been completely overtaken by Blackcaps, and on the far side of the road, a line of Pinkcaps lay dead, their blood spattered on the wall above them, like bursts of red paint.

"They were armed," the Blackcap said simply as she followed Grey's gaze. "You were not."

As the Blackcap yanked open the doors of the transport van, obscuring the dead Pinkcaps from sight, the implication of her words sank in. Regardless of cap or code, the woman had purposefully kicked the rifle under the dumpster, not to disarm them, but to save them.

Roz's mouth fell open as she glanced at Grey in surprise, but before she had a chance to speak, the Blackcaps shoved them both into the back of the empty van. With a heavy thud, Roz and Grey landed on the steel floor, and before they could scramble to their feet, the doors slammed shut behind them.

ACKNOWLEDGEMENTS

On New Year's Eve, 2014, I called out into the void and asked for a story to write. To my delight, the void answered. When I awoke the following morning, *Pieces of Pink* had burrowed its way into my imagination. Of course, it was only with the help of some amazing people that I was able to polish that spark of an idea into the novel it is today. So, from the bottom of my heart, thank you to:

Mom and Dad. There isn't enough blank paper in the world to thank you for the role that you both played in making this book a reality. Mom, thanks for listening to countless dramatic readings over the years. Dad, thank you for the Poppy Driscoll stories. Know that you are both very much loved and appreciated.

To Sharon Rose for your generosity. All of my writing comforts: lounge sweaters, "go suck a fart" mug, and feminist-agenda tote bag, are thanks to you. Whenever I use them, I feel like a total badass.

To Rebecca McBride for being the reigning queen of my fan club. You've edited some wild stories over the years, and I don't think anyone else has ever loved—or understood—my characters the way that you do. Your enthusiasm inspires me, and I am so lucky to have you as a cousin.

Annelise Driscoll

To Ben Swett for being my drama police. I can't even begin to thank you for the countless hours, energy, and passion that you have poured into this project. From the first draft to the final copy, you have encouraged and motivated me to chase my dreams and see this story through. Without you, I think Grey (character, not husband) would still be standing in line at a registration center in the rough draft of chapter one. Merci mille fois.

To Jenna Wilson for being my navigator extraordinaire. It's hard to believe that five years ago, we were cruising around the country, sleeping in parking lots, and living off of cheeseburgers. And while I'm not entirely sure where the idea for this book came from, I know you were right there with me when it hit. Maybe it was that tuna-bagel with fire sauce—or that hilariously awesome park ranger at Harper's Ferry—but whatever sparked this story, our road trip fed the flames. So, thank you for being my first sounding board in all things pink. And most importantly, thank you for being my friend.

And finally, to Grey (husband, not character) for being my tea-fetcher, dance partner, and shelter from pigs on the wing.

Made in the USA
Middletown, DE
09 March 2020